She was pinned beneath his body and could not get away.

After a few moments she stopped struggling. "Let me up," she said, laughing. "We'll both be soaked."

She opened her eyes, blinking the snow from her lashes. When she looked into his face, so close to her own, she could see a new expression in his eyes. An expression Meagan had never seen before.

"Josh? What is it? Have I made you angry?"

"Dang it, Meagan, do you know how pretty you are with your cheeks all red, your eyes so bright and your lips all red and shiny and just waiting like a juicy winter apple to be tasted?" He gave a little sob deep in his throat and knew in that moment that all the judges and courts in the world couldn't stop him.

If he couldn't taste those sweet lips, he'd surely die…!

Dear Reader,

This month we're celebrating love "against all odds" with these four powerful romances!

Since her debut with Harlequin in 1991 with *To Touch the Sun*, Barbara Leigh has written several more historical novels, but none of her previous romantic leads have had to overcome the kind of obstacles that Josh and Meagan do in *The Surrogate Wife*. Meagan is wrongfully convicted of murdering Josh's wife, and is sentenced to hang. In a moment of mercy, the judge orders her to a life of servitude to Josh, a single father in the Carolinas of 1790. So when the flame of love ignites between them, it's a matter of life or death that they keep it hidden....

The Midwife by Carolyn Davidson is the poignant story of a midwife who agrees to help out a stern farmer with his newborn after his wife dies in labor. They marry for convenience, yet later find a deep love, despite the odds. And don't miss *Lady of the Knight* by the talented Tori Phillips, about a courtly knight who buys a "soiled dove" and wagers that he can pass her off as a lady in ten days' time. Yet the more difficult charade lies in hiding his feelings for her!

Keep a hankie nearby while reading about past lovers Lily and Tristan in Catherine Archer's medieval novel, *Winter's Bride*. Long thought dead, the now amnesiac Lily is hired to care for Tristan's daughter—*her* daughter. Love shines anew as Lily's memory slowly dawns....

Whatever your tastes in reading, you'll be sure to find a romantic journey back to the past between the covers of a Harlequin Historicals® novel.

Sincerely,

Tracy Farrell
Senior Editor

Please address questions and book requests to:
Harlequin Reader Service
U.S.: 3010 Walden Ave., P.O. Box 1325, Buffalo, NY 14269
Canadian: P.O. Box 609, Fort Erie, Ont. L2A 5X3

BARBARA LEIGH

THE SURROGATE WIFE

HARLEQUIN®

TORONTO • NEW YORK • LONDON
AMSTERDAM • PARIS • SYDNEY • HAMBURG
STOCKHOLM • ATHENS • TOKYO • MILAN • MADRID
PRAGUE • WARSAW • BUDAPEST • AUCKLAND

ISBN 0-373-29078-0

THE SURROGATE WIFE

Copyright © 1999 by Barbara L. Jones

Visit us at www.romance.net

Printed in U.S.A.

Books by Barbara Leigh

Harlequin Historicals

To Touch the Sun #98
Web of Loving Lies #177
For Love Alone #254
For Love of Rory #297
The Surrogate Wife #478

BARBARA LEIGH

Born and raised in Nebraska, Barbara Leigh lived on both coasts before settling in California. She loves to write, read, travel and tramp through mansions, museums, ghost towns and castles. If it's old, there is bound to be a story there somewhere.

Barbara raised her family under the premise that there are only two gifts you can give your children: one gift is roots, the other, wings. So now that the children have grown up and flown the coop, Barbara shares life with her one-and-only husband, a bodacious cat, a precocious dog, her collection of Artists' dolls, the diverse activities of fifteen assorted grandchildren, and a vivid imagination.

To Vivian Doering

Chapter One

"We find the defendant, Meagan Anne Reilly, guilty of murder."

The jury foreman stared at the floor as he spoke, and jumped noticeably when the judge slammed his gavel down on the top of the big oak desk. There was no other sound in the schoolhouse that served as a courtroom, except for the nervous buzzing of the flies and the tiny gasp of the young woman who stood before the judge.

Judge Harvey Osborne rubbed his hand over his face. He hated this whole situation. It was bad enough sentencing a man to death, but hanging a young woman was definitely against everything he believed. Still, there was little choice. He took his watch from his pocket and opened the case as though looking at the time; however, it was not the hour Harvey Osborne was seeking, but reassurance. Silently he read the inscription: Let justice be done, though the heavens fall.

As always, the words gave him courage to do what must be done. Still, Judge Osborne cleared his throat twice before speaking. "I have no choice but to sentence you, Meagan Anne Reilly, to death by hanging and—"

He got no further, for Meagan Anne Reilly fell to the floor in a dead faint and heard no more.

In the rush that followed Meagan was lifted to a chair and held there while one of the village women waved a burned feather under her nose. As the fervor quieted the jury foreman raised his hand, waving it tentatively until he got the attention of the judge.

"Y-your Honor," he stammered, "the jury would like to suggest mercy for the defendant. We don't feel that Miss Reilly killed Lily Daniels on purpose. She had no motive to do something like that. Most like it was an accident of sorts."

Immediately the prosecutor was on his feet. "Your Honor, I object. This woman has committed murder. In an unprovoked fit of rage Miss Reilly struck Lily Daniels and shoved her down the stairs, leaving a bereaved husband and a motherless child. She refused to admit her guilt, although it's been proved beyond all reasonable doubt, and the murderess shows no signs of remorse. She must be punished!" The man warmed to his theme. "Think of the poor widower who must cook and clean and milk and plow while he tries to raise his child alone, without the help and succor of his beloved wife." He raised his hand, index finger pointed upward. "In the name of Josh Daniels and his daughter I demand retribution."

The attorney looked over the room as though expecting applause. There was a buzz of voices, and again the judge brought down his gavel as Meagan's lawyer jumped to his feet.

"Your Honor, my client cannot admit something of which she is not guilty. No one, including Meagan herself, saw Mrs. Daniels fall to her death. You cannot sentence a woman to hang for something even the jury doubts that she has done intentionally.''

''I have no doubt that she did it,'' The voice of Ruth Somers rang through the schoolroom. ''I saw her standing over poor Lily's body. I know what I saw!''

The crack of the gavel echoed above the sound of voices. ''Be quiet, all of you. Let me think on this a few minutes.''

Judge Osborne leaned back in his chair and scowled at the crowded room. The girl didn't deserve to die. It seemed as if her only crime had been one of panic. In all probability the ladies came in unexpectedly and caught the girl pilfering. In her haste to get away Meagan Reilly had likely knocked the fragile Lily flying as she tried to push past her and escape down the stairs.

If Meagan Reilly had lived in Banebridge for any length of time it would have been an entirely different matter, but the girl had been there but a few weeks, with little to recommend her other than good manners, a cheery disposition, a decent education and her willingness to work.

He sighed. Judge Osborne was not an exceedingly clever man, but he prided himself on being fair, and he didn't feel that sentencing the girl to death was fair. Unfortunately, he was unable to come up with a satisfactory alternative.

Justice was the name of the game—as it said in his watch case—and it was justice he was sworn to uphold. An eye for an eye. A life for a life.

His eyes fell on the bent head of the newly widowed husband. It would be difficult for the man to carry out the duties of his farm and family without the help of a woman, and women were few and far between. The child had been sent east to stay with relatives during the trial, but the man would want her back soon.

What Josh Daniels needed was a hired girl.

Judge Osborne's head jerked up and the room fell silent as surely as if he had struck his gavel.

"After taking the recommendation of the jury, as well as both lawyer arguments, under consideration, I have come to a decision." He paused dramatically and was pleased to see that the defendant had recovered enough to listen. "Having been found guilty of murder, and having the jury recommend mercy, in similar circumstances a man would be sentenced to life in prison. However, we have no prison facilities for women in the Carolinas. I therefore sentence Meagan Anne Reilly to serve her sentence by working for Josh Daniels and his family in such manner as they see fit. She will work without remuneration, other than bed and board and such clothing as is necessary."

"Why, that smacks of slavery!" one of the women said in an outraged whisper.

"You can't send a young woman to live with a single man," Meagan's lawyer burst out. "It's immoral!"

"I can and I will!" the judge shouted. "I cannot comprehend a man having sexual relations with the woman who killed his wife, but should Meagan Reilly manage to seduce Josh Daniels in an effort to lighten her lot, I will be forced to revert to the prescribed sentence of hanging, and Mr. Daniels will be held in contempt of court." With that the gavel fell again and the judge pushed his chair away from the teacher's desk and smiled in satisfaction.

Yes, sir, he'd done it again, thought Judge Harvey Osborne. Josh Daniels had a helpmate who would work right alongside him for the rest of her life and it wouldn't cost a cent, and Meagan Reilly wouldn't hang after all. He was still congratulating himself when he left the courtroom, oblivious to the shock, disbelief and hostility on the faces of the man and woman most directly involved.

"I refuse to have that woman in my house!" Josh slammed his fist on the table with such force that the pictures trembled on the schoolhouse walls.

"Would you rather see the girl hang?" Will Carmichael asked. He had served as Meagan's lawyer despite his close friendship with Josh.

"No! I don't want to see her hang." Josh pulled his fingers through his thick blond hair. "I don't want to see anybody hang. I'm sick of death."

Half the settlers in Banebridge Valley had passed on to their rewards during the past year. Lily's death had been only one more cross to bear. It was so senseless. So unnecessary.

"How dare the judge saddle me with a woman who suffers from fits of temper and refuses to admit her weakness?" Josh wondered aloud. "How dare he suggest that I leave my daughter in the care of the woman who is responsible for my wife's death."

"Just talk to the girl, Josh," Will suggested. "She isn't a bad sort. She's young and strong and looks to be healthy enough." He paused. "If you don't have her I'm going to ask the judge to let me take her into my home, but I'll tell you straight out, I don't think I have a chance. Judge Osborne has his mind made up. And the woman's life is on the line."

Josh sighed in resignation. "Abbie will stay with her grandparents until summer's end. I'll talk to the girl. If I can abide her presence I'll take her home with me. She can take over the chores. If she doesn't work out, I'll bring her back and you can deal with her."

"Josh, you know that half the people around these parts have served an indenture for one reason or another. There's hardly a family that doesn't have a servant who has been found guilty of some crime, and the settlers pay good money for their services."

"I've paid for this woman," Josh reminded him. "Paid with the loss of my wife."

Will nodded, breathing a silent prayer of gratitude that Judge Osborne had not known Lily Daniels, that he had considered her to have been a helpmate to her husband rather than a lovely hothouse flower. Had her true demeanor been known, the judge's decision might have been different. Especially since it was Josh who had done the baking, cooking and cleaning, as well as the chores and farming, while his wife had spent her time visiting the neighbors, playing the organ and haphazardly watching Abbie.

Most certainly, Josh would find having a helpmate a completely new experience.

Meagan stood as Will approached. The deputy stepped away to afford them some privacy, but Meagan's voice echoed through the room.

"I will not go!" she said firmly. "I would rather be dead than spend the rest of my life as a slave in punishment for a crime I did not commit."

"And that is exactly what will happen," her lawyer told her. "If you don't go with Josh there is no way I can save your pretty neck."

"I'll not be any man's slave," she reaffirmed, but her declaration fell on deaf ears, for the sentence had been handed down and the room cleared.

Will Carmichael took the girl's arm and guided her

from the schoolhouse. "Come, we'll get your belongings."

Josh Daniels watched them from across the schoolroom. He still intended to try to talk to the judge, if he could find the man before he was too deep in his cups to listen to reason. Surely Judge Osborne would see that the sentence he had imposed was impossible. Not that Josh wanted Meagan to die. Never that. It was just that he did not want her living with him, reminding him that if it wasn't for her, Lily would still be alive. Meagan's presence would be as great a punishment for Josh as the enforced service would be for her.

And, despite her size, Meagan was little more than a girl, with her bright brown eyes and golden brown hair. She was almost as tall as Will. She looked strong and capable. Perhaps that had gone against her. Not only with the court, but in Josh's mind, as well.

Lily had always looked as though the slightest breeze would blow her away. Josh knew he had been a fool to bring his wife into the wilderness and expect her to survive, much less thrive, in its harshness.

Meagan Reilly would survive. Her life might not be a happy one, but she would stay alive and earn her keep, and that was something. It was more than Lily had been granted.

As he glared at her across the room, Josh felt anger surge through his body, hard and unyielding, like molten steel.

Meagan stood in the doorway, clutching a bundle containing all her worldly possessions.

Will Carmichael was giving her some last-minute instructions. His voice droned on. Meagan no longer heard it. Her mind—her whole being—was focused on the man behind her. She could feel his eyes burrowing into her back. She could sense the hostility, the anger, the hatred.

She wanted to tell him that she had done nothing to deserve his hatred. She wanted to beg him to forgive her for being in the wrong place at the wrong time, but more than that, she wanted to slap the smug expression from his face. He was so self-righteous in his capacity as the bereaved widower, the grievously wronged party who suffered in silence. But Meagan had also been wronged.

She turned and her eyes caught his and held them with a question that seemed also to be a challenge.

Without dropping his gaze, Josh came toward them and stopped when Will Carmichael's hand dropped on his shoulder.

"She is young and strong, and should be a good worker," Will reminded Josh. "She can cook and sew and bake...." The unspoken premise that Meagan could do all the things Lily had not been willing to master hung in the air.

"I still don't want her in my house," Josh ground out the words.

"Let her sleep in the barn." Will laughed. "The judge didn't say she was to be treated as an honored guest. But Josh—" he sobered as he spoke "—don't be too hard on the girl. There is a question in my mind as to whether or not she is guilty. Something smacks of deception, but I was unable to ferret it out in the few days I had to build my case."

"You heard Ruth Somers," Josh fired back. "She knows what she saw. And she saw this woman kill my wife."

"Ruth saw what she wanted to see," Will grumbled, "just like she always does. It's just too bad Meagan hired on to help with Ruth's children. If she hadn't been there Ruth wouldn't have had such an easy scapegoat.''

Meagan gave Will a look of gratitude. But before she could speak, Josh grabbed her elbow and steered her toward the street, neither asking nor wanting to hear what Will Carmichael had meant by his words. A burst of laughter from down the street told him it was already too late to approach the judge.

''Get in the wagon,'' Josh ordered. ''And you can stop making sheep's eyes at Will Carmichael. He can't help you anymore.''

And neither can I, he added silently.

When it came right down to it, Josh Daniels suddenly realized he was unable to help himself, for when he touched Meagan Reilly a bolt of unwanted attraction shot through him that boded no good for either of them.

He drew a deep breath and climbed onto the seat of the wagon. God knew he wouldn't have such untimely, and unwelcome, surges had Lily been able to fulfill her duties as his wife. But ever since Abbie's dangerous birth she had been unable to receive him as her husband. And now Lily was dead, and the law of the land had given to Josh a young woman bursting with life and health and, God help him, an earthy sexuality to which a man would have to be dead not to respond.

If he were smart he would follow the judge and demand that, drunk or sober, the man rescind his order and give the girl over to Will Carmichael and his wife, with whom she had stayed while waiting for the judge to arrive to preside over her trial.

But where women were concerned, Josh Daniels was not a smart man. There was no question about the fact that he needed the help. Nor was there a question that he would have accepted assistance from any soul on the face of the earth rather than Meagan Reilly.

He wondered how long she would stay with him before bolting into the wilderness. Personally, he knew he would take his chances with the Indians before he'd work as another man's slave. He glanced down in time to see Meagan toss her bundle into the back of the wagon. She was about to follow when his voice stopped her.

"Get up here on the seat beside me," he ordered brusquely. "I don't want to get home and find you gone."

He clucked to the horses as she scrambled into the seat. The wagon hit every rut as they followed the road out of town.

Meagan was perched on the very edge of the seat, putting every available inch of room between herself and Josh Daniels. With each jolt of the wagon he expected to see her disappear over the side and fall beneath the wheels, or run for open country. He pulled the wagon to a halt.

"Look, Miss Reilly, I don't want to be responsible for your death either through an accident if you fall off the seat and under the wagon wheels, or through your foolishness should you decide to try to run away. Now get enough of your body on the seat so that I can be sure you're not going to kill yourself on this bumpy road, or I'll be forced to tie you in the back of the wagon."

Meagan shot him a venomous look but she did allow herself a bit more of the seat. They rode through the afternoon, stopping only to rest the horses and allow them to drink at the plentiful streams.

Meagan's eyes scanned the horizon. How she longed for the sight of her brother. But Reilly had gone to join his mother's people and it was doubtful that he would have heard of her plight. Still shocked and confused by the situation that had ended in her conviction, Meagan tried to focus on anything other than the unbelievable circumstances in which she found herself.

Josh reached into his haversack and brought out some bread and cheese, which he thrust toward her. "Chew it slowly," he cautioned, "and make it last. There will be little else until after we get home."

"Home," Meagan repeated as though the word were new.

"What did you say?" Josh asked.

"I said *home*. I don't remember ever going home before."

Josh raised his eyebrows. "Surely you must have had a home somewhere."

"Father was a schoolteacher. When I was small we often lived on the school grounds, or in the school itself. Perhaps if my mother had lived we would have had a real home, but after her death Father decided he had a calling to educate the Indians. We lived in a tepee with an Indian woman for a while. She was the mother of my half brother."

"Is that why you killed Lily?" he asked without taking his eyes from the road. "Because you were jealous of her home?"

His words hit her like a face full of cold water. "I didn't kill your wife, Mr. Daniels, and I've never seen your home. You will remember that it was at the house of your neighbor, Ruth Somers, that your wife went to her reward."

Josh jerked the reins so abruptly that the team shied in confusion. "Death was never meant to be a *reward* to my wife. She was filled with life and vivacity."

"Apparently everyone didn't see her in quite the same light," Meagan commented, positive that her words would be lost in Josh's efforts to control the panicked horses.

Josh managed to quiet the animals. Then he turned to Meagan. "If we are to keep from leaping at each other's throats, Miss Reilly, I suggest we keep our opinions regarding my wife's death to ourselves. I believe you are responsible for her death, either deliberately or by accident."

"And I believe you are a bigger fool than you look to be," Meagan fired back.

"If I turn you back to the judge you will hang," he threatened, though he knew the words to be beneath him.

"You need someone to work your land and tend your house and care for your daughter," Meagan reminded him. "There are no single women within a hundred miles of here, and a man would want a full share for the work you'll get from me for nothing. I don't think you can afford to send me away."

Josh's jaw hardened, along with his heart. The girl was too damned smart for her own good. He did need help, and the presence of a woman who could cook and clean, as well as tend the livestock, would be a tremendous asset. "Very well, then," he grumbled. "You will stay as long as you put in a fair day's work. I don't expect you to do any more than I do."

"That sounds just," she agreed.

"I am up an hour before dawn. You will be ready to help with the morning chores."

Josh Daniels continued talking, but Meagan didn't respond to his words. Her mind had traveled back in time to the days of her childhood. Life in the Indian village had been relaxed and carefree. As the only white child, she was looked upon as somewhat of a curiosity. The Indian children enjoyed teaching her their games and skills. Her father, a teacher, was a respected man in the tribe and his choice of taking one of their women as his wife was accepted with favour.

Then smallpox had all but wiped the tribe from the face of the earth. Even Meagan's stepmother had died, but Meagan, her father and half brother were not touched by the sickness. The Indians—what few there were left—began to look upon them askance. Why had the white man and his children been spared?

The day the old chief died, James Reilly took his children and left the village. His wife and his credibility had gone before him, and it was prudent to move on. But while the Indians had been willing to accept and share their lives with the little white child, the white people were not willing to share their lives, or, for that matter, their towns, with a half-breed Indian boy and his family. And they certainly did not want the boy's father teaching their children.

When Meagan was old enough she hired out, taking care of children and helping the women with their spring and fall housecleaning. After her father's death Meagan's brother decided to leave the world of the white man and return to his mother's tribe. Having been educated by her father, Meagan was qualified to supply an education to the children of a household as well as carry her share of the work.

She had come to Banebridge hoping to obtain a permanent position teaching children. Her search had taken her into the wilderness where Ruth Somers had offered employment. During Meagan's first week, Lily Daniels had pitched down the Somerses' stairs. Meagan had run from the kitchen to help and was bending over the unfortunate woman when Ruth began screaming for her husband and accused Meagan of murder.

And now Meagan was going to a place that would be her home and her prison.

Meagan had always thought that someday she would have a man and a home of her own. Now that dream would never come to pass. Slaves didn't have homes. Indentured servants weren't allowed the freedom of choosing a husband. Her life was over before it had a chance to begin.

She closed her eyes and tried to squeeze out one more prayer for salvation, aware that the prayers with which she had barraged heaven over the past weeks had apparently fallen on deaf ears. Surely the Lord hadn't received her messages, for he hadn't taken the time to answer.

The horses, tired at the end of the day, slowed to little more than a walk as they pulled the heavily laden wagon up a steep hill.

Meagan wouldn't have tried to jump from the wagon as they clipped along the road coming out of town, but now she might—if she could jump clear and somehow make her way through the woods to the Indian village where Reilly, her half brother, had gone.

As the horses crested the hill, Meagan threw herself from the wagon and ran for the woods. The air burned like fire in her lungs as she raced through the trees and across the streams.

Josh crashed through the brush behind her. Closer, ever closer, as Meagan's breathing became increasingly shallow and the pain in her side caused her to favor her right leg.

Meagan was younger than her pursuer. There was no reason why she shouldn't be able to outrun him. But his persistence defeated her, and in the end she looked back to see him less than ten feet behind. Then, she missed her footing and plunged down an embankment into the icy water below.

She could hear his ragged breathing even before he pulled her from the stream.

"What in the hell possessed you to do such a damn fool thing?" he asked as he set her on her feet.

She brushed a muddy hand across her face and tried to fight back the tears.

"If you were going to run away, why didn't you run when you were closer to a settlement? There's nothing out here. There's no place to run. You wouldn't last the week. If the Indians didn't get you, the animals would." He gave her a little push and marched stoically along beside her, his hand grasping the thick rope of hair that had fallen down her back. "I thought I was doin' you a favor by keeping you from hanging. Are you crazy or something?"

He grumbled with each step he took and became more verbose as his breath returned right along with his anger.

But his fury was no match for hers. She was angry with him, angry with herself and angry at the world in general.

"No, Mr. Daniels, I'm not crazy. No more than you. I just don't want to spend the rest of my life working as your slave."

Josh stopped and turned the girl toward him. She was a sorry-looking sight, with her dripping clothes, muddy face and red-rimmed eyes.

"If you'll remember, Miss Reilly, I didn't ask for your indenture. And, I guess if it were me, I would have done the same thing. But I'm a man, and at least I would have had a chance of survival in the wilderness. You don't!

If I thought you did, I just might let you go and save us both a lot of grief.'' He sighed as he realized she was shivering noticeably. "As it is, if I don't get you warmed up, and quick, neither of us will have to worry about you ever being an indentured servant because you won't live long enough for me to get you home."

Again he nudged her forward. "Now get a move on. We'll camp in the clearing near the wagon."

Meagan did as she was told. She knew she had been foolish to try to run away, but even her senseless act did not affect her as much as did the words Josh had spoken in trying to quiet her as they walked back.

What sort of man was this who would actually admit that not only did he understand the reasoning behind what she had done, but in like circumstances, he would have done the same? She watched him from the corner of her eye, wondering what the outcome of her failed escape would ultimately be. But the expression on Josh Daniels's face told her nothing, nor did the tone of his voice, which was flat and without emotion as he told her to gather kindling so he could get a fire started.

Before she could move away she heard him give a deep sigh, and with a look of resignation on his handsome face, he looped a rope around her waist, giving her several yards of slack before securing the other end about his own body.

Meagan was unable to suppress the sob that rose to her lips.

"What's wrong now?" he demanded impatiently.

She lifted the rope in her hand. "Now I truly feel like a slave," she replied.

Josh looked at Meagan. He looked at the rope and then he said, "So do I!"

* * *

With Meagan lashed to his belt, Josh managed to turn the horse out to graze, make a fire and distribute the last of the pemmican and bread between them. He then spread blankets on the ground and motioned Meagan to lie down on one of them while he stretched his body across the other.

"You can't expect me to sleep there," she squeaked as she realized his intention. "The judge specifically forbade us to sleep together."

Josh looked at the girl. At first he thought she was trying to pull a fast one, but the concern on her face and the tears reflected in her eyes told him different.

"We're not sleeping together. You have your blanket, I have mine. Now be quiet and go to sleep." He handed her an extra blanket, but Meagan remained standing, unsure as to the exact meaning of Judge Osborne's orders.

In pure exasperation, Josh gave the rope a tug and toppled the girl over onto him.

"Jumpin' Jehoshaphat, you're freezing!" He jumped to his feet, dragging her with him. "Get out of that wet dress," he ordered. Then, seeing the look on her face, added, "You got something more to wear, don't you?"

Meagan had other clothes, but she certainly couldn't change into them while bound to this man's belt like a partridge.

"You'll have to untie me so I can change," Meagan told him. "I can't get my clothing off or on trussed up with this rope."

Josh grumbled all the way to the wagon as they retrieved her bundle. The minute he untied Meagan he expected her to run. "Will you give me your word that you won't try to escape again?"

Meagan's eyes searched the shadows. The fact that she did not care to explore the dangers of the night reflected in her expression. "I won't try to run away," she promised.

"Very well." He thrust the bundle of clothes into her arms and untied the noose about her waist. "If you try to run this time I'll never believe another thing you say."

"You haven't believed anything up to now, so what's the difference?" she asked aloud, but for some reason, there was a difference.

With all her worldly possessions in her arms, Meagan had actually given consideration to trying once more to escape. Nothing had seemed as devastating as spending the rest of her life in virtual slavery. But Josh's threat never to believe her brought her up short.

It mattered that Josh should know he could believe her. It mattered that he might someday be willing to trust her, regardless of the circumstances that had thrust them together. "I told you I wouldn't run away again," she said defensively, and slipped behind the questionable protection of a small bush where she changed into dry clothing.

After spreading her dress near the warmth of the fire, Meagan realized that Josh had taken her at her word and spread her blankets on the side of the fire opposite his. With a grateful smile she lay down and pulled the blanket over her shoulders. Even with the warmth of the little fire the night was cool, and her teeth continued their incessant chattering no matter how she tried to silence them. The dress she wore was lightweight gingham and did little to protect her from the cold.

The tribulations of the previous weeks had taken their toll, and even though Meagan fell into a troubled sleep her thoughts would not allow her to rest.

As the night wore on a light rain began to fall. Josh

cursed under his breath. Above the sounds of the night he could hear Meagan's teeth chattering and the little sobs she emitted during her sleep.

Picking up his bedding, Josh got to his feet and went over to awaken the girl. "Come with me," he ordered once she opened her eyes, her expression a mixture of bewilderment and dread.

Obediently Meagan followed, half dragging her damp blankets. Josh threw an oilcloth under the wagon and quickly spread his blanket over it. "Get under there." He shoved her toward the wagon and she obeyed without argument.

Even when he joined her beneath the shelter of the wagon she did not speak. It never occurred to Josh that she had clamped her mouth closed so he would not hear her teeth chatter. But Meagan could not hold her mouth closed forever, and before she could be certain Josh was sleeping her teeth again began clacking in her mouth and her body shook so violently she could have sworn it shook the ground.

She felt the tears squeeze from her eyes and burn down her cheeks. Then a hand closed on her shoulder and rolled her onto her side.

Without a word Josh pressed her against the warmth of his body. Within minutes his body heat permeated her clothing, skin and bones. She wanted to object to the close proximity. She knew she should object, but his warmth was like a narcotic. The chill dissipated from her body, leaving it soft and pliable against his. Her whole being relaxed as she inhaled the scent of buckskin, brandy and man.

For the first time since the death of her father, Meagan was able to relax. Her fate had been decided for her. Her future laid out without any possibility of deviation. She might spend the rest of her life serving this man and his family, but she would never stop trying to prove her innocence. The very fact that she was to remain near the scene of Lily's death gave her hope that someday she would find a way to clear her name.

She felt herself drifting off to sleep and forced herself to whisper drowsily, "The judge said we shouldn't sleep together."

Josh absently patted her arm. "Don't worry about it," he said. "I'm not going to sleep." And he knew it was true, because the sweet agony of again holding a woman's soft body in his arms was enough to keep him from batting an eye—especially a woman who had caused his wife's death. The memory would no doubt haunt him for many sleepless nights to come.

Chapter Two

They rose with the sun. After breaking their fast, Meagan gathered up her dress and climbed up onto the wagon seat where Josh waited. Without a word they started off down the rutted road toward their destination. But the day was all but spent when Josh finally drew Meagan from her reverie. "There it is," he said.

Meagan's eyes swept the valley below.

The land was rich and fertile. The green of the grass and trees was vibrant, and the earth black and rich.

Josh skillfully guided the horses along the narrow road, opened the gates and stopped the wagon between the house and the barn.

Meagan glanced around. The outbuildings consisted of a barn, chicken house, several covered stalls for animals, a smokehouse and outhouse. The double cabin was really two buildings connected by a dogtrot.

She wondered if Josh would actually make her stay in the barn as had been suggested before they left town. She glanced at him surreptitiously but he paid her little mind as he climbed from the seat of the wagon and started toward the house, every line of his body alert for whatever he might encounter.

He pulled the nails from the boards that held the doors and windows shut. Putting the nails in his pouch, he stacked the boards beneath the steps and turned to Meagan.

"Get yourself down from there," he ordered. "Seems safe enough."

"Safe from what?" Meagan asked as she clambered from the wagon and grabbed her belongings.

"Indians! What else?"

"Oh," she scoffed. "Indians. I've never had any trouble with them."

"Then you've never met Old Howling Dog." Josh pushed the door open and went inside.

Meagan hesitated on the porch before following.

Josh didn't bother to look at her as he threw open the shutters on the windows, allowing the fresh breeze to stir the dust in the room. "Indians aren't going to ask who you are or whether you like them. They aren't real happy that we're living on their land. Old Howling Dog wants us gone, and I'm expecting him to make a move to try to see it happens real soon now."

Meagan swallowed, her false bravado lost in the reality of his words. "I'll keep my eyes open," she managed, realizing for the first time the vast difference between what her life had been and what it would be now.

Without another word she took off her bonnet and surveyed her surroundings. A musty, cloying odor permeated the air and Meagan decided that perhaps sleeping in the barn wouldn't be so bad after all.

There was a thin film of dust on the floor mingled with a sprinkling of mouse droppings. The room boasted a fireplace, bookshelves, wooden chest, two armchairs, a table and a desk. Near the window stood a little organ, and it was all Meagan could do to keep from crying out in joy over the discovery.

Before she could speak, Josh opened a small door on the far wall opposite the fireplace. Meagan followed more slowly. It seemed odd that a home could show so little sign of being lived in, for her trial had taken very little time, considering everything, and Josh couldn't have been away long enough to account for this stuffiness.

She followed him, wondering how to ask about the room when she found herself on a little dogtrot. A second door opened onto the rear cabin, which Meagan had thought to be a shed since Josh had piled logs for the fire down the side.

She crowed with delight when she popped her head into the smaller room. This one was steeped with warmth from the sun and the spicy smell of life.

There was a fireplace with a cook oven built into the brick. Pots and pans, along with metal utensils and wooden basins, hung from the wall and were stacked neatly on the shelves.

A heavy wooden sink beckoned invitingly as Josh picked up a bucket and headed toward the stream some distance away.

The table was polished to a warm hue. The chairs were solid. A heavy blanket hung along one wall and when Meagan peeked behind it she saw two beds. In the far corner on the other side of the room there was a straw mattress covered with a knit shawl.

A chill ran through her body. It was almost as though Josh Daniels had been expecting to bring her back. But of course, that was ridiculous. He could not have known the judge would give such an order.

''Start a fire and get some water boiling. There's cornmeal in the keg over by the dry sink." He looked at her and took a deep breath. "You know how to make mush, don't you?"

Meagan felt the color rise in her cheeks. "Yes, sir, I do." She set her jaw and took the kettle from the hook.

"Fine, then make it."

Josh went outside, unhitched the horses and set them loose in the pasture nearest the house as Meagan washed the pot. The fire was burning brightly when he stopped at the narrow back door.

"Good," he said as he saw her progress. "I'm going to go down to the river and bring back the livestock."

He caught her questioning look. "I drive them down there when I'm going to be gone a spell. There are good strong pens and the Indians aren't likely to bother them there."

"Do you want me to go with you?" Meagan was aware that he hadn't let her out of his sight for more than a few minutes.

"You goin' to run?"

"No. What good would it do me?"

Josh nodded his head. "Wouldn't be no help to either one of us," he told her. "You got any questions before I leave?"

Megan's eyes scanned the horizon. Her eyes lit on a thin spiral of smoke rising above the treetops some distance away. Was this evidence of Indians? Perhaps a neighbor. Perhaps it was someone who had not heard the accusations and would judge Meagan for herself, not condemn her because of a vindictive woman's lies. Meagan tried to smother the hope that sprang up within her.

"What is that smoke in the distance?" she asked.

"That's from the chimney of my nearest neighbors,

Rafe and Ruth Somers.'' Without looking back Josh went out the door and through the yard toward the river.

The hope fluttered and died in Meagan's heart. It was bad enough being the slave of a man who hated her for something she hadn't done, but having as her nearest neighbor the woman whose testimony had brought her to such dire straits was the last straw.

Meagan measured the cornmeal and water into the pot, put it on the crane and swung it over the fire. There had to be a way to prove her innocence, and somehow she was going to find it, or die trying.

Much to Meagan's dismay, it wasn't long before Ruth Somers made her way to the Daniels cabin.

Ruth was a short woman, with a body that reminded Meagan of the masthead on a ship, full-figured and solid. Her dark hair was pulled into a tight bun on the back of her head. Her eyes gleamed with malevolence as she swept from her wagon and advanced on the house.

Meagan didn't want to face the woman and took as much time as possible before going to the door. It was obvious that Ruth Somers was familiar with the living arrangements of the Daniels house because she bypassed the parlor and went directly to the door at the far end of the dogtrot, where she hammered her fist against the heavy boards, demanding admission.

Reluctantly Meagan opened the door and faced her nemesis. She didn't speak, but Ruth Somers did.

''So, you haven't run away after all. I was about to go to the fort and set up the hue and cry.'' She swept past Meagan into the room.

''I'm sure that would have given you a great deal of satisfaction,'' Meagan commented.

"It would also have made you look like a fool." Josh's voice suddenly rang through the room.

Ruth swung around at the sound of his voice. Her haughty attitude diminished somewhat in his presence. As a woman with a dominant and volatile husband, Ruth knew her place where men were concerned.

"Josh, I thought you'd be out working the land," she managed.

"And so you came to intimidate my servant, is that it?"

"I simply dropped by to make sure the girl was doing her job and hadn't poisoned you with her cooking, or stabbed you in your sleep," Ruth protested, but the words were said with a brittle smile.

Josh went to stand near the hearth where a pot of stew simmered on the hob. He wondered why he was standing up for Meagan against his wife's friend.

Without being asked, Ruth sat down beside the table. "I'll have a cup of tea." She tossed the words at Meagan, who cast a quick glance toward Josh before taking the water kettle from the back of the fire. "Now, what did you mean when you said I would look like a fool?" She folded her hands over her belly and leaned back in the chair, looking like a well-dressed beetle.

Josh softened his attitude toward the portly little woman. After all, Ruth had been Lily's best friend. It was to be expected that the woman would wreak vengeance on the person she deemed responsible for Lily's death.

"Meagan often works the fields with me. Sometimes we're away from the house from dawn till dusk."

Ruth gave a derisive sniff. "That will all end when little Abigail returns, I assume. Although I wouldn't allow an indentured felon the care of one of my children."

Meagan literally bit her tongue to keep from saying that had it not been for Ruth Somers, she wouldn't have been convicted in the first place. She longed to ask the woman why she had made such wild accusations and was almost ready to do so when Josh guessed her intent and shook his head, silently warning Meagan to be silent.

Ruth was oblivious to the whole situation and continued her harangue regarding the return of Josh's little daughter.

"I think you should let the child come and stay with me. I could give her a good home and a warm and natural family life. She'd even have children of her own age to play with." Ruth warmed to her theme, throwing her sons into the bargain. "Far better off with me than living in her father's house with a murderess."

"Abbie won't come back until the end of the summer. By that time most of the work will be done and I will be here in the house to keep an eye on things." And then he asked what Meagan had not dared to. "Why are you so hostile toward Meagan? You admitted that you hardly knew the girl when you took her to your home, and that you had thought to hire her permanently if she had shown herself to be a good worker."

Ruth dabbed her eyes with a wisp of linen. "The girl caused the death of my friend. What's more, she did so in my home. I cannot abide the sight of her." She glared in Meagan's direction.

"Then turn your back, Ruth, because I'm afraid that as long as she causes me no trouble, Meagan is here to stay."

"I'd be more than willing to speak to Judge Osborne," Ruth offered. "Perhaps I could talk him into hanging her instead of leaving you saddled with a criminal for the rest of your life.''

The teacup rattled against the saucer as Meagan placed it on the table. She took a deep breath. The hatred and something more that she couldn't name emanated from the guest. How she wished that Josh would say something more on her behalf, but he only shrugged his shoulders. Perhaps he felt the same way and managed better to contain his anger and his hatred for his indentured servant. Meagan had no way of knowing. Surely his demeanor toward her had been clipped and abrupt as he had given orders as to what he expected done about the house.

Meagan had done what she could to avoid making Josh repeat his instructions, and only asked questions when she did not fully comprehend what he had said. He had no quarrel with her work or her willingness, and she knew it. However, he apparently had little compassion for her plight, for rather than refute Ruth's suggestion about having Meagan hanged, he simply went on talking about the crops and the livestock and then to ask about her husband, Rafe.

A pot of tea later, Ruth prepared to leave.

Josh helped the woman into her wagon and held the reins as she arranged her ample posterior across the seat. ''I want you to know that should there be any question of Abbie's safety I will expect you to bring her to me right away. And see that you remember,'' she admonished as she wagged her finger at him, clucked to the horses and was on her way.

Josh started back toward the house where Meagan stood framed in the doorway.

''Now what do you suppose *that* was all about?'' they

said in unison. And, realizing what they had done, their laughter, also in unison, echoed over the little valley.

A short distance down the road Ruth Somers caught the sound and pulled her horse to a halt to listen. Of course, she couldn't be sure it was laughter she heard, but Meagan *was* attractive and Josh was still young. She would have to keep an eye on them. After all, Judge Osborne had said that should Meagan Reilly seduce Josh or, most likely any other man, it would mean the hangman's tree for her.

Yes, Ruth would have to keep her eyes open, but more than that, she would have to make sure she kept her own husband far away from the Daniels household. For the girl was young and pretty, and Rafe Somers was only a man.

Life in the Daniels house had fallen quite easily into place. Josh was not a vindictive man, and while he resented the girl's presence to a certain degree, he could not deny that her willingness to work and make the best of a bad situation had made life a great deal easier for him. He often wondered what she was thinking as her great dark eyes followed him. She could be spunky, as he had discovered on their trip home from Banebridge. Josh saw no reason to make the situation any more difficult for either of them, so he did not question her any further about her part in Lily's death. Instead, he went about his own business and made sure she tended to hers.

It had not taken Meagan long to discover that the cozy little room at the back of the house was the hub of the home. The front room had apparently been used only on special occasions. She dreaded going into the musty

shadows to sleep even though it had the best feather bed
in the house.

She lay stiffly on the bed, jumping at every creak and
snap of the night-filled house. She dared not say a word
about her nervousness, for Josh would surely believe her
fears were caused by a guilty conscience rather than her
inherent fear of being alone in the dark. A fear she had
not been able to outgrow since childhood.

The only thing she feared worse was a storm. The
apex of her fears struck before the week was out.

The wind was already moaning through the trees
when she hurried across the little dogtrot and closed the
door. The room was tight and sound. She would close
her ears to the storm and pull the blankets up over her
head and go to sleep, she promised herself.

Meagan pulled the blankets up, but the wind whined
and sobbed, and then began lashing the house when it
failed to disturb the human creatures who dared build a
house in its domain.

For all Meagan's promises she found her eyes wide
open and her hands clenched against the feather bed. The
wind and rain continued to strike the house. Tree
branches bent and cracked as they whipped the house in
fury. The wind seemed to come from all sides as it
fought to find a chink in the walls. At the height of the
storm Meagan heard the sound.

It groaned through the room. First one note, then two,
and finally a full chord resounding in ghostly pleasure
above the storm.

Meagan leaped from the bed. She stood in the middle
of the floor as the lightning lit the night in unearthly
splendor. The sound faded as Meagan backed toward the
door, her eyes locked on the area where she knew the
organ to be.

Once again the notes began, increasing in intensity until they drowned out even the wind. As they reached their highest intensity Meagan gave a yelp and dashed into the night.

Many times she had heard the Indians speak of the souls of the dead who found no peace and walked the earth during the storms. And though she knew no guilt in Lily's death, she had been forced by the living to assume the blame, and she wasn't about to see what punishment the dead might conceive.

The rain blew against her with full fury as she threw herself against the door to the room in which Josh slept. Her fingers slipped from the wet latch. She beat against the wood.

"Josh! Josh! Let me in!" she screamed. She rattled the useless latch as she hollered and banged, aware that the organ continued to sound out its ghastly melody.

"What in the hell is going on here?"

The door burst open against her pounding hands, and Meagan fell into Josh Daniels's arms. She could feel the smooth warmth of his skin against her hands and buried her face against his chest to try to escape the sound that seemed to follow her. She felt his hand press ever so gently against her head, stroking her hair as though she were a frightened child. His other hand rested on her back, firmly, holding her against him as she relished the warmth and safety she knew when he enfolded her. The hair on his chest brushed her cheek and tickled her nose but she only burrowed closer, desperately trying to shut out the terror of the night. Her sobs quieted and she fought to gain control of herself, to curb her childish fears. She longed to stay with him as she had the night they had spent under the wagon, but she would be happy to sleep next to the fireplace in the kitchen if he was nearby to fend off the fearsome sounds of the night. But it was not to be, for although Meagan found safety in the arms of Josh Daniels's, his reaction to Meagan was the exact opposite.

The lightning brightened the night and he could see the tears of terror on her face. "What is it?" he asked more gently.

"The organ...someone's playing the organ. I heard them."

"Nobody ever played that thing except Lily," Josh said in exasperation. "What you heard was the wind."

He wanted to push her away from him. He wanted to separate himself from the vibrant body that molded its lush, young curves against him. He wanted the cool softness as far away as possible before the spark dared to ignite and destroy them both. He could feel her face against his chest. Her hand brushed his taut nipple before her face burrowed into his chest.

He stroked her hair hoping to comfort her and restore her self-confidence so that he could put her from him and send her back to her room.

She trembled and he felt her legs wobble. He pressed her more closely against him, taking deep breaths, willing his body not to notice that her breasts had warmed and were burning orbs of fire against his naked chest. His hand slipped down her back, following the curves of her body, tracing them ever so gently but in a way he knew he would never be able to forget.

How could a man forget the resiliency of her skin, which was even more exciting through the thin, wet material of her cotton nightdress? How could a man forget the touch of her breath against his skin, heated with promise forever unfulfilled?

She sagged in his arms as her fear began to leave her. He moved to hold her weight and his leg was suddenly encased between the heat of her thighs. His head swam with desire. His blood pounded above the sound of the storm as it raced through his body, erasing the threat of punishment, any hope of reason or memory of decency in the headlong sweep of passion.

Oh, God, it had been so long since he had burned for a woman, and never, never as he did in this moment, with this woman whose body was like a torch that ignited his whole being. Blood surged through him, blocking out the ability to think. He didn't want to think. He only wanted to feel. To feel her, to know her, to become part of her and to hear her cry out in her passion for him as she cried out for his comfort against her fears.

Her fears! If she feared the sounds of the storm, how much more greatly would she fear the gallows tree? And he would bring her to it, to be faced alone by the sick desire of a man for the murderer of his own wife.

With his last ounce of resolve, and dredging the depths of his soul for hard-held decency, he placed his hands on her shoulders and pushed her from him.

He looked down into her face, taking in her eyes wet with tears, her cheeks flushed with fear and her lips parted, begging to be kissed. His body throbbed with his need for her. Were it not for the judge's order, Meagan would be his, now, right here on the dogtrot, and again on the bed, and...

God in heaven, he was going mad. She was driving him wild. The whole situation was too much to bear, and if he could get his hands on Harvey Osborne he'd tear him limb from limb for imposing such an impossible sentence on a heretofore law-abiding, God-fearing man.

"I don't hear anything," he managed. And the Lord

knew that was the truth. The blood was pounding so loudly in his head he couldn't have heard a full-fledged Indian attack.

He took a few steps down the dogtrot, dragging the reluctant Meagan with him.

"Somebody was playing the organ," Meagan gasped. "I heard it."

"You heard the wind in the trees," he assured her. "Now go on back to bed. We'll have a long day tomorrow cleaning up after this storm."

He shoved her inside the room and closed the door, desperate to put as much distance between them as possible.

Meagan started toward the bed, but before she reached it she heard the first note begin to swell.

This time she hit the door full tilt and stood shivering in the middle of the dogtrot. It would do no good to appeal to Josh. It was obvious he wanted as little to do with her as possible. Ignoring the pounding rain, she ran out into the storm.

Josh lay back on his bed and closed his eyes. He shut out the storm and the vision of Meagan's face as she had looked into his eyes…into his soul.

He could still feel her flesh against his hands, cool and firm. His body ached to hold her again. He longed to go to her, to ease her childish fears of noises in the night. But he knew he did not dare. He would shut her from his mind, and in the light of day the night's desires would evaporate like the shadows.

He forced himself to concentrate on the chores that would need to be done after a storm of this magnitude. There was always damage from the rain. The streams would be up and the trees down. They would have their work cut out for them for some days to come unless he missed his guess.

He took deep breaths as he mentally listed the tools he would need. His heart had stopped slamming against his chest as some semblance of sanity returned. He welcomed the relief sleep offered and allowed himself to drift on the edge of slumber until a persistent banging caught his attention.

Irritated, he pulled the pillow around his ears. He did not want to leave his bed again, but the pounding did not cease.

At first he thought it might be Meagan hammering at the door for admittance, but as awareness became prevalent he realized the sound was too distant. There was a hesitation but just as he relaxed it began again. Something had broken loose and was banging against the house.

He rolled over and sat on the side of the bed. Josh had to see what had happened and if it could be curbed before it did more damage. He pulled on his breeches and opened the door. The storm still raged, but Josh saw immediately the source of the sound.

With a curse, he crossed the dogtrot to where the door to Meagan's room swung back and forth in the wind. It didn't take him long to make sure that he was correct in his assumption. The room was empty. Meagan was gone.

Chapter Three

"From now on you can sleep behind the curtain in the larger bed," Josh told Meagan the next morning as he sat drinking coffee and resting his head in his hand, his eyes bleary with lack of sleep. "I'll take the cot out here."

He'd searched half the night, believing that she had run away. Expecting with every step he took to find her lying dead in the mud and rain. Blaming himself for not having more control of himself and sending the frightened girl to face her fears alone when she had come to him for help.

The rain had disappeared with the night, and as the watery sun fought its way through the tops of the trees, Josh had wearily made his way to the barn. The cow had to be milked and the chores done. He'd never tell her how relieved he was when he saw her curled up under a blanket in the hay. He'd never admit that he stood there and just feasted his eyes on her as she slept in exhausted innocence. But he would never allow himself to forget that he had promised the good Lord that if he found her safe he'd never take another chance on being alone with her in a situation that might lead to dishonor and death.

And so, in the dim light of morning he burned her sleeping image into his mind and his heart, knowing he would never again dare hold her in his arms.

Even now, in the broad light of day, with the homey sounds and smells of breakfast surrounding them, Josh could hardly bear the pain of denial. He fought to keep his mind on his grits and eggs and off the woman who had prepared them.

"I don't mind sleeping in the barn," she was saying. "Besides, I have to get up early and start breakfast and…"

He shook his head. "There's no need," he told her. "I'm used to rising before anyone else is up. Lily was never one to rise with the sun. It takes me a bit to get myself together." He paused and gave the matter some thought. "In fact, I'd be more comfortable if you didn't bother to get up at the first crack of dawn. I'll go out and start the chores. You can make breakfast, and have it ready when I come in. After that we'll both start our day."

Meagan nodded in agreement. But before she could speak he added, "And you will sleep behind the curtain."

The blanket that separated them was adequate, and while Meagan was sure that Josh could not see through it to where she slept, Meagan was able to see him outlined against the light of the fire as he pulled his shirt over his head and got ready for bed.

The night was warm, and Meagan knew that sleeping near the fire must be uncomfortable. But it was his choice. She closed her eyes and drifted off to sleep. It seemed but a few minutes when she was awakened by a sound.

Through a chink in the curtain she could see Josh moving around the room. He stirred the fire and swung the hob with the kettle on it over the flame. She realized it must be morning and was about to get up when she remembered his instruction. Silently she lay back on the bed, but sleep would not come and she found herself watching Josh as he moved about the room.

She followed the movement of his body as the light of the flames touched his chest and arms, his rippling muscles, flat belly and smooth skin that looked so warm and delicious in the firelight. She closed her eyes. The very fact that she dared allow such thoughts to exist was dangerous, if not life-threatening in her situation.

But her eyes would not stay shut. They devoured the man with a mind of their own, and she forgot even to breathe as he placed a basin on the table and washed his face and chest.

The firelight caught the droplets of water that clung to the golden hair across his chest. Like tiny jewels, the water tempted her. She felt the urge to run her fingers through his hair and take the water onto her own skin, still warm from his.

The thought made her squirm. The rope tether that cradled the mattress on the frame of the bed gave a muted groan and Josh looked toward the curtain, but Meagan had rolled over and pulled the comforter over her head in an effort to smother the shameful thoughts proximity with this man had placed in her mind.

She allowed herself the painful pleasure of remembering the feeling of warmth and security she had known when Josh had taken her into his arms that night as she lay shivering beneath the wagon. She had tried to forget.

Heaven knew, she had tried to put the whole thing out of her mind. And, for the most part she had done so. It wasn't her mind that refused to obey. It was her body. Her sinful body remembered every moment, every touch, every bit of wonderful warmth that seeped through the barriers between them and melted her heart and her soul.

How she wished she had met Josh under other circumstances. How she longed to have him look at her without the glimmer of sorrow in his eyes, and the accusation in his heart that was forever between them. And yet, she realized that his wife would have stood between them, alive or dead. According to all that Josh believed, had it not been for Meagan, his wife would still be alive. Meagan could not help but wonder how things might have played out had she been far away from the Somers household the day Lily fell down the stairs, and what Josh's opinion of Meagan Reilly might have been if she had been introduced to the new widower as an eligible woman. But fate had dealt her a lethal blow and, try as she might, she could not resign herself to it.

Meagan blinked back the tears. She had waited all her life for such a man, and now she would never dare look further than serving as his slave for the rest of her life. Yet, she had begun to realize that even living as his servant was better than living without him.

She would work for him. She would work *with* him, and she would work harder than she had ever worked in her life. Perhaps then, as her reward for her toils, she could fall into a sleep that carried no dreams of life with—or without—Josh Daniels.

She heard the bar lift on the door. There was a swish of air through the cabin and she knew Josh was gone.

With her vow in the forefront of her mind, Meagan dressed for the day and went to start breakfast.

As the summer heat gave way to the crisp mornings of fall the lives of Meagan and Josh began to assume a pattern of cautious camaraderie. Together they tended the land and the animals, rejoicing in the harvest and the abundance their toils had produced. Josh could find little fault with Meagan. When he chose to carry on a conversation with her he found her informed and intelligent. Without intending, Josh found himself asking her advice and listening to her opinion.

With the end of summer came the time for Josh's daughter, Abbie, to return.

It was Will Carmichael who would retrieve the little girl from her grandparents. He stopped at the Daniels farm to tell Josh that he was planning a trip to Albany and would pick up the child on his way back.

"You had some reservations about leaving Abbie with Meagan when she first came to live with you," Will reminded him. "Have those been resolved?"

"Meagan's a right smart young woman. Has a lot of book learning. She's going to be able to teach Abbie a lot of things I couldn't," Josh said. "I can't fault her."

If there was any fault to be had it was within Josh himself. He found himself listening for the sound of her voice as she sang while she hung out the laundry or called out to the chickens and ducks as she fed them. He would hurry in from the fields, embellish his accounts of little things that happened during the day to make her laugh and hold his breath at night to hear her gentle breathing behind the curtain across the room. But all these things were locked tight in his heart and he did

not share them with his friend, although Will stood waiting for Josh to continue.

The silence lengthened until finally Josh added, "I'm
sure that Meagan will get along nicely with Abbie and
with the winter coming on I'll be around the cabin most
of the time. If there is any problem I'll know about it."

Will nodded. "That will be best," he agreed, cutting
short his own thoughts as he became aware from his
friend's expression that Josh had something more to say.
"What is it, Josh?" he asked. "Has Meagan done something to upset you?"

"Other than being prone to accidents, and afraid of
the dark, she seems fine," Josh admitted.

"Accident-prone?"

"Just little things, mostly," Josh said as he thought
back. "Except for the other day when the big cast-iron
pot we make the soap in fell off the shelf and darn near
knocked her head off."

"What was a soap cauldron doing on a shelf in the
first place?" Will asked.

"Danged if I know." Josh gave it some thought.
"Never saw it up there before, but it was sure there that
day. On the shelf right above the washtub."

"Is Meagan all right?"

"She managed to jump out of the way, but it about
scared the life out of me. She seemed to take the whole
thing in stride." There was a hint of approval in Josh's
voice as he spoke of the incident that wasn't wasted on
Will Carmichael.

"Is that all?" Will asked.

"Well, that and the night Meagan thought the organ
was haunted."

"The organ? The one in the parlor?" Will reiterated.

"That's the one," Josh admitted. "She was sleeping

in there on the daybed and swore she heard it playing in the middle of the night. The girl's got a real good imagination. Guess she was afraid of the rainstorm and didn't want to admit it.''

"Does it happen often?" Will was playing for time. He had wondered where the girl slept and was fairly certain it wasn't the barn. He wondered if he should remind Josh of the judge's warning. For that matter, he had been wondering if she should warn Meagan, but since they slept in separate buildings he needn't worry. He gave a sigh of satisfied relief as Josh answered his question.

"It won't happen anymore. She stays in here with me and sleeps behind the blanket there."

That did it! The time had come to speak out. "You remember what Judge Osborne said."

"I remember." Josh didn't bother to hide the resentment in his voice, and Will didn't know whether to bless the judge, or blast him to hell.

"Besides, it isn't Meagan that worries me—" Josh wiped the back of his neck with his hanky "—it's Ruth Somers."

"Has she heard the organ playing too?" Will asked innocently.

Josh gave his friend a dirty look and continued. "Ruth stops by here right often. A bit too often, if you ask me. It was different when Lily was alive. Lily enjoyed entertaining and couldn't seem to get enough of it, but with both Meagan and me off in the fields it's kinda unnerving to come home and find Ruth sittin' here waiting."

"What does she want?"

"Far as I can see she just wants to make trouble. She says she wants to make sure Meagan is doing her job and hasn't run off, but she's sure got a funny way of doing it. Guess I kind of resent Ruth playing God as far as Meagan's concerned." Josh rubbed his neck again. "You don't suppose she knew the girl from somewhere before, do you?"

"I wouldn't know where it could be, but I'll surely see what I can find out."

"That will be fine," Josh agreed. "I doubt that there's anything to it, but it just doesn't make sense that a woman could harbor so much hatred toward another. Seems like it should almost be the other way around. I mean, if what Meagan claims is true, she should be mad at Ruth for getting her convicted for something she says she didn't do."

Will could hardly avoid showing the satisfaction he felt on hearing Josh's words, because Will had never believed Meagan was guilty of the crime. He had expressed his opinion openly until it became obvious that championing Meagan was costing him clients among the women who liked and believed in the stalwart Ruth Somers. Ruth was one of the cornerstones of the widespread community and given a great deal of credibility by the other members.

"I'll let you know if I learn anything," Will promised. "Ruth has always been something of a busybody."

"It's just that she seems to have a real mean streak when it comes to Meagan and I don't want the woman hanging over our heads like a nesting vulture when Abbie comes home."

The comparison of Ruth to a vulture caused Will to burst into laughter. Josh joined him and they were both in the throes of jocularity when Meagan joined them.

"Is it a private joke?" she asked.

Josh wiped his eyes. "We were just talking about Ruth Somers."

"There must be something I missed about the woman," Meagan said in confusion, "because I swear I've yet to see anything funny about her."

This sent the men into another gale of laughter. Exasperated, Meagan started back toward the house. "I'll get you both something to eat. Unless I miss my guess, you've already had enough corn whiskey."

"Do you think we should tell her?" Will asked as the door closed.

"No use worrying Meagan over something she can't do anything about. Ruth hates her, and that's a fact. And I don't think anyone but Ruth knows why."

"Well, we'll see what we can find out," Will promised as he followed Josh back to the house where the scent of fragrant stew permeated the air.

Abbie Daniels proved to be a very precocious little girl, with a sharp mind and insatiable curiosity. However, she could not be described as a beautiful child.

Meagan liked children, and Abbie was no exception. But to say that the child's appearance came as somewhat of a shock would be an understatement.

Having lived in close proximity with Josh Daniels for the better part of the summer, Meagan recognized the fact that he would be considered a handsome man. His features were strong and even. Nothing about him seemed out of proportion.

Meagan was the first to admit that she had not seen Lily Daniels at her best; still, Lily had been a woman who, even in death, had held exceptional beauty. So Meagan was prepared to welcome an attractive child.

To her amazement, the little girl was small for her age, with a pensive, intelligent face. Otherwise her features were unexceptional. Her hair was pulled back so tightly her eyebrows looked to be permanently raised above her blue-gray eyes. But it wasn't until the child removed her bonnet that Meagan realized she was indeed faced with a challenge.

The afternoon was warm and while Josh and Will talked on the dogtrot, Meagan, Abbie and Will's wife, Phoebe, went into the house.

Meagan was happy to see the woman who had given her shelter during the time before and during her trial. Phoebe had been a bulwark against adversity and despair, and Meagan was pleased that she had come to help break the ice with Josh's daughter.

"Are you the new hired girl?" Abbie asked bluntly.

"You could call me that." Meagan caught Phoebe's eye and gave a sigh of relief. Obviously the child hadn't been apprised of Meagan's true situation. "Actually I am going to be helping you with your lessons as well as helping your father with his work."

"That's good." The child nodded. "Papa needs help sometimes and I'm too small." She poked around the room as Meagan prepared tea. She peered, prodded and finally decided that there had been no major changes of which she didn't approve.

Phoebe was telling Meagan about the trip she and Will had taken to Albany when Abbie settled herself at the table.

"Would you like some tea?" Meagan asked as the little girl looked at her expectantly.

"I'd rather have buttermilk," Abbie told her.

"There's some in the ice house," Meagan replied. "Can you carry the pitcher by yourself?"

"Of course," Abbie said importantly as she dashed out of the room.

Meagan watched the child from the window, making

certain she was able to manipulate the heavy door that Josh had built to keep in the cold. A few minutes later, Abbie returned. She placed the pitcher on the table and brushed the perspiration from her forehead.

"It's warm today, isn't it?" Meagan remarked as she poured the thick liquid into a cup. "Why don't you take off your bonnet? There's no need to wear it in the house."

Phoebe uttered a gasp of protest, or perhaps it was a warning. Regardless, it came too late, for the child pulled the ribbons of her heavy cotton bonnet, jerked it from her head and handed it to Meagan. Then Abbie lifted the cup of buttermilk to her mouth, closed her eyes and began to drink.

Meagan's hand went to her lips as she saw the reason why the child wore the heavy bonnet, for Abbie's ears stuck out on either side of her head like two foreign appendages.

Before the child finished her drink, Meagan turned away, denying the child any glimpse of her face.

"Why don't you go and see if your father wants some buttermilk?" Meagan suggested.

Abbie wiped her mouth on her forearm and ran out the door. Meagan turned to Phoebe.

"Why didn't someone tell me?" she asked.

"I'm sorry, Meagan," Phoebe apologized. "I just assumed that Josh would tell you about Abbie's...ears. It didn't occur to me that you didn't know until you told her to remove her bonnet."

"Does she wear a bonnet all the time?" Meagan asked, her heart going out to the little girl.

"I've seldom seen her without one." Phoebe fiddled with her teacup. "Lily thought it was a hopeless case. The only thing the doctors could suggest was to keep tight-fitting bonnets on Abbie's head and hope her ears would somehow benefit from the pressure.'' She shook her head. ''I don't think it helped a bit, but Josh has always insisted she wear them.''

Before Phoebe could continue, Josh appeared at the door. ''Come along, honey,'' he urged, ''I'll help you get your bonnet back on.'' He gave Meagan a wilting look. ''Abbie always wears her bonnets, Meagan,'' he said in a matter-of-fact tone. ''Day and night.''

''I understand,'' Meagan said quietly. She wanted to shout at him that he hadn't told her and she had no way of knowing about his daughter's ''affliction.'' Then she saw the anguish in his eyes and held her peace.

Josh tied the ribbon under his daughter's chin. ''There! Now you look like Abbie again.'' He grinned and tweaked her nose before his smoldering gaze fell again on Meagan.

''Abbie again…Abbie again…'' The little girl danced about the room, basking in her father's approval. She stopped in front of Meagan. ''I have lots of bonnets,'' she told her. ''I'll show them to you if you like.''

''I'd like that very much.'' Meagan smiled, aware that the child had made the first gesture of acceptance. She looked at Phoebe, expecting approval, but there was only a little worried frown that creased Phoebe's forehead.

It was obvious to Phoebe that Josh Daniels could not keep his eyes off his indentured servant, just as it was obvious that Meagan was unaware of the explosiveness of the problem.

The Carmichaels spent the night, using the trundle on the daybed. The morning mist had not yet faded when they made their farewells.

''If you need us, let us know,'' Phoebe said as she

impulsively embraced Meagan. "We'll find some way to come to you."

And before Meagan could ask what she meant, the woman allowed her husband to help her into their buggy. As they were leaving, Meagan stared after them, wondering what had prompted the woman's words.

It wasn't long before Abbie had reestablished her place in her own home and Meagan found herself hardpressed to keep up with the little girl.

"My mama never made me tell her where I was going," she protested as Meagan brought her in from an impromptu trip to the barn.

"Abbie, you need to tell someone. Your father worries when he comes in and doesn't know where you are. He is working the fields all alone right now, and if you refuse to tell me where you are going, I am going to go back into the fields to help him and you'll have to come along, whether you want to or not."

"Well, I don't want to go with you," Abbie protested. "And I don't want to tell you where I go. My mama never made me do anything like that."

"Your mama never made you do anything you didn't want to do." Josh's voice boomed. "But your mama isn't here. Meagan and I are. And you're gonna tell one of us where you're going, or you are not going to go."

Abbie put her hands on her hips, a vision of indignation, but there was no submission in her father's face. He wasn't going to change his mind no matter what she tried. Abbie surrendered to authority. "I'll tell you or Meagan, but then I'm going to go where I like," she asserted.

"Only if you have permission," her father reminded her.

The little girl turned on her heel and marched out the

door. She hadn't left the porch when her father called after her, "Abbie! Where are you going?"

"I'm going back to the barn."

"Do you have permission?"

She stopped.

"You know where I want to go," she fired defiantly.

"And you know you're supposed to ask for permission," he said again.

"My mama never had to answer to anybody when she wanted to go somewhere," Abbie shouted at her father.

Angered at the defiance in his daughter, Josh spoke rashly. "Maybe if she had she wouldn't be dead now."

His words brought a simultaneous gasp from the lips of both his daughter and Meagan. Before he had a chance to utter another sound, Abbie ran back through the door of the house and burrowed herself into her bed behind the curtain.

Josh did not try to talk to her. He looked at Meagan and shrugged before returning to the fields. It was Meagan who went to the child.

"I guess you pretty much had the run of the place when your mama was alive," Meagan remarked as she took her place on the side of the bed.

"Mama knew I wouldn't get into any trouble." Abbie sniffled into her pillow.

"Your father knows you aren't going to get into any trouble," Meagan told her. "It's just that he wants to know where you are. I don't think he really knew how much freedom your mother was giving you around here. I tell him where I'm going so he won't worry, and he does the same for me."

The little girl lifted her head and looked at the young woman. "Is that because you love him?" she asked.

Meagan was taken aback. Loving Josh Daniels was

the last thing in the world she would ever dare admit to, even if it was true, which of course it was not. It would be foolhardy to love someone who could never love you back.

"That's because it's the best way to do things when people live out here," she said. "What if there was a fire, or an Indian attack, and your father didn't have any idea where you were?"

"He never knew where my mama went, or what she was doing, and nothing bad ever happened." Abbie sat up and crossed her arms over her chest.

Meagan stood up, her back toward the girl as she straightened some of the articles on the chest of drawers. "Well, that's not quite the way I'd look at it."

Realizing her mistake, Abbie was about to try to retract her words, but the look on Meagan's face told her she wouldn't get away with it.

"All right." Abbie scuffed her foot under the rag rug beside the bed, "I'll tell you or Papa where I'm going. But I'm not going to like it."

"Abbie, life is just full of things we don't like," Meagan told her. "It's all part of growing up."

Abbie jumped off the bed and looked down her body at the distance to her feet. "Do you think I'm growing up?" she asked.

"I think you're growing up faster than you know," Meagan told her.

"My grandma called me her baby all the time," Abbie admitted. "It didn't make me feel grown-up."

"I think grandmas are allowed to say things like that because they are so much older than everybody else," Meagan confided. "I guess everyone seems like a baby to them."

Abbie's face brightened. "I guess I can be Grandma's

baby as long as I can be grown-up here at home.'' She gave an assertive nod as she threw back the curtains and headed once more for the door.

"Abbie," Meagan called out, "just remember, you have to earn the right to be treated like an adult, and the first thing you must remember to do is—"

"Tell you where I'm going." Abbie finished the sentence for her and sighed a deep sigh. "I'm going to the barn to look for baby kittens. The cat has babies every spring and fall." The little girl stopped, a new thought springing to her mind. "Do you know where they are?"

Meagan wiped her hands on her apron. "As a matter of fact, I do. There are five and they're about a month old. If you like, we can bring one into the house and keep it for your very own."

Abbie flew across the floor and grabbed Meagan's hand. "Come on," she urged. "Let's go now! Why didn't you tell me you knew there were kittens? If you had, we wouldn't have had all this trouble."

Meagan stifled a laugh. "Why didn't you tell me kittens were what you were looking for?"

"I thought if I told you, you wouldn't let me go. My mama always said kittens were dirty, sneaky little things and she didn't want me to play with them. One time when I showed her where they were she took the kittens out of the barn and put them in a bucket of water."

Meagan knew drowning kittens was a common practice, but she couldn't help but give a little gasp of disapproval. "What did you do?" she asked, wondering if the child had cried over the loss of her treasures.

Abbie swung Meagan's hand as they crossed the yard. "I waited until Mama had gone into the house to lie down and then I ran back and took them out of the water and laid them in the sun. As soon as they dried out, all but one of them came back to life. Mama never even noticed and Papa never knew.''

''Well, I don't think we should trouble your father about it now,'' Meagan said, and the little girl cast her a look encompassing friendship and trust that, given a chance, could last a lifetime.

Chapter Four

Much to Abbie's disappointment the kittens proved to be too young to leave their mother, but the child was allowed to visit them often. She was returning from one of her little sojourns to the haymow when Ruth Somers stopped her.

"What are you doing out here alone?" the woman demanded. "Isn't anyone around to take care of you?"

"I was up in the haymow playing with my kitten," the little girl told her.

"Why wasn't someone with you?" Ruth demanded.

Abbie backed away, anxious to be free of the woman's persistent questioning. "Usually Meagan comes with me, but she's churning right now."

"Nonetheless, you shouldn't go wandering about alone," Ruth declared, not considering that her children ran wild from dawn to dusk, never answering to anyone for their whereabouts as long as they showed up at mealtime.

"I'll have to speak to your father about this," Ruth said. "Now run along and play."

And Abbie was more than happy to do so as she turned and hurried toward the house.

Meagan was rinsing the wooden churn when Abbie came running toward her.

"How are the kittens?" Meagan asked the breathless girl.

"They're fine, and Aunt Ruthie is here," Abbie gasped.

Meagan straightened up and glanced toward the front of the house. A wagon stood at the hitching rail and the horse looked longingly toward the grass a short distance away. Ruth was nowhere in sight.

"Did Mrs. Somers go into the house?" Meagan asked as she wiped her hands on her apron and gathered up the bowl of butter and the pitcher of buttermilk.

"She said she was going to talk to Papa," Abbie volunteered as she trailed behind Meagan toward the house.

"She'll have a time finding him," Meagan observed with some private satisfaction. "He's gone down to check the animal pens by the creek."

Abbie's saucy smile told Meagan that the little girl didn't like Ruth much more than Meagan did.

In all truth, Meagan was nervous over Ruth's persistent visits. There was always the chance that the woman would tell Abbie the real reason Meagan was working for the Danielses, and Meagan could not bear to see the friendship and trust in the little girl's eyes replaced by fear and loathing.

Meagan hadn't had time to store the milk and butter when she saw Josh and Ruth coming toward the house.

Abbie rushed toward her father and was swept up in his arms.

"Look who's come to see you." He laughed as he acknowledged Ruth's presence. "Your Aunt Ruthie is here."

"I know," Abbie said, burying her face in her father's neck.

"Now don't be so shy," he urged. "You haven't seen Aunt Ruthie for a long time."

"Yes I have," the little girl insisted. "I saw her when I came out of the barn. She said she wanted to talk to you and sent me to the house."

Ruth laughed. "What an imagination that child has," she asserted. "Why, I barely got here when I saw you go into the barn and went to meet you."

"That's not true," Abbie protested. "You were here before Papa came back." Suddenly the little girl looked stricken and began squirming in her father's arms. "You didn't hurt my kittens, did you? Let me down, Papa! I have to go see my kittens."

Josh let the child drop to the ground and she ran off toward the barn before he could stop her.

"You see," Ruth said, "the girl is completely out of control. Imagine living in fear that someone is going to harm a bunch of barn kittens. That's what comes of allowing her to live in the same house as a murderess. You should let me take her home with me where she'd know she would be safe. If anything happens to that child there will be the devil to pay."

Josh removed his wide-brimmed hat and replaced it on the back of his head. "It's funny," he said casually, "but Abbie never had any worries about the kittens before today. Could be she's afraid you might want to take them home with you the same way you want to take her."

Ruth drew herself up in outrage. "How dare you insinuate that I might have done something to disturb the child! I have nothing but her welfare at heart. And after the way she lied about seeing me…"

Meagan had heard most of the conversation and came forward. She didn't understand Ruth's intentions, but she certainly wasn't going to allow the woman to drive a wedge between Abbie and her father. She smiled as she came toward them.

"Hello, Mrs. Somers. I see you found Josh. How lucky that he came back so early. I wanted to tell you that he had gone down to check the pens near the creek when Abbie told me you'd arrived, but you were no-where in sight."

Ruth was taken aback for a moment. Meagan was trying to ruin her credibility. Her mind worked desperately as she endeavored to think of some way to detract from Meagan's tale.

Finally it came to her and she twisted her lips into a superior smile. "Of course I was nowhere in sight. If you didn't see me it's obvious I wasn't here." She turned to Josh. "This is ridiculous. Meagan is trying to cover up for Abbie's lies. They're conspiring together against you."

Meagan spoke up before Josh had time to form an answer. "Well, maybe you weren't here, Mrs. Somers," Meagan admitted, "but your horse and wagon have been hitched to the rail ever since before I finished churning and that was quite a while ago."

Ruth had forgotten about the horse, and the fact that it could be seen from the house.

"I can see that my presence isn't appreciated here," she fumed. "I just stopped by to see that Abbie was all right, not to be interrogated over the time of my arrival."

"Now, Ruth," Josh chided, "I'm sure you're reading more into this than is necessary. You seem to be the one who is touchy about how long you've been here." He was irritated that the woman had implied that Abbie lied.

"If you don't have time for a cup of tea I suppose you should be starting back home. Meagan and I have to get back to work."

With a jerk of her head, Ruth marched to her wagon and, without a word of farewell, went on about her business, leaving Josh and Meagan to wonder as to the woman's motives.

Meagan returned to the house and picked up the butter crock when Josh reached out and stopped her. As his hand touched her arm he felt the resilience of her flesh all the way to his toes.

"I just wanted to thank you for coming to Abbie's defense," he said, knowing it was only a half-truth.

Meagan had been real spunky when she stood up against Ruth in defense of his little girl, and he had wanted to whoop for joy. For once, someone besides himself had championed the child. Even Lily had seldom found a good word for their daughter. It had embarrassed the lovely Lily to have given birth to a child who was less than perfect. Making Abbie wear the bonnet was a constant reminder that there was something wrong with her appearance, and when the bonnet was removed Lily had found it almost impossible to look at her daughter.

And now Meagan had come along and seemed completely oblivious to the imperfection that set Abbie apart.

Meagan never accused Abbie of lying to draw attention to herself. And, to the best of his knowledge, Meagan never made fun of the girl because of the angle at which Abbie's ears stuck out on each side of her head.

Josh wanted to do more than say thank-you to Meagan. He wanted to take her in his arms and tell her how wonderful he thought she was, but he knew that was the last thing he dared do.

Meagan smiled at him somewhat hesitantly when he

did not take his hand from her arm. He wanted to say something more, but he simply released her and stepped back.

"And Abbie thanks you too," he said lamely, as Meagan, sensing potential danger, scurried out the door.

It was almost dark when Josh saw Meagan again. By that time he had gotten a rein on his emotions and greeted her in an offhanded manner as she entered the barn.

Abbie darted past her and ran to the stanchion where Josh was milking the cow.

"Squirt me some milk," the little girl demanded, and her father laughingly aimed the udder toward her opened mouth. The first stream of milk missed and splashed against Abbie's cheek and onto her bonnet. She shrieked with delight as the second hit her open mouth.

"Sorry about getting milk on her bonnet," Josh called over his shoulder.

"Don't worry," Meagan answered laughing. "Bonnets will wash."

The cow lowed restlessly. Josh checked the trough and asked, "Meagan, will you go up in the mow and toss down some hay?"

"I'll go first and make sure the kittens aren't in the way," Abbie volunteered as she whisked up the slat ladder and disappeared into the loft.

"Hurry, hurry," Meagan urged. "I'm right behind you."

Abbie's delighted giggles were punctuated by a gasp and the clap of one piece of wood striking another. Josh turned from his milking to see Meagan tumble to the ground.

Exasperated at having her milking turned into a circus,

the cow kicked the bucket the moment Josh let go of her udder.

Meagan groaned as she tried to catch her breath while Abbie's anxious little face peered from the top of the ladder.

Josh knelt down beside Meagan and lifted her into his arms. "There, there, now. Take it easy. It's going to be all right. Are you hurt? Do you think you busted anything?"

Meagan's head was spinning but she wasn't certain whether it was because of the fall or the touch of Josh's hands as he ran them along her body searching for broken bones. Had she been alone she would probably have climbed to her feet and waited until the pain in her hip and the dizziness subsided, but with Josh cradling her against his body she lost any desire to move.

She opened her eyes and waited until she was able to focus on the thick blond hair and strong features so unbearably close to her.

She nestled her head against his shoulder as he brushed back the hair that had fallen over her face.

"What happened, Papa?" Abbie demanded from her perch. "How did Meagan fall off the ladder?"

Josh looked up. One of the wooden slats that served as a rung swung free on one end. "I guess one of the slats came loose." Josh barely glanced at the ladder, for his full attention was on Meagan, who was still trying to catch her breath.

"Are you hurt?" he asked again. "Do you have pain anywhere?"

"No," she managed. "Nothing like that. Just knocked the wind out of me. Is Abbie all right?"

"She's up there." Josh indicated the cavernous hole above their heads without taking his eyes from the woman in his arms. "Looks like you cracked your head real good." He brushed his hand over her forehead, gingerly touching the rising lump.

"Papa! Lift me down!" Abbie demanded. "I'll go get some cold water for Meagan's head." The little girl's perception amazed her father.

Reluctantly, he released Meagan and held his arms up to his daughter. It was while he stood in this position that he saw the fresh marks against the aging wood. He put the little girl on the ground and turned back to the ladder.

"You haven't been trying to repair this ladder, have you?" he asked.

"I didn't realize there was anything wrong with it." Meagan struggled to a sitting position and attempted to get to her feet.

"There probably wasn't anything wrong until the nails came out." He bent down and ran his hands through the straw on the floor of the barn. Nails were hard to come by and he wanted to find them if possible.

"What made you think I was tinkering with it?" Meagan asked.

"Marks here along the edge of this board." He pointed to the fresh gouges. "Looks like somebody was either trying to put it up, or take it down."

"Abbie runs up and down that ladder all the time and she's had no trouble," Meagan pointed out.

"Abbie weighs next to nothing, but once either you or I hit that step we were going to take a fall."

"But how could something like that happen without either of us noticing?" Meagan wondered aloud.

"Maybe it just happened today," Josh said thoughtfully as his eyes met Meagan's in concerned contemplation.

Meagan's eyes opened wide. "You don't think Ruth could have gone up into the loft to look for you and knocked it loose, do you?"

"Something like that could have happened," Josh said noncommittally. "Now let's get you back to the house so I can clean up this mess."

Meagan looked beyond Josh and realized the fruit of the days' milking was spilled across the floor. She pulled herself to her feet, her head spinning. "Oh, Josh, I'm so sorry," she said. "I should have been more careful."

"Don't let it fuss you," he said reassuringly. "I'll take care of it. You go back to the house. I'll make sure there aren't any more unpleasant surprises before I come in and we'll try to sort this whole thing out later."

Abbie came across the barnyard, a dripping wet dish-cloth trailing behind her like a banner. "I got it!" she hollered. "A nice cold cloth for Meagan's head."

The child was somewhat taken aback when she realized her potential patient was already on her feet, but she thrust the cloth into Meagan's hand and smiled proudly at her achievement.

Meagan wrung out the cloth and pressed it against the lump. "Thank you, Abbie. That feels much better. Now if you'll just help me back to the house, I think I'll sit a while before I put supper on the table."

Abbie would have preferred to stay in the barn with her father, Meagan knew, but the little girl made no argument. If there were other accidents waiting to happen, Meagan and Josh wanted to be certain Abbie was not the next unsuspecting victim.

There was nothing else that posed a threat, and life returned to normal. As normal as life could be for a man and a woman who were trying to hide their attraction from each other, as well as from themselves. With the approach of the harvest they worked from sunup to sundown.

Abbie stayed on the edge of the fields playing with her kitten. Buttermilk was a fat, yellow feline, lazy beyond belief, who didn't care what position he was in as long as he was cherished and fed. Abbie dressed the little animal in doll clothes and carried him in a basket, feeding him a continual bounty of tidbits she had brought for his gratification.

Because the little cat occupied Abbie so completely, Meagan and Josh were able to accomplish a great amount of work and by the end of the week Josh felt he could take time to go hunting to fill the larder.

"I could butcher a pig," he told Meagan, "but I'd rather wait until the cold weather sets in. There's plenty of game out there and thanks to you and that lazy cat of Abbie's I have the time."

He left early the next morning, promising to be back by nightfall.

Meagan and Abbie listened throughout the day, occasionally catching the echo of a shot from his gun. Meagan put dinner on the table and saw to it that Abbie ate a healthy portion. She stored the rest on the back of the fire for Josh.

The days were growing short, and Meagan reminded herself of that fact as she got Abbie ready for bed. Once the child was settled, Meagan sat on the dogtrot in the warm summer night and watched the shadows chase the moonlight across the yard.

A twig snapped somewhere in the distance. Instantly alert, Meagan watched for Josh's familiar figure to come through the trees.

The smile on her face froze, and the greeting in her

throat was silenced when she realized the figure that emerged from the woods was not Josh Daniels, but an Indian.

She jumped to her feet and was about to run into the house when a familiar voice called out, "Meagan? Meagan? Is that you?"

In the next moment she was across the yard, hurling herself into the arms of her younger brother.

"What in the devil are you doing way out here?" he asked as he tried to embrace her and get a look at her at the same time.

"Oh, Reilly, how I've hoped you'd find me." The tears ran down her cheeks and she was on the verge of blubbering.

He jerked the scarf from around his head and wiped her cheeks, then he thrust it in her hand. "Blow your nose and tell me what happened."

Meagan did as she was told. "How much do you know?" she asked.

"I heard that a white woman was found guilty of murder and made a slave of the man whose wife she supposedly killed. I never thought it might be you." He hesitated and looked through the moonlight into her eyes. "It is you, isn't it, Meagan?"

"Yes, it's me." She sighed.

"Tell me—" he ordered "—all of it."

"After you left I heard of a possible position with the Somers family. The woman said if I pleased her she would hire me to teach her children and help with the housework. I was carrying some supplies to her kitchen when I heard a scream and a thumping sound. I ran into the parlor and found a lady lying at the foot of the stairs. As I bent over the body to try to help the woman, Ruth Somers started screaming that I'd killed her friend. She said I had pushed her down the stairs. Reilly, I'd never even been upstairs, but it was Ruth Somers's word against mine and no one believed me.

"The jury found me guilty, but asked for mercy because there was no evidence, and no motive. Just Ruth's testimony that I'd pushed Lily Daniels down the stairs."

There was a moment of silence, then Reilly urged, "And…"

"There is no prison for women in the Carolinas, and rather than—" she swallowed once before forcing out the word "—hang me, the judge sentenced me to work for Josh Daniels, the dead woman's husband."

"And…" Reilly prompted.

"I tried to get away. To find you, somehow. Josh caught me and brought me here. I think he would have let me go had it not been for the threats of the judge."

"So you live with him and take his wife's place, is that it?" The anger built in Reilly's voice.

"I take care of Abbie, Josh's little girl, and I help with the chores and the housework." She swallowed again, realizing the core of her brother's concern. "I don't share Josh's bed," she finished weakly.

"Of your choice, or his?" Reilly persisted. The whole situation regarding his sister was so bizarre he couldn't believe it had happened.

"Judge Osborne said that if I did anything more than work for Josh the original sentence would be carried out. I would hang and Josh would be jailed for contempt of court."

Meagan watched as her brother's already swarthy face grew dark with anger. "I'm beginning to understand why the Indians delight in taking the scalps of white men," he growled. "Where is this bereaved widower now? Why isn't he here protecting his *property?*"

"Josh went hunting. He should be coming back any time now."

Reilly's eyes scanned the shadows. "Get your things, Meagan. Come with me, now."

"I can't leave Abbie here alone. She's just a little girl."

Reilly grabbed his sister's arms, squeezing them firmly as he gave her a little shake. "Listen to me, Meagan. I'm on my way to a powwow. Old Howling Dog wants the white man out of these mountains. Many of the Indians are joining him. There's going to be trouble come spring. If you won't go with me now, be ready to leave when I come back through here or it won't matter what the judge said. When Old Howling Dog goes on the warpath, no one is going to be spared."

"But shouldn't you tell someone, Reilly? Think of all the people who will be killed."

"I can't tell what I don't know. The white man doesn't believe half-breeds. I must have proof. That's why I'm going. If you can hold your jailer at bay until I get back I'll take you to my mother's people. They live at peace with the white man. You would be made welcome there until we can find some way to prove your innocence, or change the judge's mind." Reilly touched the hilt of his knife as he made his statement concerning the judge's mind and Meagan gave a little gasp.

Reilly had a ruthless streak in him that their father had spent his life trying to eradicate. It seemed the old man hadn't been successful.

"You don't understand," Meagan told him. "If I leave here they will hunt me down like an animal. They'll hang me, and most likely you too, if you help me escape."

"You don't understand, sister," Reilly said with a twinkle in his eye. "I don't intend to be caught."

"But..."

"No 'buts,'" he said. "Be ready to leave when I return. There won't be much time. If for some reason the attacks start before I can reach you, go to the fort. I will find you. I will not allow my sister to live out her life as a white man's slave."

"Reilly, I can't leave Abbie. She's not like other children. She needs..."

She got no further, for Abbie's sleepy voice called out, "Meagan? Who are you talking to? Is that my papa?" Abbie wandered toward the door. Her bonnet had slipped from her head and hung down her back and her ears stood out like small white saucers on either side of her face.

Reilly gave a muffled snort. "You're right, Meagan. She is definitely unique." His hand moved over his face as though wiping away the mirth he had momentarily experienced. "Does she resemble her father by any chance?"

Meagan looked at the little girl who moved toward them. "No, Abbie doesn't really resemble Josh," she said somewhat defensively. "Josh Daniels is a very handsome man."

Reilly placed his hand beneath his sister's chin and looked into her eyes. "Handsome, or not, be ready to leave when I return, and make sure the man understands that he must get himself and that child to the fort." He kissed his sister on the forehead and faded into the shadows as Abbie, still groggy from slumber, reached the door.

Meagan hurried toward the little girl and scooped her up. "There now, sugar pie, your papa's not home yet, but I'm sure he'll be coming along anytime. You get back in bed and when you wake up he'll be here.'' She carried the yawning child back into the house, and when she returned to the door her brother had gone. But a whole batch of new problems had just begun.

Chapter Five

The first light of dawn had barely touched the sky when Meagan awakened Abbie. "You'll have to get up now, child," she told the sleepy girl. "We're going out to look for your father. He must have shot so much game he couldn't carry it all home by himself. He needs our help."

Meagan didn't believe her words, and she was fairly certain Abbie didn't completely believe it either. She watched the horizon as they started out, hoping to see signs of a campfire in the distance. She even went so far as to hope that Josh had taken shelter with Ruth and her husband if he found himself too far away to reach home before darkness set in.

Abbie rubbed her eyes and lagged behind, ignoring Meagan's urging. Apparently the child had not slept any better than Meagan, who had found herself fully awake with every creak of the house. The girl gnawed on a biscuit as they went along.

They had only been out a few minutes when a shot shattered the morning silence. Meagan took Abbie's hand and started toward the sound.

"I hope that's Papa." Abbie quickened her pace.

"And I hope he doesn't think we're a deer and shoot us."

"I hope so too," Meagan answered, but her mind wasn't on the little girl's fears; she was too obsessed with her own. There was the chance that someone else was out hunting, and that whoever it was might see their movement and take a shot at them. There was an even greater fear that Josh had been injured and was trying to attract attention.

They reached an area where Meagan often went to gather herbs and pick berries. The little estuary flowed into their creek and a well-beaten path ran alongside the water. Near the bank lay a man.

Meagan gave a little cry and ran to him, ignoring Abbie who clung to her skirt.

"Josh! Can you hear me? What happened?"

"Meagan…thank God!" He tried to move, but fell back as the pain caught him. "Caught my arm in a trap. Don't know what the damned thing was doing out here in the first place. I stopped by the stream to wash my hands and face and it got me."

Meagan helped him to a sitting position and examined his arm.

"The trap is rusted fast. The bleeding has stopped, but I haven't been able to pry the trap loose." He grunted in pain as he moved.

"I'll go find something to wedge into it." She turned and almost fell over the wide-eyed child, who squatted behind her. "Stay here with your papa, Abbie. I'll be right back," Meagan promised.

How she wished Reilly was still in the area. Even with Josh's help it would be difficult to open the trap. She chose a chunk of tree limb, good solid oak, about the size of a man's arm.

By the time she returned the sun had peeked out over the trees and she could see that Josh's pallor had not been in her imagination. He had lost a great deal of blood. His skin was pasty and cold.

Ignoring his tightly closed lips and the murmurs of pain he could not suppress, Meagan forced the tree limb through the jaws of the trap and using the barrel of the gun for leverage, wedged the trap open. Josh managed to lift his arm from the trap. He moved it as though it were a foreign object.

Meagan jerked off her blouse and wrapped it around his forearm, completely oblivious to the fact that she now stood before him in her chemise.

"Help me to my feet," Josh ordered. "You can help me get to the house, then come back here for the game I shot. I fought animals off it all night, and I'm not about to lose it now."

Meagan almost laughed aloud at his declaration. It was so typical of him not to give up what was his.

Josh leaned heavily against Meagan's strong young shoulders as they made their way back toward the house. "As soon as I get this arm soaking in some hot water I want you to go back and get that trap. It isn't mine and I don't understand how it got there. No trapper in his right mind would leave a trap that close to a well traveled path. Probably some damn fool Indian that didn't know what he was doing. I thought I saw some Indians prowling around here during the night. They didn't bother you, did they?"

"I didn't see any strangers." Meagan chose her words carefully. It was the truth. Reilly was certainly no stranger, and she wasn't about to tell Josh of his visit at this time.

"Let me take care of you first, then I'll go back and get the trap," Meagan assured him.

Surely Reilly wouldn't have set a trap hoping to get back at the white man who held his sister prisoner. No, of course not! Reilly knew that more than likely it would be Meagan who would go to the easily accessible area of the estuary. But if it wasn't Reilly, who could it have been? They hadn't had any visitors other than Ruth Somers.

Meagan was still mulling over the possibilities when they reached the house.

Meagan eased Josh down onto the bed near the fireplace and went to fill the iron teakettle with water.

Carefully she cut the shirt from his arm and soaked away what was left of the sleeve adhering to the wound. The trap had cut to the bone and for all Meagan knew, the bone might be fractured, although she could see no break. Carefully she took out needle and thread and after cleaning the wound as best she could and dosing both Josh and the wound liberally with whiskey, Meagan painstakingly stitched the edges back together, hoping that somehow the tortured flesh would hold and heal.

She fed Abbie and got the little girl ready for bed. The child was exhausted from the tension of the long day, but she clung to Meagan's hand as she tucked the covers around the child.

"You aren't going to let my daddy die, are you?" Abbie all but choked on the words.

"Not if I can help it," Meagan replied. "Now don't you worry. I've never seen anybody die from a cut arm. He's going to be all right. He'll probably wake up tomorrow as right as rain."

"And if he doesn't?"

"Then I'll leave you here to tend him and I'll run

over to the Somerses' place and see if they can go for the doctor,'' Meagan promised.

But the following morning, Josh was burning with fever, and Meagan dared not leave him as he hovered on the edge of delirium.

She bathed him with tepid water. His arm became red and swollen. She forced him to eat bread beaten into broth to give him sustenance, but it did little good. She could see the pain reflected in his eyes and in the lines around his mouth.

''Josh,'' she said, placing her hand on his shoulder as she spoke, and nudging him gently. ''Josh, I'm going out to gather some herbs to try to get the poison out of your arm. I want to leave Abbie here with you. Can you watch her for a few minutes?''

''I'll watch her,'' he mumbled. ''I should get up. The fields, the crops…all our work.''

''Don't worry about that right now,'' Meagan soothed. ''Just talk to Abbie until I get back.''

With that she sped out the door, the herb basket over her arm.

Abbie crept near her father's bed. She sat down on the stool Meagan had used and stared at him.

Josh tried to keep his eyes open and focus them on her. He tried to think of something to say. He tried not to scream with the pain that throbbed from his arm and extended itself through his whole body.

''It's going to be all right, honey,'' he assured the little girl.

She nodded solemnly. ''That's what Meagan said when you didn't come home. I didn't believe her either.''

He reached out toward her and the strain sent shivers

of pure white pain jolting through his body. "Holy Mother of God," he whispered.

"What did you say?" Abbie moved closer and cocked her little head.

"Nothing, baby," he managed. "I was talking to myself."

Abbie nodded again. "Meagan does that too. She was talking to herself the night you didn't come home. I woke up and thought you were here, but when I got to the door it was just Meagan."

Josh pulled himself to some semblance of alertness. The Indians. He had seen Indians as he lay caught in the trap. Maybe Meagan had seen them too. Maybe she had lied. "Why did you think I was here?" he asked his daughter.

"I thought I heard you talking, but when I got to the door there wasn't anyone there but Meagan."

"Where was she?"

"Out on the dogtrot." Abbie pointed indifferently as she spoke, obviously losing interest in the subject.

"You're sure there wasn't anyone else there?" he prodded.

"I didn't see anybody else, and Meagan came in and picked me up. There wasn't anybody with her."

"Did Meagan go back out?"

Abbie shook her head. "No, we went to bed." She got up and walked across the floor to the cupboard. A moment later she returned. "This is my reading book. Meagan is teaching me," she declared with obvious pride. "Now, I will read to you." With a flourish she resumed her seat and opened the book.

As her voice piped through the room Josh came to grips with the doubt that had suddenly filled his being. Why would Meagan lie to him? If the Indians had come, surely she would have told him. He closed his eyes and drifted in a dark world of doubt. It seemed an eternity before he heard Meagan's voice.

"What a good little helper you are," she crooned to the child. "And how clever to read to your papa and help him forget his pain."

Josh opened his eyes. The woman was lovely. Like a beam of light or a breath of fresh air, she brightened the whole room with her presence. How could he have thought that she would lie to him? And how could he help but continue to wonder if she had lied?

He watched as she placed horsetail in a sieve over a pan of boiling water. Once it was piping hot she placed it in a piece of clean linen and wrapped it around his arm.

Although Meagan changed the compress every few hours, the arm was no better the next day.

"I'm going to go into town to get the doctor," she said as she wiped her hands on her apron.

"I don't need a doctor," Josh complained fuzzily. "I need to get out into that field."

"You can't stand on your feet with your arm the way it is now," Meagan told him. "At least let me go to the Somerses' place and see if..."

"If Ruth will go to town and tell the constable that we need a doctor and that you have run away?"

"But I haven't run away," Meagan protested.

"If you show your face at her home, Ruth will say you ran and it will be up to you and me to prove you didn't. I don't know whether I'll be in any shape to help you, Meagan."

"If I'm here with you when the doctor comes, I couldn't have run away," Meagan protested, but her words were lame even in her own mind, for she knew that Ruth's word was believed whether she told the truth or not. Meagan had no defense against the woman, and she had the horrible feeling that Josh didn't either.

"Meagan, what's a doctor going to do?" Josh asked. "Bleed me? Hell, I lost enough blood the night I was caught in the trap."

"But surely a doctor…" Meagan began lamely.

"The first, last and only doctor they had at the fort got his training through the army to tend to the needs of the horses. He proceeded to pull the teeth of the soldiers when necessary, and last year got to the point where he applied leeches and started bleeding people. He could set bones, but hell, so could practically any man in the settlement."

Meagan didn't know what to say. Her father had never dealt with a doctor who didn't have a medical degree. And, although degrees were not to be had in the colonies, they were readily available in England and on the Continent. It was beyond belief that Meagan herself might have more knowledge of how to heal than the man who had hung out a shingle claiming he could treat the people who settled around the fort.

"Meagan, I want you to try to help me." Josh's voice was husky with the need to keep her with him and make her accede to his wishes.

"Very well," she agreed, "but I don't know a great deal—"

"I know some things about the healing of a wound. Between us, we should be able to lick this thing." He gave her what was meant to be a smile and turned out as more of a grimace, but Meagan met it bravely.

"We'll take care of it somehow," she agreed, but her words sounded empty to her own ears when she removed the bandage and saw the creeping red line of infection had set in during the night.

Infection was one thing Meagan knew how to cope with. Heaven knew, Reilly always seemed to have an infected scrape somewhere on his body.

Josh's fever was mounting so Meagan took Abbie with her as they searched for the kidney-shaped leaves and greenish-yellow flowers of lady's mantle that she had seen along the edge of the pasture. When they returned to the house Meagan crushed the leaves with the rolling pin. Then she applied the pulp to Josh's arm and wrapped it with a cloth.

She could feel Josh's eyes on her, watching her, even after she left his side to fix dinner.

Once their meal was over, she washed the wound with clear water and left it open to the air until it was time to apply the poultice and repeat the process. But the fever had gotten the best of Josh, and he tossed and turned, mumbling incoherently. What would happen to Meagan if he died? Would they send her to Will and Phoebe, or would they say she had let him die and take her life in return?

In his more lucid moments she bathed him with tepid water and dosed him with horsetail tea. She tried to remember the herbs that Reilly's mother had used for fever, but there were few that she could recall.

The best she could do was to force liquid down him and try to keep him quiet. She dosed him with whiskey when the pain became too great, and applied poultices of whiskey to his arm when it became inflamed. She fanned him against the heat of the day and kept him covered at night. She shooed away the flies. Other than that there was little she could do for him personally. When Meagan wasn't caring for Josh she was looking after and reassuring Abbie as the child followed her about while she did the chores.

The cow had to be milked, the livestock fed and watered, the milk churned and the clothing, bandages and bedding washed. Abbie must be fed and good rich broth must be ready at all times on the chance that Josh would call for food. Meagan did everything other than the harvesting of the late crops. She dared not leave Josh long enough to go to the fields.

On the third day Josh's fever broke. He asked for water, food and more whiskey. She gave him what he wanted and he fell into a deep, healing sleep.

Meagan dropped beside his bed in a heap of exhaustion.

When she awoke she could feel his eyes upon her and lifted her head to find it only inches from his face. She got to her feet, stumbling over the stool on which she had been seated as she backed away.

"I'm sorry. I didn't mean...that is to say, I guess I must have dozed off."

His arm was afire. Hell, his whole body was on fire thanks to that rusty trap. But his head was no longer filled with cotton. His mind was clear. "Did you go back and get the trap?" he asked.

Meagan gave a little start. "I forgot," she admitted. "With everything else I just totally forgot."

"No matter," he told her. "You can see about it tomorrow. Doesn't seem right that someone would leave a trap there and not have it sprung in all the time it would take to get it rusty."

"No, it doesn't," Meagan agreed as she cut a crust of stale bread into pieces and added the bread and walnut-sized chunk of butter to a pot of boiling water. After whipping the mixture to a gruel she offered it to him.

Josh ate obediently but when the food was gone he remarked, "Tomorrow I want meat and potatoes."

"And you shall have them," Meagan promised, not bothering to hide the relief in her voice.

Meagan was up before dawn. When Josh awoke he saw the fire burning in the yard and knew she was boiling the bandages she had used on his wounds. By the time the sun topped the trees Meagan had fixed breakfast, washed the dishes and headed for the field.

Abbie was left to watch her father and told to get Meagan should anything unusual happen. Unfortunately, no one told the child what was to be considered as unusual, so when Josh pulled the poultice from his arm and left it exposed as he drifted into a troubled sleep, Abbie saw nothing of concern and continued to play with her kitten just outside the open door.

Meagan came in from the field just after noon. With a cry of alarm she rushed across the floor, swatting at the flies that blackened Josh's arm.

"What's wrong? What's happened?" Josh came awake with a start.

Meagan was almost in tears. "There were flies all over your arm," she told him.

"Don't get fussed about it," he said as he tried to soothe her. "A few flies aren't going to make any difference. The dang things are everywhere." As he spoke he noticed that there were dark circles beneath her eyes. She was exhausted.

Though weak, Josh was determined to make himself useful, if not in the fields, at least around the house. Although clumsy with the use of only one hand, he managed to get a pot of potatoes and sausage simmering over the fire and just collapsed on the cot when the door burst open.

"I knew it! Loafing again!" Ruth Somers's voice rang out over the room. "You worthless girl. Get back to work and stop trying to make everyone believe you're sick."

Josh jumped to his feet, his head reeling with the sudden movement. He grabbed the table to steady himself as Ruth slammed back into the wall.

"Josh! What ever are *you* doing here?"

"I live here, Ruth," Josh reminded her dryly. When he caught himself on the table he had jostled his arm and now held it tenderly against him. "What do you want?"

"I came to make certain that wretched girl was doing her job. Where is she?"

"She's out working in the field."

Ruth smiled. "It's about time you came to your senses and quit treating her as though she were a trusted servant."

"I'd be out there myself, but I had a little accident."

"What happened?" Ruth glanced about the room, obviously annoyed that it was clean and neatly kept.

"Got caught in a rusty trap. Dang near took my arm off," he told her.

"Where on earth would you find a trap out here?" Ruth demanded. "Heaven knows, traps are dear, and those of us who have them keep close track of them."

"It was in the water at the head of the creek. I never knew it to be there before. It was right by the side of the road. You must have passed the spot a hundred times. Maybe even stopped there to water your horse."

"No, no, I'm sure I never have," Ruth said somewhat nervously. "I would have noticed something as large as a trap. Besides, I have to go. I just stopped by to check on Meagan and get a cup of tea.'' She sighed and glanced about, hoping he would offer her a cup.

''Kettle's on the hob,'' he told her. ''You're welcome to make yourself some tea.''

Ruth moved closer to the man, her eyes riveted on his arm. ''What's that black stuff on your arm?'' she asked. ''Surely that stupid girl isn't packing the wound in mud, is she?''

''That's just flies.'' He brushed them away. ''They're a bother but there's no keeping them away.''

''You get that lazy girl to go out and pick some mint leaves and rub them on your arm. The flies will go away quick enough,'' Ruth assured him.

She placed her handkerchief against her nose and drew nearer, peering at his arm with avid curiosity. ''Doesn't look like it's infected to any great degree,'' she observed. Then, turning to the fireplace she swung the crane forward and lifted off the kettle. ''I'll fix us a nice cup of tea before I go down to the field.''

''No need for you to go to the field, Ruth. Meagan doesn't have time to chat with you.''

''Oh, I don't want to chat,'' Ruth busied herself with the teapot. ''Rafe is down there and I have to fetch him before I go.''

Meagan kept the scythe swinging in a steady rhythm despite her aching shoulders and back. Once the grain was cut she would bundle it together. Sweat ran into her eyes blurring her vision, but when she brushed it away she noticed a movement near the edge of the field. Annoyed that Josh had tried to come out so far, Meagan stopped working and laid the scythe down, determined to scold him. But then she realized that it was not Josh but a stocky, heavily muscled man who watched her. When she turned toward him, the man stepped out into the sunlight and Meagan's breath caught in her throat.

She stood perfectly still and the man started across the field toward her. "I thought to find my friend Josh here." Rafe Somers glanced around as though he expected the man to appear at any moment.

There was no need to pretend she didn't know who he was. Meagan had seen Rafe Somers often enough during her trial. And, even though he was a good half day's ride away, he was the nearest neighbor, though to the best of her knowledge the man had not taken the time to call at the Daniels household since Meagan came. Until today of course.

"Mr. Daniels is up at the house," Meagan said. "He had an accident a few days ago. I'm trying to finish up the harvesting before the bad weather sets in."

"I just got my crops in a few days ago." Rafe puffed out his chest with pride. Then his demeanor quickly changed. "What sort of accident?" he asked. "Indians?"

Meagan shook her head. "He got his arm caught in a trap. It happened right off the road by the beaver pond. You must have passed by the spot when you drove up."

Rafe's dark brow furrowed. "I noticed some blood on the grass, but I just thought some animal had been eaten there. I usually stop there and let the horse drink. This time the animal wanted nothing to do with drinking. Now I know the reason."

"You never set a trap over there, did you?" Meagan asked boldly.

Rafe hooted with laughter and slapped his thighs. "You are a spunky one. You accuse me of setting my trap where it will likely catch the nose of my horse? I think not!'' He settled down and crossed his arms against his chest. ''Where is this trap? I would like to see it.''

''I don't know,'' Meagan admitted. ''I went back after it once I was sure Josh would be all right, and the trap was gone.''

''Ah!'' Rafe hooted again. ''The phantom trap that jumps out in the night to catch unsuspecting victims.''

Meagan felt her cheeks redden under his teasing. She bent down to pick up the scythe. As she turned, Rafe took the tool from her hands.

''You go back to the house. See to your patient and fix some dinner. I will finish the field.'' He turned and swung the scythe a couple of times to get the feel of the tool.

Meagan took a couple of steps before she stopped and asked, ''Did Mrs. Somers come with you today?''

''Most sure she did,'' he said as he started down the field, setting a steady rhythm.

Meagan's shoulders slumped. She longed to get back to the house and see to Josh and Abbie's welfare, but not with Ruth there. ''I think I'll stay here and finish bundling the sheaves,'' she told him.

Rafe gave the girl a glance that encompassed sympathy and compassion. ''Keep well back,'' he warned. ''I cut a deep swath.'' His laughter echoed across the land.

''Why didn't you let me know you were in need?'' Rafe chided gently as the men drew on their after-dinner pipes. ''I would have come to help you.''

''I would have sent Meagan, but there never seemed to be time. Been outta my head with fever up until just the last day or so. Hadn't been for Meagan I would have died sure.'' Josh drew deeply on the clay pipe and exhaled with slow satisfaction. "You got any idea how that trap might have got there?''

Rafe's eyes narrowed. "I was a trapper before I was a farmer. No one would leave a trap so close to the road, for he would catch his neighbor before he catches the beaver.'' Now it was Rafe's turn to draw on his pipe. "Unless it was the neighbor he wanted to catch.''

"What a stupid thing to say," Ruth interrupted. "Rafe, sometimes I don't know what ails you. Who would want to hurt poor Josh? It must have been Indians. They're all over the place.''

"You seen any lately?'' Josh tried to sound casual.

"No sign of Indians around my house. I watch for them, but I haven't seen anything in many weeks. Do you see Indians, little one?'' Rafe asked Abbie.

"I woke up one night and thought I heard people talking but it was only Meagan.'' Abbie liked the robust Frenchman and sidled nearer to him.

"You heard Meagan talking to Indians?'' Ruth was instantly alert.

Abbie wished she had kept silent. "I don't know anything about Indians. All I heard was Meagan talking to herself.''

"How do you know she wasn't talking to your father?'' Ruth persisted, well aware of the child's discomfort.

"Papa wasn't here. It was the night that Papa got hurt. We didn't find him until the next morning.''

Abbie had said all she was going to say and slipped behind the curtain to play on the bed with her kitten.

Ruth narrowed her eyes in speculation. This would take some looking into, and the girl would take a bit more watching. Perhaps Meagan was planning to sell them out to the Indians to save her own scalp.

"You'd better watch that girl, Josh," Ruth warned. "She may have set the trap herself to try to get rid of you."

"If Meagan had wanted to get away she'd be long gone by now," Josh told her. Then he chuckled. "I'm sure she wanted me hurt so she could do all the work by herself, finish up the harvest, do the chores, get the vegetables ready for winter storage, plus take care of the house *and* Abbie *and* me. Woman would have to be a regular glutton for punishment."

"Well, I still say she should be watched." Ruth sniffed derisively. "And if you won't, I will!"

Rafe leaned forward and knocked the ashes from his pipe into the fire. "The girl is a good, steady worker. Leave her alone, wife."

But Ruth tossed her head, and both men knew she would not heed her husband's words.

"I appreciate you helping with the field," Josh told Rafe. "Meagan says the work is done for the most part."

"That is so," Rafe agreed. "Unless I hear from you, we will see you at the fort for the Harvest Festival next month." He got to his feet and took his wife's arm, hauling her up to join him.

Meagan looked up from the dishes she was washing, surprised that they weren't going to spend the night. But Josh said nothing and it wasn't Meagan's place to do so.

While Ruth fussed at Josh with her goodbyes, Rafe made his way across the room. "You come get me if you need me, yes?"

"Yes, Mr. Somers, and thank you." Meagan smiled.

Rafe was about to turn away when he added, "And you don't worry about the little varmints you will find in Josh's arm. They will eat away the dead flesh and keep the gangrene from setting in. It is a good thing. Just wash it clean. I know these things. Josh Daniels will heal well.''

Before Meagan could inquire as to his meaning Ruth opened the door. A gust of wind wrenched it from her hand and slammed it back against the wall. Through the opening they could see the storm clouds billowing above. Before they could do more than shut the door, the rain came clattering down.

Like it or not, Ruth and Rafe Somers would stay the night.

Chapter Six

Ruth glanced about the room in disdain. Abbie was already in her nightclothes, a plain cotton sleeping bonnet on her head. The little girl kissed her father goodnight and disappeared behind the curtain where Meagan waited to tuck her into bed. It was obvious the sleeping arrangements were not to be altered.

"I suppose Rafe and I will have to sleep in the barn." Ruth sniffed disparagingly. "I certainly don't intend to spend the night in the same room with a murderess."

Rafe scowled but made no other move to silence his wife. Josh, however, in deference to the fact that his daughter was in the same room, made certain his guests understood the rules of the house. "There will be no such talk in my house, Ruth," he warned. "As for your sleeping quarters, I'm sure you'll be comfortable in the parlor. There is a trundle along with the daybed. Meagan can make it up for you."

He glanced toward Meagan and she slipped out onto the dogtrot, happy to put as much distance between herself and Ruth as possible.

Meagan hesitated before opening the door to the parlor. She had not entered the room after dark since the night she had run out so abruptly in an effort to escape the eerie sound of the organ. A sound that had ultimately sent her into Josh's arms, to be held in his warm, wonderful—dangerous—embrace.

There was no sound tonight.

Meagan took the linens from the chest and made up the beds in record time. One note out of the organ and there was no power on this earth that could force her to return. With a sigh of relief she finished her task and closed the door behind her, returning to the main part of the house.

The rain was coming down in earnest. Meagan rushed into the room as Ruth peered out the door. It was obvious that even the thought of going down the covered dogtrot was distasteful. She held back, seemingly waiting for Meagan to make some move. Finally, Ruth could hold back no longer. "Aren't you going out to the barn to sleep?" she asked.

"Meagan sleeps with Abbie." Josh had had enough. He was exhausted. Sparring with a woman who was obviously trying to undermine every positive step he and Meagan had been able to make in their living arrangement had sapped his strength. Nothing would make Ruth happier than to see Meagan miserable.

"Well, I never," Ruth protested.

"You have now," Josh returned.

Rafe took his wife's arm and steered her toward the door, but Ruth was not to be denied. She would have the last word.

"Why didn't you make Meagan sleep in the parlor?" she inquired.

"Meagan couldn't sleep in there," Josh said. "She was uncomfortable."

Ruth snorted. "Well, I should think so. If Lily was

anywhere on earth it would be in that room. All of her belongings are in there. It's a wonder poor Lily doesn't come back to haunt the person who wronged her.''

It pleased Ruth to see that Meagan noticeably paled and her hands shook ever so slightly as she finished putting away the dishes.

Without another word Ruth marched out the door and followed her husband down the dogtrot.

It was sometime after midnight when the storm reached its peak. Meagan thought she heard the moaning of the organ, but the sound was muted and she assured herself it was only the wind in the trees. She pulled the blankets over her head and remembered the warmth of Josh's strong arms as they had closed about her the night she had been so frightened. She relived the wonder of his touch, the safety she had known, if for only a few moments.

Meagan closed her ears to the sounds about her, and her mind closed to Ruth's suggestion that Lily Daniels's ghost roamed the parlor. She was on the edge of sleep when she heard Josh rise from his bed. She heard the doors slam and the creak of the Somerses' wagon as Rafe pulled it as near to the door as possible.

''I thought Ruth would like sleeping in that room,'' Josh said, stifling a yawn. ''She and Lily were always such good friends.''

Rafe's dark eyes shifted toward the parlor.

''I cannot say what is in that room,'' Rafe told Josh while Ruth wrapped herself in a piece of borrowed oilcloth. ''The organ, it plays in the night. Ruth will not go back inside, and this time I agree.'' He wiped the rain from his face. ''We will go home. I would rather be drowned in the darkness than hounded by the dead.''

And even though Josh graciously offered them his

own bed, the Somerses couldn't leave the house fast enough. Rafe whipped the horse to a brisk trot despite the muddy roads.

Josh went out and made sure the parlor door was securely shut. He listened, but heard no sound other than the storm. Whatever it was that had chased his neighbors away was silent now. When he returned, Meagan peered from behind the curtain.

"Is something wrong?" she asked, knowing full well their guests had gone.

"Ruth and Rafe went home," Josh told her. He sat down on the bed and stared into the embers of the fire. It was several minutes before he spoke again. "Meagan," he called softly, "are you awake?"

The sound of his voice sent her heart racing. "Yes, I'm still awake," she managed.

"I wanted to apologize," he offered. "About thinking you were daft after the way you carried on over hearing organ music. Ruth and Rafe heard it too. That's why they left."

Meagan wrapped her shawl about herself and came from behind the curtain. "What do you suppose it is?" she asked softly.

Josh smiled. "I'm sure there's some reasonable explanation, but we'll never be able to convince Ruth and Rafe of that. They think it's Lily's ghost playing her organ."

"And what do you think?"

Josh traced the smooth skin of Meagan's cheek with his knuckle. Her eyes were dewy with sleep and her lips full and moist and parted, begging to be kissed.

How he longed to feel her young, strong body pressed against his. To shut out the sounds of the storm with the hammering of his heart.

"I think we'd better get some sleep. Storm means a lot of cleaning up has to be done. If Lily wants to spend eternity playing the organ I don't know what I can do to stop her."

Meagan disappeared behind the curtain as Josh lay back on his bed, propped his arm on a pillow and closed his eyes, unaware that she had paused before she let the curtain drop between them. He looked so young, so handsome. How she would have loved to go to him and brush back the hair that fell across his forehead as she had done when he was caught in the ravages of fever. But it must not be. It must never be. For to love Josh Daniels was to flirt with death. Yet before the curtain dropped she kissed him with her mind. And he lifted his hand and touched his lips as though he felt the pressure of her thoughts.

As Josh began to mend he took on the responsibility of cleaning and dressing his own arm. Meagan still prepared the poultices and ointments and washed and boiled the bandages.

Each day when she came into the house she sniffed the air for the first scent of decaying flesh that would mean the onset of the dreaded gangrene. She knew there had been infection. But as the days passed the scent of decay did not infiltrate the little cabin and a feeling of relief permeated her whole being.

Overburdened with her own work as well as the work Josh had done before his accident, Meagan had all but forgotten Rafe Somers's words until one morning when she returned to the house just as Josh was changing his bandage. The arm was healing from the inside out and the decaying flesh that would most likely have caused the arm to be amputated had been consumed. The maggots had done their work.

But Meagan, through the mere reputation of the little creatures, felt that she had somehow failed to give Josh the nursing he needed. She had failed to keep his arm clean enough and, in her failure, might have lost him. She ran out behind the smokehouse where she could not be seen from the cabin itself.

Once there she buried her face in her hands and cried. Perhaps Ruth was right. Perhaps Meagan was a worthless girl and shouldn't be left alone with the responsibility of a house and a child, much less that of a sick man.

If, through her stupidity in not knowing, or seeing, what was happening to Josh's arm, she had been responsible for his death, what would have happened to Abbie? And, with Josh gone, what would have happened to Meagan herself? She knew without a doubt that Ruth would have pushed the judge to carry out his original sentence.

Even over the sound of the blood pounding in her head as she tried to silence her sobs, Meagan was aware of someone stopping nearby. Josh's warm, strong body came to occupy the space beside her on the rock on which she sat. His arm, gentle and comforting, wrapped around her shoulder and turned her slowly until her head rested on his broad shoulder. He tenderly stroked her hair.

"There's nothing to cry about, Meagan. You did everything right. The whole situation couldn't have worked out better," Josh said.

"I didn't do enough." She managed to choke out the words. "I should have taken better care of you."

"You gave me the best care I could ever have had," he assured her.

"But those…those…" Meagan couldn't make herself say the words.

"Those little varmints saved my arm. If this had happened in the winter I wouldn't have had a chance. Dead flesh won't grow back to more dead flesh. It would have rotted and gangrene would have set in."

Meagan looked up into Josh's eyes. "Why didn't you tell me?" she asked.

"You'd have screamed and fainted and cleaned the varmints out, and I would most likely have lost my arm."

"You don't know that I would have done that." Meagan drew herself up with indignation.

"And you don't know that you wouldn't," Josh reminded her. "Now we don't need to worry about it because it's almost over. The only thing we need to worry about is whether or not I can get the use of my hand back, but that isn't as important as just knowing it's still there at the end of my arm, and for that I thank you."

He wanted to say more. He wanted to tell her that he admired her bravery and her stamina. He wanted to let her know how much he appreciated her uncomplaining demeanor and her ability to smile through the deepest adversity, but most of all, and more than anything else, he wanted to bend down and kiss her tears away. His jaw set as he fought the urge, almost too overpowering to bear.

Keep talking, he told himself. *Think of something, anything, to say.* But his mind was focused on the tear-streaked face and to save his soul, he could hold no other thought.

To his disappointment and relief, Meagan turned

away, and Josh knew it was in the best interest of them both not to call her back.

There was a period of time before the coming of winter and after the fields had been harvested when the settlers went into to town to buy, sell and trade their wares and their excess produce for the supplies they would need during the winter.

Josh and Meagan had finished loading the wagon and Abbie was dancing with excitement as they made ready to leave, when Meagan made her plea.

"Perhaps it would be better if I didn't go into town with you," she said. "I should stay here and tend the stock. Leaving them down by the creek could be a problem should the weather turn bad."

Josh looked at her. She was pale and wan. She had worked harder than any woman he'd ever known, bringing in the last of the harvest single-handed while she'd kept up with the household chores. If anyone deserved a holiday it was Meagan.

"I'm not leaving you here alone," he told her in a firm voice.

"I wasn't planning to run away." She wasn't planning on it, but had Reilly turned up while Josh was away Meagan would most likely have gone with him. Staying there with Josh was a source of constant heartache. Leaving him would be worse, but at least he would not be threatened by what might happen should they stay together.

As though catching the whisper of her thoughts Josh watched her speculatively. Was she thinking of escape? Obviously the thought had entered her mind, or why else would she have mentioned the possibility? It made little difference. Meagan would go into town with Josh and Abbie.

Will Carmichael and his wife were expecting them, and while Josh would have been the first to admit that Meagan would be somewhat of a curiosity to the other settlers, as soon as they realized that she was carrying her weight they would accept her presence.

"Come along." Josh gestured toward the wagon. "The house is boarded up and I don't intend to take the time to open it up until we get back."

"I could stay in the barn," Meagan bargained.

"You could get in the wagon," Josh said firmly. Meagan gave up and did as she was told. "You'll be surprised how quickly people forget, Meagan," he assured her.

Meagan thought about her half brother. No one ever forgot that he was half Indian, and no one ever let Reilly forget it either.

"And you'd be surprised how long they remember," she countered.

Josh helped her into the seat and swung up beside her while Abbie squeezed in between them rather than sit in the place they had prepared for her in the back.

"All right," Josh said with a sigh, "have it your own way. We're going to be staying at the Carmichaels' place, and you don't have to show your face the whole time we're there." Having spoken, Josh closed his mouth and stared at the road. He wanted Meagan to come. She deserved to relax for a few days, but it hadn't really occurred to him that going among the people who had convicted her of murder might not exactly be Meagan's idea of fun. However, it was the best he could do.

Josh knew that the Carmichaels would never allow anything unpleasant to happen to Meagan and he had come to feel the same way. As long as Meagan was with Josh, heaven help the man who spoke against her. His jaw set and he didn't relax until he heard Meagan whisper "Thank you."

There were some questioning glances when Josh Daniels's wagon entered the town, but the only voices that were raised were those that called out greetings as he guided his team toward the Carmichael house.

Many of the settlers had no close friends in the settlement and had provided for themselves by pitching tents and lean-tos. A veritable village had risen. Josh was pleased that he did not have to join them. His friendship with Will Carmichael had held him in good stead, and a grin split his face as he pulled up in front of the Carmichael house.

Will lived in the middle of the town. His home also housed his law office and the printing press where he edited and printed the small weekly paper, which was the only source of printed information for miles around.

Hearing the wagon, Will went to the door to greet his guests while Phoebe ran around from the garden where she had been choosing some late vegetables for their meal.

"And I'm glad to see you, Meagan." Will helped Meagan from the wagon after greeting Josh.

"And me, too, Uncle Will." Abbie giggled as she held out her arms to be lifted from the bed of the wagon.

"And you, too." Will swung her around. "And don't you look pretty today. Looks like you're sporting a new bonnet."

"I have lots of new bonnets," Abbie affirmed. "Meagan makes them for me. With lots and lots of lace and ribbons."

Meagan took the little girl's hand as the child skipped along at her side on the way to the house. Phoebe was genuinely happy to see Meagan again. The woman had grown quite attached to Meagan during the time she had been forced to stay with the Carmichaels while awaiting her trial.

Before Meagan could reach the house a crowd of well-wishers had gathered, coming from the doors of the business establishments that surrounded Will's office. They greeted Josh with enthusiasm and true pleasure and their acknowledgment of Meagan, while cool, could hardly have been called unfriendly.

Meagan's feeling of well-being was shattered when she spied Ruth Somers sailing down the street, the feathers on her bonnet standing straight up in indignation.

"How dare you bring that creature here." She shook her fingers at Josh.

"What did you expect me to do with Meagan?" Josh asked. "Leave her home alone?"

"You could have locked her in the shed until you got back," Ruth asserted. "It would have served her right after what she did to Rafe and me. Chasing us off in the middle of the night during the worst storm of the season."

Everyone paused. Conversation ceased. Heads went up.

"That's silly, Ruth." Josh tried to brush the whole situation aside. "Meagan was nowhere near you that night. You were the one who insisted on leaving."

"Any God-fearing woman would have left when she was shut up in a haunted house," she said snorting, the feathers nodding in assent to her claim.

"I've never seen or heard any ghost," Josh said firmly. "If I remember correctly it was you who said

Lily would probably come back to haunt the people she didn't want using her things. Maybe you fell into that category.''

Before the situation could get completely out of control, Will Carmichael stepped forward, neatly edging Ruth off to the side and drawing Meagan forward.

''Why, Meagan, I believe you look a bit the worse for wear.'' He turned to Josh. ''The judge didn't say you were supposed to work her to death,'' he chided. His lips formed a smile, but it didn't extend to his voice.

''Oh, goodness no,'' Ruth purred as she paused beside them. ''We surely wouldn't want to work her to death, would we?'' But the malice in her eyes belied her words.

Will ignored the woman and frowned as he scrutinized his friend. ''Come to think of it, Josh, you don't look so good yourself.''

''I had an accident,'' Josh admitted reluctantly. ''Got myself caught in a trap a while back. Danged near lost my arm. Meagan got stuck doing most all the work for a spell. Couldn't have handled it better myself. She brought in the last of the crops along with most everything else that got done around the place, plus nursing me and taking care of Abbie.''

Will put his arm about Meagan's shoulders. ''Looks as though you have a right to look a little tired.''

''I'm fine, Mr. Carmichael,'' Meagan protested. ''Really, I am. Josh has been able to help with the chores for the past couple of weeks and we're coming along just fine.''

''Nonetheless, we're going to see that you get a well-deserved rest for the next couple of days while you're here, and maybe pamper you a little, too.'' He gave her shoulder a fond pat. ''Maybe you should let the doctor take a look at your arm, Josh. He might have some suggestions on how to get your hand to working a little better.''

Josh blushed. He had hoped his disability was not that noticeable and kept his thumb looped through his belt. He knew his friend only wanted the best for him. After casting an apologetic glance in Meagan's direction, he acquiesced.

''I guess it wouldn't hurt to ask. Gets sort of tedious trying to milk the cow with one hand.'' Both men laughed, with Meagan and Phoebe joining in. Only Ruth did not see the humor in the situation.

Instead, the woman gave a little gasp of outrage, turned on her heel and blasted her way back toward the general store, where Rafe waited calmly, whittling a piece of wood as he sat on the porch. ''I just can't understand why that creature should be allowed the comforts of a fine house like the Carmichaels' while we are relegated to a tepee at the edge of town,'' Ruth complained.

''Maybe if you hadn't insulted most of the women in this town at one time or another we would have better accommodations,'' Rafe remarked. ''I don't mind staying in the tent,'' he continued. ''Leave the girl alone. Her life is difficult enough without you making it worse.''

''Are you criticizing me?'' Ruth was aghast.

''I am just pointing out a possibility,'' her husband said as she disappeared into the store and slammed the door.

Meagan could barely suppress the sigh of relief as she realized Ruth had gone into the store and no longer spat insults from the porch.

"What's this about the house being haunted?" Phoebe's interest wasn't to be denied.

Meagan looked around for Abbie and saw that the little girl had gone to join her father and Will. It was safe to speak without frightening the child.

"It's the organ in the parlor."

"What about it?" Phoebe urged.

"Sometimes it plays when there's nobody around."

Phoebe placed her handkerchief over her mouth and coughed gently into it. "It does?" she managed, hardly able to contain her mirth.

"It's not funny, Phoebe," Meagan assured her. "I've heard it and it about scared me out of my wits. Rafe and Ruth Somers had to spend the night because of a storm. The organ began to play and the Somerses got up and left."

Phoebe threw her apron over her face and sank into her rocker. Her shoulders shook with mirth. When she managed to pull her face out of her lap she took one look at Meagan's face, let out a whoop and dissolved into another fit of laughter.

"I take it Josh hasn't found the time to move it away from the window," she said as she wiped her eyes.

"Is that how the ghost gets out?" Meagan asked softly.

Her question sent Phoebe into another laughing spell.

"Don't you worry about that organ," Phoebe told her. "Next time I come out I'll exorcise your ghost for you and you won't have any more trouble." She wiped her eyes and patted Meagan on the shoulder. "Now, come along and I'll show you to your room. You'll share with Abbie. I didn't think you'd mind."

"Abbie and I are used to sharing," Meagan assured her as they mounted the stairs.

"After you get settled in and cleaned up, we'll have some supper and see if we can find you something suitable to wear to the autumn social." Phoebe bustled along the hallway, but Meagan stopped dead in her tracks.

"I can't go to any social." Meagan fought to keep her voice from shaking. "With Ruth Somers in town there's no telling what the woman might say."

"She'll hold her tongue," Phoebe told her. "Besides, it's a masked affair so no one's likely to figure out who you are until the party's about over, and by that time, if you like, you can come home."

Meagan beamed. Oh, yes! There was no doubt she wanted to get dressed up and go to a party. She wanted to look pretty for Josh and see the approval in his eyes, if only for a moment.

"A Masque!" she echoed. "What a wonderful idea!"

"Thank you." Phoebe preened pointedly. "It was my idea and I thought it rather marvelous myself."

Meagan was still smiling to herself as she poured water from the flowered pitcher into the washbasin. Her heart was lighter than it had been since before the death of her father. She would go to a party incognito. A party! She savored the word. She had never thought to go to a party again, especially one where no one would recognize her. They wouldn't be in town all that long. If she kept to herself and stayed inside the Carmichael house, everything should be all right. After all, what could possibly happen that would cause her to make a spectacle of herself? She smiled to herself again as she whispered the words, "Absolutely nothing can go wrong this time."

The dress was the color of cranberries, rich and shimmering. Phoebe fussed and nipped and tucked, talking constantly despite a mouth full of pins.

"It wasn't as though Lily married beneath herself," Phoebe declared as she jabbed a pin into the material. "Josh comes from good stock. He's a hard worker and has gone out and built a good place for himself.

"To the best of my knowledge Josh was never much for book learning. He learned just what he had to know to cipher and read or write a list of supplies. Beyond that I doubt he's ever willingly picked up a book except to move it out of his way. But he can build or repair anything, and there's no better backwoodsman in the area. Most any woman would feel lucky to have a man like Josh. Even Lily.

"It was just that Lily was a town girl. Born and bred in Boston, and she didn't adapt easily to the rough and sometimes rather frightening life on the frontier."

Meagan listened, not daring to so much as breathe for fear the woman would stop talking. Though at the rate Phoebe went on there seemed little possibility of that.

"I can tell you there were times when Lily would come into town and complain about how lonely she was out there in the middle of nowhere." She sighed. "I can't say that I blame her. There's been many a time when I've thanked my lucky stars that Will is a lawyer and must hang his shingle out where people can see it. But Lily knew that Josh didn't want anything more than to work the land. He never made any bones about it and she never objected until the past year or so. I guess that was when they realized the honeymoon was over and hard times set in."

Phoebe sighed again and followed her persistent pinning with some basting stitches without taking the dress from Meagan's body. "'Course it was just one thing after the other from the time Abbie was born. I guess Lily wasn't really cut out to be a mother, but she stuck it out for a good long time before it became obvious she had little interest in Abbie. Of course, I doubt the child will ever be a beauty, but she has many lovable characteristics that could easily make someone overlook those unfortunate ears.''

The woman shook her head and Meagan wondered whether there was something wrong with the fitting of the dress, or if it was the memories her soliloquy had evoked.

''You couldn't really say it was a natural situation when the first thing the mother did on seeing her new-born daughter was laugh aloud. 'Get those things off her head,' she said, and tugged one of the baby's ears. Poor baby didn't know what had happened and screamed at the top of her lungs. Lily was contrite, but she never so much as looked at the girl again unless Abbie was wearing a bonnet.''

''What about Josh?'' Meagan ventured.

''What about him?''

''I mean, he loves Abbie. How did he cope with the situation?'' Meagan had lived most of her life without knowing her mother, but she knew she would rather have it that way than have a mother who laughed at her or a father who allowed her to do so.

Phoebe paused a few moments before speaking. ''Lily put out the word that the child was subject to earaches and had to keep her ears covered. The fact remains that the woman never had another child. 'You can't make a boy wear bonnets for the rest of his life,' she used to say, and even Josh couldn't argue with that statement.''

Phoebe stood back contemplating her efforts and finally proclaimed herself satisfied.

"I'm going to get pink ribbon for the trim," she said as she put on her bonnet. "It should set it off just right. Do you want to come along?"

Meagan looked wistfully at the main street. She longed to go out but the stares that would follow her held her back.

"No, I'll stay here."

Understanding her reluctance to appear in public, Phoebe did not argue as she bustled out the door and hurried off down the street.

Meagan removed the lovely dress and hung it carefully in the armoire. She could hear the sounds of the children playing along the side of the house as she buttoned her everyday dress and sat down on the window ledge to enjoy a moment of relaxation. Her room on the second floor butted against a huge old tree and she opened the window to enjoy the early autumn beauty.

So far everything had gone beautifully. The doctor had said there was nothing he could do for Josh's arm, and all it needed was daily use to build the strength back up to normal. Abbie had made friends with some of the village children and had hardly been able to finish her breakfast before bolting out the door to join them.

Meagan closed her eyes and allowed herself to drift on dreams of the dance that would take place that evening. It was the change of the tone of the children's voices that caught her attention.

The squeals and laughter of play quickly changed to the raucous tones of teasing. Above it all Abbie's voice rose in a terrified wail. "No! No! Don't take my bonnet! Leave it alone!"

Meagan threw her legs over the windowsill and eased herself out onto a branch of the tree. She edged her way across as she and Reilly had done as children, and dropped easily to the ground, landing in the midst of the startled children.

"It's the murderer!" one of the boys yelped, releasing his hold on Abbie's bonnet. "Don't let her get me!"

He turned and ran, the others following in his wake.

A moment later Meagan and Abbie stood alone in the now silent yard.

Chapter Seven

Abbie buried her face in Meagan's skirt. "They were going to take my bonnet," she wailed. "Then they'd see my ears!" She sobbed out the last word like the curse her ears had proved to be.

Meagan hugged her tightly. "But they didn't get your bonnet, and they didn't see your ears. Now come back into the house and we'll see if we can find you some bread and jam while we talk this over."

The little girl sniffled, somewhat appeased that she would be given a treat despite her ridicule by the children of the town. Meagan led her into the house, waiting for the child to ask about the words of the boy describing Meagan as a murderer, but Abbie apparently had not heard the accusation. However, Meagan had heard, and the words were burned into her soul. She blinked back the tears that stung her eyes. Sometimes it seemed almost as though hanging would have been the better choice, rather than to live branded as a criminal for a crime she did not commit.

The children gave the house a wide berth and Abbie stayed inside, until Phoebe returned.

"Why aren't you out playing?" the woman asked.

"Meagan said I didn't have to," Abbie replied stoically.

Phoebe turned to Meagan. "What happened?"

"They tried to take my bonnet," Abbie volunteered before Meagan could speak. "They wanted to make me cry, but Meagan wouldn't let them."

The little girl looked at her benefactor with pure worship in her eyes. It wasn't wasted on Phoebe. She put her hand on Abbie's head and steered her toward the door. "Meagan's right, you don't have to play with them. Now go on down to the cook and tell her you want some pumpkin bread and whipped cream. Meagan and I will be with you in a little while."

Abbie didn't try to hide her joy over the promised goodies. She skipped out of the room without another word.

Phoebe turned to Meagan.

"There was nothing I could do," Meagan told her. "They would have taken Abbie's bonnet and her dignity. She would never have regained the latter. I couldn't let that happen. I was sitting upstairs in the window in my room. I heard it all. When I realized they were threatening Abbie, I climbed out onto the tree branch and scooted over until I could swing down. You should have seen them scatter when I dropped right in the middle of them. You'd have thought I was the devil himself."

Phoebe had no doubt that to the children, Meagan had seemed nothing less than what she had proclaimed herself to be.

"Let's just hope word doesn't reach the wrong ears, or there'll be the devil to pay, and that's gospel," she asserted. "Now climb back into this dress and we'll see if we can get finished before suppertime."

* * *

Meagan turned and swayed before the floor-length mirror, while Phoebe sat back on her heels, her hands clasped in satisfaction.

"You look as pretty as a day in May," Phoebe exclaimed as she surveyed her work. "Let me go and get the teakettle and steam the wrinkles out of the material and you'll be the belle of the ball." She hurried out of the room while Meagan waltzed back and forth, admiring her image.

Meagan could see it all. She would drift down the stairs, her lovely feathered mask in place, the gorgeous cranberry-colored dress billowing about her. She would take Josh's arm. Of course he would know who she was, but he would be so overcome by her beauty he would never think of revealing her secret. He would hand her into the coach and they would sit side by side, their legs and arms touching as they drove toward the festivities.

Once inside, Josh would not be able to hide his anxiousness to hold Meagan. To dance with her across the shining oak floor. The music would start and they would find themselves locked in each other's arms. They would dance, their steps matched so perfectly that everyone else in the hall would stop in their tracks to watch.

Josh's eyes would soften in the reflection of her beauty. He would know, beyond a question of a doubt, that he could not live without her. In the end he would join Will Carmichael in going before the judge to have her proclaimed innocent of Lily's death, and she would ride back to the cabin as Josh's wife.

Meagan closed her eyes as the lovely image of her fantasy bloomed before the eye of her imagination, but when she opened her eyes, she knew it could never be. No matter how lovely she was in her borrowed gown, Josh would never love her, never want to wed her and never want her to be anything more than his indentured servant.

She wiped her tears away before they could fall and stain the lovely watered silk of her gown. The sounds of men's voices and doors slamming echoed through the house and before she could cover her gown with her cloak, Josh entered the room with Will hard on his heels.

"Get into your traveling clothes," Josh ordered. "We are returning home within the hour. Phoebe is packing Abbie's things."

Meagan stared in stunned silence. "But what about the social?" she managed.

"You destroyed any hope of that when you dropped into the midst of the village children like an avenging angel. Ruth Somers is crying for your incarceration for threatening half the children in the territory. The sooner we get you out of here, the better."

Before he could say more, there was a hammering on the door. Will answered it, but he was no match for the bodacious Ruth, who bounded into the house.

"I told you so! I told you that woman was up to no good," she shouted. "She nearly frightened the feathers out of half the children here, not to mention what she did to my own sons."

"I doubt Meagan would know your sons if she saw them." Josh tried to defend Meagan.

"That doesn't matter! My children know who Meagan is. They know she is a murderer and shouldn't be allowed around decent people."

To Josh's astonishment, Meagan stepped forward. "If you want your boys around decent people you should teach them to behave decently," she said. "You should teach them not to tease and torment Abbie and try to steal away her bonnet and embarrass her."

Ruth huffed herself up. "My sons wouldn't do such a thing."

"Yes they did! Yes they did!" Abbie came running down the hall.

Josh caught his daughter in his arms. "Are you sure?" he asked.

"Yes, Papa, I'm sure," the little girl answered solemnly.

Josh hardly gave Ruth another glance as he threw his bags and supplies on the wagon. The woman's harangue continued as she hardly paused for breath. Finally, realizing that none of her threats was being taken seriously, she went for the jugular. "And you don't need to bring your family around to my home for the Christmas celebrations either," she shouted. "I won't have that felon in my home. And Abbie is becoming just like her." She huffed like a ruffled hen.

"You needn't worry," Josh returned. "You'll not see hide nor hair of us on your property. I expect the same courtesy from you, Ruth. If you or yours set foot on my property from this day forth, I'll set the dogs on you." And without further ado, he backed her out the door and closed the portal in her face.

Josh was still shaking when he turned to see Will Carmichael watching him.

"I don't want to hear it," Josh said.

"The Somerses are your nearest neighbors," Will pointed out.

"The Somerses are troublemakers," Josh returned. "We're better off without them."

"It's going to be a long, lonely winter," Will reminded his friend.

"It'll be all right," Josh assured him. "We have each other."

''You also have a very vocal enemy,'' Will said as he gave Josh's shoulder an encouraging squeeze before the two men picked up the remaining bags and carried them toward the wagon.

Meanwhile, Meagan's heart was singing. Josh had defended her. He hadn't understood or approved of what she had done, but he had defended her nonetheless, and even though there would be no ball for Meagan, she didn't care.

From the moment Josh had shoved Ruth out the door, Meagan knew she could no longer deny her love for him any more than she could keep from hoping that he loved her, too. Yes, she loved him and wanted his love in return, though it threatened her very life.

Abbie sat silently in the bed of the wagon during most of the trip home. They were well into the afternoon of the second day when Meagan finally managed to get the little girl to speak, and it was Meagan's apology that brought forth the reply.

''I'm sorry you didn't get to play with the children a bit more.'' Meagan turned on the wagon seat to speak to the child. ''I'm sure they would have been more charitable once they got to know you better.''

''Daniel Somers tried to take my bonnet and he knows me. He's just mean.''

''Rafe's boy?'' Josh entered the conversation.

''That's him,'' Abbie said in a flat little voice. ''He's always teasing me and trying to get the other kids to tease me, too.''

Josh gave a sigh. It didn't seem like such a big thing to him. ''That's the way boys are, Abbie.''

''Were you like that, Papa?'' The child looked up at

her father in disbelief and Meagan tried hard to keep from smiling.

"I don't rightly remember," Josh admitted. "Most likely I was, but you have to remember that we never see ourselves the way other people see us."

"Well, I don't like to be teased," Abbie asserted. "It hurts my feelings. I don't care if I never see Danny Somers again, ever. He's a mean boy."

"You won't have to worry about seeing him for a while," Josh told her. "I told Ruth not to come to our house until she could control her temper and her tongue. I guess we won't be going to the Somerses' place for Christmas the way we usually do." He glanced at the little girl, trying to gauge the depth of her disappointment. Josh was surprised to see that she was concentrating on adjusting the dress on her doll.

She looked up to find him watching her. "I didn't guess we'd be going to Aunt Ruthie's for Christmas anyway, even if Mama had been here."

Abbie seldom made reference to her mother, and both Meagan and Josh immediately gave the child their undivided attention. "Why would you think a thing like that?" Josh prodded gently. "Most everybody that's settled for miles around ends up at the Somerses' house for Christmas dinner."

Abbie plucked at the lace on her doll's petticoat, obviously uncomfortable over her disclosure. "One day when we went to visit, Aunt Ruthie and Mama started shouting at each other real loud. I went over by the door and heard Aunt Ruthie say that she never wanted to see Mama in her house again."

Josh was speechless. He'd had no indication of bad blood between the two women.

"What did your mother say to that?" Meagan asked.

"Mama just laughed, kinda mean, like the way she always did when I took my bonnet off. Then she said not to worry, that she'd make sure Aunt Ruthie'd never *see* her."

"Did you ever go back to the Somerses' house again?" Meagan persisted, disregarding the pressure of Josh's leg as he tried to silence her.

"Oh yes, we went back, but Aunt Ruthie never was there until the day she came home with you—"

Josh cut her off mid-sentence. "I'm sure hungry. I think we should pull over by that little pond and have something to eat."

Meagan could have screamed. It seemed as though the child had been about to reveal something that might have helped to clear Meagan's name and Josh had stopped her.

The minute the little girl was out of earshot Meagan approached Josh. "Why didn't you let her speak?" she demanded. "Apparently things weren't exactly the way Ruth led everyone to believe at my trial. Abbie might know something that would—"

"Abbie is just a little girl," Josh said flatly. "I don't want her upset thinking how her mother fell to her death." He paused. "I don't want Abbie to have to live it all over again. You will not encourage her to talk about her mother's death. Do you understand?"

"Yes, Mr. Daniels, I understand and I'll abide by your wishes. And I'm sorry your wife is dead. But *I* didn't kill her!" And she lifted the basket of food from beneath the wagon seat and went to join Abbie, who was floating sticks on the edge of the pond.

The trip into town proved to be the last of the good weather. With the exception of a few isolated days the rains had definitely come and it was time for repair and stocking up for the winter ahead.

With Ruth's proclamation that the Danielses were not welcome in her home, Meagan set her mind to make Christmas in the Daniels house a time to remember.

As the weather turned more hostile, Meagan taught Abbie to hem a handkerchief for her father. A few weeks before Christmas day itself, they ferreted through the supplies in the pantry and came out with currants, raisins, porridge, nuts and freshly made sausage, which, along with eggs and the spices Meagan had managed to unearth, would add flavor to the treasured Christmas pudding. This delicacy would be stored for five weeks, after which time they would wrap it in a cloth and steam it.

On Christmas day they would smother it with brandy sauce and set fire to it when it was served.

"Our very own Christmas pudding," Abbie said for the tenth time as she slowly stirred the concoction. "We never had our own Christmas pudding before. We always had to have a bite of Aunt Ruthie's pudding. She puts lots of peel in her pudding and I don't like peel, but I had to eat it because Mama wouldn't let me spit it out."

Josh remained quiet as he sat near the fire painstakingly carving a piece of wood. Meagan knew from experience that he did not like to talk of things that made it seem as though Lily had been an incompetent wife and mother.

"Well, there won't be any peel in this pudding," Meagan said gently.

"That's right, this will be the best pudding ever," Abbie bubbled. "I wished it would be the best when I stirred it. What did you wish for, Papa?"

Everyone took a turn at stirring the pudding, and by doing so was allowed to make a wish. Josh had given it little thought, but since the child was so exuberant over the prospect, he came up with an answer.

"I wished I could get my hand to working better, and I'll bet by this time next year my wish will have come true. I'm already able to use both hands when I milk the cow." He cast a smile across the room. "But I thought you'd wish for something for yourself, Abbie."

"Oh, I wished for that, too," Abbie assured him. "I wished my ears didn't stick out anymore." The little girl tugged at her bonnet impatiently. "I get awful tired of wearing bonnets."

She didn't look at her father when she spoke, and he didn't look at her.

"I hope your wish comes true," he said without enthusiasm. Then he turned to Meagan. "And what did you wish for?" he asked.

"I wished that both of you would get your wishes," she smiled, but Megan knew that if Abbie was to get her wish it would be up to Meagan to find some way to make it happen.

The days grew shorter and Meagan spent the daylight hours doing the household chores. With the spat between Josh and Ruth there were no visitors. But it mattered little to Josh. Catching the spirit of the season, he went about choosing a goose to grace their dinner table with all the enthusiasm of a host about to welcome a table full of guests.

A few days before Christmas he accompanied Meagan and Abbie through the snow as they gathered greens to decorate the house.

They found cranberries and evergreens. They cut

branches that would be woven into garlands and made into wreaths. They laughed and breathed in the pine fragrance that seemed to permeate their clothing. As Josh and Meagan pulled the hand sled piled high now with greenery, Abbie followed along behind, occasionally pelting one of them with a handful of snow that fell apart on impact and sparkled like fairy dust in the sunlight.

But one well-sent missile hit a tree branch heavy with snow and managed to move it enough that a good deal of the white powder fell down Josh's neck.

"That did it," he shouted in mock anger. "Now you're in for it!" And he took off running toward the little girl, who shrieked in delight and dashed away.

Abbie dodged from one side of the sled to the other, giggling and yelling in delight. Just as it looked as though Josh would catch the child, Meagan jumped into the fray.

"No fair!" she admonished. "You're bigger than she is. Pick on someone your own size." And she pelted him squarely with a handful of snow.

Now it was two against one. Meagan felt her heart pounding wildly as Josh took off running across the snow and disappeared into the trees.

"You go that way, I'll go over here. Holler when you find him." Abbie gave the orders like a drill sergeant and hightailed it into the bushes.

But it was Meagan who found Josh when he leaped out at her. She tossed the last of the snow into his face and turned to find herself at the top of a little hill. Without a moment's hesitation, Meagan grabbed the edge of her cloak and slithered down the hill on her on her backside.

Josh caught her halfway down, and they rolled to a stop as they reached the bottom of the incline.

"Let's see how you like having your face washed in snow," he said as he swiped his mittened hand over her face.

Meagan shoved snow down Josh's back, but she was pinned beneath his body and could not get away.

After a few moments she stopped struggling. "Let me up," she said laughing. "We'll both be soaked."

She opened her eyes and blinked the snow from her lashes. When she looked into his face, so close to her own, she could see a new expression in his eyes. An expression Meagan had never seen before.

"Josh? What is it? Is it your hand? Have I made you angry?"

"Dang it, Meagan, do you know how pretty you are with your cheeks all red, your eyes so bright and your lips all red and shiny and just waiting like a juicy winter apple to be tasted, again and again and again." He gave a little sob deep in his throat and knew in that moment that all the judges and courts in the world couldn't stop him.

If he couldn't taste those sweet lips he would die of starvation just as sure as if he never again allowed food to pass his lips.

"Lord, have mercy," he whispered as his lips fell on hers with heated urgency.

Her lips were as cold as his own, but they parted and the sweet warmth of her breath caressed his mouth as he ran his tongue over those cool, inviting lips and felt them give way until he reached the warm cavern that was her mouth.

His blood was singing in his veins. His head hammered with a need greater than he had ever imagined. She drew him deeper into her warmth, as though breathing him in. In that moment, there was no law greater than the one they had discovered—their full and abiding love for each other. A love that could not be assuaged until they were granted the ultimate fulfillment, no matter the cost.

"Meagan! Meagan! You promised!"

Was it the wrath of God, shouting down upon them? Had the good Lord sent down an angel to protect them from certain doom?

"You said you'd holler when you found Papa, and you didn't," the little girl accused as she crested the hill and started skidding down the side.

Josh took a shaky breath as he stood and extended his hand to help Meagan to her feet. "I'm afraid Meagan got the breath knocked out of her," he told his daughter. "We came pelting over the hill and our feet came out from under us. By the time we came to a stop, I landed right on top of her. Wasn't much chance of Meagan saying a word."

Abbie looked up into Meagan's flushed face and then back to her father. "I don't guess we'd better snow-fight anymore," she told him as she brushed the snow from her mittens.

"Are you worn out?" he asked as he swung her up onto his shoulder and grabbed Meagan's hand.

"No," she said as they started back to where they'd left the sled, "but I think Meagan is tired. It looks as though she's been crying."

Josh slowed his steps and turned to look at Meagan. She didn't look as though she was crying to him. He saw a woman who returned his love in kind. Josh had thought he'd never love again. Thought he'd never want to share his life to the fullest extent with another human being. Not from the day when Lily had let him know that she no longer wanted to share any part of herself with the man she had taken as husband.

At first he had thought it must be due to her fear of childbirth, but as the time went on, he realized that the life they lived was not the life that Lily Daniels desired. Josh had invested everything in his land. He had no choice but to stay and make it work, but Lily would not try to understand and refused to do anything other than haphazardly watch Abbie while Josh was working in the fields.

Again he glanced at Meagan. Her eyes were bright and alert with excitement. She was laughing with Abbie, but he did not hear their words, nor did he share in their cheer, for the very life that shone so brightly in Meagan's eyes was the life of which his love would rob her.

"Papa! Papa!" Abbie's voice piped. "Aren't you going to sing? We're going to sing all the way back to the house. Aren't you going to sing?"

"Yes." He pushed the dark thoughts from his mind. "I'm going to sing." He patted her leg and swung her down. Somehow he must make certain nothing like this ever happened again. If Abbie had come upon them, there was no telling who else might accidentally discover them in a like situation.

No, it must never happen again, for it could mean Meagan's life, and his happiness. It must be enough to enjoy her presence, and know that in her heart she cared for him, just as he cared for her.

Oh, yes…in the name of heaven, sing! For if they did not sing Josh didn't know whether he could keep from telling Meagan that regardless of how she might view his future treatment of her, he loved her, and most likely he always would.

"You girls start singing and I'll join in," he promised as they plodded through the snow toward the house.

The house smelled of pine and spices. Every available inch had been decorated with greenery and hung with berries. Abbie skipped about the room inspecting each bough while Meagan took a sheet of cookies from the oven and sprinkled them with sugar she had dyed with cranberry juice.

At Abbie's cry of joy, Josh came over to inspect their handiwork. He had helped cut the bells and stars out of the rolled cookie dough, and had even tried his hand at cutting out a little cookie man.

"I'm afraid Abbie will be too excited to eat much," said Meagan, laughing. "I don't know whether it will be worthwhile to make any supper."

"I'm hungry enough for all of us," Josh replied. "I'll eat her share."

"I could eat a cookie," Abbie offered.

"Not until tomorrow," Meagan reminded her. "We're going to use them for decorations." And she proceeded to place the cookies among the greenery, adding a bit of color.

Abbie clapped her hands. The child couldn't keep still and it took both adults to contain her.

Meagan silently thanked God for Abbie's excitement. It kept her from having to think, or feel, or relive the precious moment when Josh's lips had touched her own.

There would be time later, when the others were asleep. It was then Meagan would be able to restore each wondrous moment and treasure it within her heart as deeply as it was burned into her memory. As it was, she hardly dared look at Josh. But what she could see told her nothing. His face was impassive and had been ever since Abbie had found them on the hill.

She touched her fingers to her lips, reliving the touch of his lips once again.

It wasn't until later in the evening that Abbie quieted down enough to crawl onto Meagan's lap. The child yawned.

"I think I know a little girl who needs to go to bed," Meagan said gently.

Abbie shook her head.

"The sooner you go to sleep, the sooner tomorrow will come," her father said.

"Papa, what do you think will happen when the Christ Child comes tonight? Will Meagan get the gift he always brought for Mama?"

Josh's face flushed. He had forgotten that part of Christmas. Lily had always received a gift from the Christ Child on Christmas Eve. It was a surprise and was left on the doorstep, or outside the window. She had seen no reason why the custom should not be continued once she had a husband and home of her own. And, in Lily's mind, the Christ Child came for her alone, and she refused to share the moment even with her little daughter.

"I don't think we need worry about the Christ Child bringing anything. He always came while we were over at Aunt Ruthie's. I expect he knows your mother isn't around anymore."

Meagan felt a shiver run down her spine as Josh's eyes swept over her. "What did the Christ Child bring you, Abbie?" she asked in a desperate attempt to change the subject.

"Oh, the Christ Child only brought things for Mama. He never brought me anything. I was too young."

Now it was Meagan's turn to cast an accusing glance in Josh's direction. He looked away, unwilling to meet her eyes.

"And if the Christ Child were to bring you a present, what would you like?" Meagan asked.

Abbie cocked her head. "I'd like a new doll with *two* dresses." She thought for a while longer and finally admitted, "But what I'd really like is not to have to wear bonnets anymore."

"Everybody wears bonnets in the winter," Meagan reminded her.

"Not in the house," Abbie returned.

Idly Meagan removed the bonnet from the child's head. The girl's hair was coarse and with a hint of a wave, probably from being braided. Still, if it were not so long and heavy...

"I think we should wash your hair before you go to bed tonight. That will relax you and you'll sleep right through till morning."

Josh was about to object. It was cold and the cabin was drafty despite all his efforts to make it snug and warm. He opened his mouth, and this time his eyes met Meagan's with an impact of a blow.

"Go stir up the fire and make sure the kettle is full," Meagan ordered without a qualm. "I've got to find something to tear into strips."

By the time Meagan came back with a handful of cloth strips, Abbie was already standing near the wash-basin.

Meagan washed the little girl's hair and then shocked father and daughter into speechlessness as she took the scissors and began to cut the child's hair.

Chapter Eight

"What in the hell do you think you're doing?" Anger and frustration rang in his voice. "Abbie's never had her hair cut before. She needs all the hair she can get to hide—"

"A foot of hair hanging straight down her back isn't going to do her a bit of good. Now let me get these rags in her hair before it gets dry." She edged him aside and ignored him as he grumbled his way back to his chair.

When Abbie's hair had been rolled smoothly around the strips of cloth Meagan carefully wrapped the end of the strip around the hair and tied each securely.

"They look like little bandages." Abbie gurgled in delight. "My hair is sick and Meagan is making it well again, just like she did my papa."

They laughed at her joke while Josh nodded his approval. With the rags in her hair, her ears were almost hidden.

"Of course you know she can't go around wearing a torn-up pillowcase on her head for the rest of her life, but I have to admit, it hides her ears as well as the bonnet did." He didn't wait for Meagan to reply as he continued. "I'm going out to the barn to make sure the animals are all right. You'd better keep an eye on the window to make sure I don't slip and fall down."

He motioned toward the window farthest from the door, and Meagan knew he expected her to watch for him there.

Abbie came out from behind the curtain, dressed in her nightgown. Every few minutes she would touch the prospective curls in her hair.

"I'm sure my bonnets will look much prettier when there are curls around them," she told Meagan, realizing there had been a certain amount of tension between Meagan and her father over the cutting and curling of the hair. "I'm just sorry that you can't have a really happy Christmas like we always had before. I mean, going to Aunt Ruthie's and playing parlor games with the others. It was my fault for screaming about my bonnet. If I hadn't, you would have been having a good time now instead of doing up my hair and waiting for Papa to come in from the barn."

Meagan's heart went out to the little girl. There was no way she could tell her the truth, but she couldn't in good conscience allow the child to take the burden of guilt onto herself.

"I would have been here all alone if it hadn't been for you, Abbie. Your Aunt Ruthie doesn't like me, and she wouldn't have let me stay at her house, no matter what!"

Abbie threw her arms around Meagan's neck. "Then it's all right." She grinned. "Because I like you, and I like having Christmas right here in my own house."

Just at that moment a light moved across the window. Meagan lifted Abbie in her arms and turned the girl toward it.

"Did you see that?" Meagan asked. "I thought I saw a light out there."

The door opened and Josh plodded into the room behind them. "Night isn't fit for man or beast," he said. "Gave the animals an extra portion of feed and...what's the matter? You both look like you've seen a ghost."

"There's something outside that window." Abbie's arms tightened around Meagan's neck. "You don't suppose it's Indians, do you?"

"I didn't see any Indians," Josh told them, barely able to suppress his smile. "Why don't we go over to the window and find out?"

He unlatched the casing and let it swing inward. A blast of cold entered the room, but even the shock of icy air could not compete with the shriek that came from Abbie's throat as she beheld the culmination of her fondest dream.

She lurched from Meagan's grasp and flew to the window. Her father took the doll from the window ledge and placed it in her arms.

"Well, I'll be danged," he said dryly, "I guess the Christ Child decided you were old enough to be remembered this year after all."

He secured the window and went back to his chair by the fire.

"She'll be up all night," Meagan chided gently, "she's that excited."

"Give her a couple of minutes and then maybe you can read the Christmas story from the Bible," Josh suggested.

"But it's *your* place to read the story of the first Christmas," she told him. Only after she'd spoken did she remember Phoebe's words and wonder just how limited Josh's literary knowledge might be.

Josh looked uncomfortable, but did not argue as he took the large family Bible from the shelf. He settled into the chair and Abbie came to sit at his feet, while Meagan sat down near them on a stool.

The fire crackled. The little girl caressed her new doll, and Meagan felt her heart sing at being allowed to be a part of this family scene, regardless of the misery that had put her here. For this single moment, unhappiness was only a memory.

Abbie leaned her head against her father's leg and had fallen into the deep sleep of contentment before Josh finished the story.

Meagan carried the little girl to her bed and then returned to straighten up the house and get ready for the next day. "That was very nicely done, Mr. Daniels," she complimented. "I would never have realized that you had memorized every word if I hadn't noticed the Bible."

"What about the Bible?" Josh stopped before placing it back on the shelf. Surely he hadn't inadvertently taken the wrong book. No, this definitely said Bible right on the cover. "What's wrong with it?"

"There's nothing wrong with the Bible, and there's nothing wrong with you. It was just that you had it turned backward. I could have read the words from where I was sitting, but you certainly couldn't have done so."

Josh stared at her for a moment. "Lots of people have memorized that particular passage, I imagine."

Meagan carried the mixing bowls into the pantry. When she returned Josh was lighting his pipe.

"Abbie needs some help with her reading. She doesn't have the incentive other children have, the competitive spirit. Do you think you'd have time to read with her during the winter months? Just until she can get off to a good start?''

Josh was about to say no. He knew what Meagan was trying to do and didn't want her to make a fool of him in front of his daughter. But when he looked into her eyes he realized that this was Meagan's way of helping him learn to read without making it obvious that he was deficient in the subject. He drew on his pipe.

''Yes,'' he said as the smoke wafted about his face. ''Yes, I think I'd like that, as long as you're around to make sure we do it right.''

''I'll be here,'' Meagan said as she disappeared into the pantry again.

And Josh could have kicked himself for reminding both Meagan and himself that neither of them had any control over the matter.

Because Meagan couldn't help but stay there with him, any more than Josh could help but love her.

The day began early. Even though it was Christmas, there were chores to be done. By the time the sun managed to squeeze through the gnarly branches of the trees Meagan had the turkey in the oven, the bread baked and Abbie was stalking the plum pudding to make certain it was cooked properly.

Meagan allowed Abbie to wear her second-best dress, pink with a white pinafore. Once the dress was in place, Abbie sat on the stool while Meagan carefully removed each rag from the little girl's hair. And, although there were several curls that had managed to tangle the hair, Abbie never flinched.

''I'm going to be just as pretty as my doll,'' she said dreamily, caressing her newest possession.

Josh hadn't wanted to falsely raise Abbie's hopes, but

kept his opinion to himself. If all else failed she could continue wearing the bonnet and nothing would be lost. He managed to keep himself busy until Meagan gleefully called out to him.

"Come and see your lovely daughter."

Josh set his jaw. The damn fool woman didn't have to be so exuberant about it. The child was perceptive. She knew she wasn't as beautiful as her mother had been. He turned slowly and his jaw dropped.

"Why, you are surely the prettiest little girl that's ever graced this house," he managed to say once he found his voice. And she *was* pretty! She really was!

Meagan had parted Abbie's hair in the middle of her head and somehow managed to situate the curls over her ears. The were tied with bows to match her dress.

Josh walked cautiously around his daughter as though expecting her ears to pop out at him at any moment. He lifted her from the stool and stood her on the floor.

"Can she walk, and everything? I mean, won't her hair go straight or something?" he asked.

"I think Abbie's curls should last through the day, and then if we decide we like them, we'll do them up again tonight."

Abbie danced across the floor, hair bouncing joyously as she gazed at her reflection in the fat silver teapot on the china closet.

"Wait a minute. I've got something better." Josh rushed from the room and returned holding a dainty hand mirror. "Now, look in there." He thrust it at Abbie.

The little girl's face exploded into a smile of pure delight. "I am! I really am the prettiest little girl here!" She hugged her papa. She hugged her doll, then threw herself into Meagan's arms.

It was when Meagan looked over Abbie's head into

Josh's face that she realized there were tears in his eyes. She wanted to go to him and ask if she had somehow erred in her judgment. The last thing she wanted was to cause him unhappiness on his first Christmas without his wife.

Before she could move they heard the sound of horses. Voices called out from the yard. Josh opened the door in time to see Will Carmichael pull up in front of the house and help Phoebe from the sleigh.

"Merry Christmas!" Will clasped his friend's hand as Phoebe embraced Meagan in an exuberant hug. "Now, you're going to have to help me unload this food because I swear this woman seems to think you're in danger of starving before the new year."

His arms were full as he entered the house, and he almost dropped his burden when he spied little Abbie dancing on her toes in delight. The curls bounced on either side of her face and the smile of joy was surely a thing to behold.

"Hello." He placed his bundles on the kitchen table and bent over the little girl's hand. "Who is this lovely young lady? I didn't know you had company." He looked around the room as though seeking her parents and then dropped to his knee. "You know, my friend Josh has a little girl. Her name is Abigail. But she's much younger than you are. Have you met her?"

"Oh, Uncle Will, I *am* Abbie." The child giggled. "It's just that Meagan made me beautiful, and the Christ Child left me this doll. And now you and Aunt Phoebe have come and this is going to be the best Christmas ever."

In her enthusiasm the child never even remembered that this would be the first Christmas without her mother.

Perhaps that realization would come later, but for now she was happy and there was no reason to remind her.

Phoebe stood back and surveyed the scene, her chin quivering in emotion. The good Lord must have had a plan when he took Lily and left them Meagan, for surely little Abbie had never been happier.

"But how did you get here so early in the morning?" Josh asked. "You didn't travel all night."

"We stopped at the Klinerts' place yesterday afternoon and left before dawn. It got us here just about right, don't you think?"

"Oh, yes." Meagan put her arm around Phoebe. "I certainly do."

Together Meagan and Phoebe finished preparing the meal. There was the bird, a roast, mashed and browned potatoes, onions in cream sauce, rice coquettes, mince pies, potato cake, and of course, the coveted plum pudding with rum sauce.

The room was a delight of scents and sounds and Meagan was about to set the table when Josh drew her aside.

"Since we have company and this is such a festive occasion I think we should eat in the parlor," he told her.

"But the table…" Meagan objected.

"I'll set up a trestle table," he told her.

"The food will get cold if we have to take it across the dogtrot," she tried again.

"Everything will stay covered and it will be fine," he assured her. "I'll take care of getting the parlor ready. In the meantime, I think Phoebe wants to talk to you."

Meagan looked around in frustration. More than anything in the world she didn't want to go into that haunted room and try to eat. What if the organ started playing during their meal? Everything would be ruined. She suspected that Josh still didn't believe any part of the organ playing, regardless of what Ruth and Rafe Somers said.

She looked at Phoebe, hoping for support. Instead, Phoebe was holding out a large box. "This is for you," she said. "Merry Christmas."

Meagan felt her knees wobble as she walked across the floor. She could see Will smiling and Josh had a silly grin on his face as he waited to see her reaction. She lifted the lid and gasped in delight.

"The dress!" she managed. "The dress I was to have worn to the social." She ran her fingers over the material, touching the flowerettes.

"It's yours now," Phoebe told her. "Come…let me help you put it on. Josh and Will can put the food on the table."

"Oh, no, I couldn't let them do that," Meagan protested. Her delight at having the dress was as great as her fear of staining it as she finished the dinner.

"Josh has done it before. I'm sure he's not forgotten how," Phoebe assured her as she drew Meagan behind the curtain and pulled it shut.

By the time Meagan was dressed to Phoebe's satisfaction, the men had managed to set up the table with linens and cutlery, put the food in serving dishes that Meagan had not known existed and place most of it on the sideboard in the parlor.

There were exclamations of approval when Meagan appeared in the parlor doorway.

"Oh, Meagan," Abbie chirped, "you look almost as pretty as I do."

Everyone laughed, but the laughter caught in Josh's throat because Meagan looked beautiful. She looked like the most beautiful woman he had ever seen and he didn't dare tell her, not with words, and not even with his eyes, because if he tried, he might not be able to stop. He might go on to tell her how much she had come to mean to him and how much he appreciated all that she had done for Abbie, and, God help him, how much he loved her.

Meagan turned slowly so everyone could admire the gown. "Isn't it the most beautiful thing you've ever seen?" she asked.

"Yes, you are," Josh said before he could stop himself. "Now let's sit down and eat before everything gets cold."

It wasn't until after the dinner was consumed and the flaming plum pudding had been acclaimed a success that everyone settled down around the table.

Meagan had brought out some fine linen napkins, embroidered with the initial C, which she had made for the Carmichaels. Abbie yawned in the euphoria that comes only on Christmas when the stomach is full, and the heart is full and the house is full of laughter and love.

"Perhaps we should sing Christmas carols," Phoebe suggested. "I'll play the organ, unless Meagan would like to." She smiled. "As the daughter of a school-teacher, I presume you have received musical instruction."

Meagan froze in place. She stared at the instrument as though it were a preying beast. "Yes, I can play a bit, but not on *that!*" Then quickly changing the subject she remarked, "I didn't know you could play the organ."

"The organ belonged to Phoebe before I bought it for Lily," Josh volunteered. "Phoebe didn't have room for it in her house, and Lily was always saying she was bored and didn't have anything to do, so I got her the organ." He turned to Phoebe suddenly. "You wouldn't take it back, would you? I don't think Meagan has any interest in the thing, and I certainly don't need it."

"Perhaps Meagan can teach Abbie to play," Phoebe suggested, casting aside her usual perception. One look in Meagan's direction would have told her that Meagan had no intention of touching the organ, let alone teaching Abbie to play it. "If you want to keep the organ quiet when we have a storm you're going to have to move it away from the window," she said flatly as she placed herself on the stool.

"What do you mean?" Josh leaned forward, his interest piqued.

"I told you when you bought it to keep it out of drafts, and the casing around that window has a couple of holes in it you could throw a cat through. When the wind blows from the east it goes right into the bellows and that's what makes the music in the first place...wind in the bellows."

"You mean it wasn't a ghost?" Meagan almost swallowed the words.

"It was the wind," Phoebe assured her. "It's done it before and it'll do it again if you aren't careful. Put it over there next to the sideboard and it won't make another peep. I guarantee it."

"Then it was just the wind that..." Josh's eyes met Meagan's. In that moment he could feel her sweet, young body nestled in his arms. He wasn't going to share even one second of that memory with anyone. "That stampeded Ruth and Rafe out of here in the middle of the night?"

"That it was," Phoebe assured them above laughter that rang from the rafters. "And that's *all* it was, too!"

* * *

For the next week, laughter and happiness reigned in the Daniels household. Neighbors dropped by from miles around, stopping on their way to and from holiday visits. They all greeted Meagan politely, Josh effusively and Abbie with stunned surprise.

"Honestly, Josh, I'm afraid if one more person tells Abbie how pretty she is it will go to her head," Meagan confided.

"But she *is* pretty." Josh defended his daughter. "Besides, I don't care if it goes to her head. She deserves to be pretty and to know it. If she gets too vain we'll just not curl her hair for a couple of days and she'll get over it quickly."

"That would be harsh," Phoebe protested over the pan of apples she was peeling.

"Life's harsh. When you least expect it, it'll take you down," Josh said philosophically.

"And then what do you do?" Phoebe asked with a smile, as though she knew the answer he would give.

Josh shrugged. "You get up and start over again."

"And that's just what little Abbie is going to do," Will told them. "In case nobody noticed, she's practicing making rag curls on her doll. If Meagan stops doing up her hair, that child's going to put them in herself."

Phoebe shook her head. "It isn't easy putting in those rags. If Abbie tries it she'll quickly realize how bad she needs Meagan."

Meagan blushed prettily and hurried across the room to see to the dinner she was preparing. She was bending over the hissing pots when Josh said quietly, "We both need Meagan. Real bad."

Will Carmichael's forehead creased in a concerned scowl, for he feared it was only a matter of time before the situation between Josh and Meagan got completely out of hand.

The Carmichaels left on the last day of the year. They would stop at the home of the Klinerts and celebrate the arrival of the new year with them.

"I wish you were coming along," Phoebe told them. "I know you'd be welcome."

Josh shook his head. "Thought we'd be welcome in Banebridge last fall, but it didn't turn out. I'm not about to put my womenfolk through all that backbiting again."

Phoebe knew better than to continue her argument. She kissed Meagan goodbye, giving her an extra little hug. "You come into town if there's any trouble, you hear?"

Meagan stopped short. What did Phoebe mean? Had she heard the rumors that Reilly had mentioned?

"What do you mean?" she asked in a voice too small for the question.

"She means you shouldn't have had to nurse Josh and take care of the farm all by yourself. She means if anything like that happens again, you let us know and we'll see that you have help," Will answered for his wife. Without giving her time to do more than hug Abbie and give Josh a peck on the cheek he ushered her out the door.

They were almost out of sight when Phoebe turned on her husband. "Why didn't you let me tell her there are rumors of an Indian uprising? They should be on the lookout for signs of trouble."

"I told Josh everything I know, and that's little enough," Will assured her. "There's no reason to upset Meagan. She has a hard enough row to hoe."

"Meagan's fine. She's not the flighty type."

"Unless it comes to haunted organs." Will laughed.

"Oh, that." Phoebe joined his laughter. "She'll be fine now that I exorcised her ghost. I'll bet she even teaches Abbie to play."

"I hope so," Will said thoughtfully. "As long as she doesn't try to teach Josh."

Phoebe paused. "Whatever gave you an idea like that? Josh would be the last man on earth to want to learn to play the organ."

Will shrugged his shoulders. "She's teaching him to read."

Phoebe swung around so quickly she almost fell off the seat. "Josh? Our Josh? Josh Daniels?"

"That's the one. And right proud of it he is, too." Will was hard put to keep from laughing. Phoebe had known Josh Daniels all her life and was well aware of his aversion to book learning.

Now it was Phoebe's turn to shake her head. "Oh Will, I'm afraid those two may just find themselves in deep trouble."

"Did Meagan say something to you?" he asked quickly.

"It was what she *didn't* say that caught my attention. That and the fact that Josh couldn't keep his mind on anything when she was around. And Meagan can't keep her eyes off Josh. She thinks he's the most wonderful man God ever created." She brushed the snowflakes from her face and burrowed down into her scarf.

"How do you know that?" Will asked sharply.

"Because I feel the same way about you." Phoebe patted her husband's hands as they held the reins. "And on top of everything else, I had to take Meagan a dress that made her look better than she's ever looked in her life."

Will clucked to the horses. "When the judge handed down his sentence I thought it was the best thing for everyone concerned. I never thought about the fact that we were putting a pretty young woman in close proximity with an attractive man, both of them lonesome and vulnerable. It seems as though the judge's decree, though merciful, in this case is next to impossible. Next time Judge Osborne comes through I'll have a talk with him."

Phoebe settled back in the seat. "Well, you'd better be prepared to talk fast and fancy."

After the departure of the Carmichaels, life at the Daniels household returned to normal. The only noticeable changes were Abbie's hair, and the evening reading lessons. It was doubtful if Abbie realized that her father was learning right along with her for Meagan always managed to be there when either of them stumbled over a word. Abbie enjoyed the attention so much she would never have questioned the motives behind her good fortune.

Shortly after the holidays the weather mellowed and some of the snow melted. Josh and Meagan took this respite to get everything ready for the final onslaught of winter.

Josh walked the fields to make certain all was well. The curious accidents that had plagued them had ended with the coming of winter so Josh did not worry about leaving her alone. When the weather was clement, Abbie went out with her father.

Meagan had just come out of the washhouse when she saw him.

Reilly stood at the edge of the copse of tress that bordered the yard. He didn't move, but waited for her to join him.

Meagan put down the basket of clothes she had been carrying and hurried to him. She had made her decision long ago. Now she must tell her brother something he could not possibly understand. "I'm not going with you," she said as she came to a stop in front of him. "And you shouldn't have come here in broad daylight. All the settlers are nervous about the Indians. Someone might take a shot at you."

He took her arm and drew her into the wood.

"The white people have reason to be frightened," he told her. "The Indians are angry that the white man takes their land. They are determined to drive them out. Old Howling Dog says he will burn every cabin from here to Banebridge."

"Doesn't he realize the settlers will only come back?" Meagan asked, wondering exactly where her brother's sympathies were in this matter.

"Old Howling Dog feels that a good settler is a dead settler."

"Are you going to go to the fort and warn them?" Meagan asked.

"No, sister," he replied stoically. "Since you cannot come with me, I'm going to let you warn them when you take the little girl to safety."

"But what if they won't believe me?" Meagan protested, remembering her last foray with civilization.

"Do you think there is a better chance of them believing me? Belief is not mandatory. Your responsibility is to take the child to safety and tell the people at the fort that the Indians have sworn to attack with the first break in the weather. They have already begun their raids on the settlers nearest their village." He put his hand on her shoulder. "If you have any influence with this Daniels man, you must make him go to the fort."

"Josh may take Abbie and leave her with friends, but he won't stay. He'll come back to his land." Meagan pulled her coat more closely about her. "Besides, how can I convince Josh without telling him you were here?"

"Why don't you tell him the truth?" Reilly's eyes took on a faraway look. "I saw him in the farthest field. The girl was with him. Her head was bare and there were curls around her face. Is this the same girl I saw when I was here last?"

"You may have caught a glimpse of her when she came to the door," Meagan admitted.

"I have heard stories of the child with the large ears who wears a bonnet and the woman who drops from the trees to defend her." He watched his sister closely. "I think the child was the girl you call Abbie and I think that the woman was you."

Meagan gave a deep sigh. "It was me," she admitted. "And it was Abbie the children were teasing. I'm doing everything I can to see that it doesn't happen again."

"Hence the curls," Reilly reiterated.

"That's right."

"You've done a good thing, sister. The child is happy. Now get her to the fort or she will lose her curls, and her scalp along with it."

"Reilly, won't you stay and speak to Josh? He'd be more apt to believe you, once I tell him who you are."

A bird called from somewhere in the trees. Reilly hesitated, then pulled Megan into his arms for a quick hug. "Go and get your things ready to go to the fort. But be aware, sister. If your Josh Daniels brings you back here to face the attack that is sure to come, I will return and take you away from this place, and from him. My sister is no man's surrogate wife."

"Reilly, I can't go."

This time her brother's fingers bit into her arms. "Meagan, the Indians do not live in a separate world. They are well informed of the white man's activities. I know of the sentence that keeps you here, and I know that your love for Josh Daniels will bring you pain and death."

"No!" She pulled away. "There is nothing between Josh and me. We live together and work together. We're a good team. That's all."

Reilly put his hand under her chin and forced her to look into his eyes. "Are you certain?" he asked.

Meagan held his gaze as long as she could, then she lowered her eyes. She had never been able to keep anything from her brother. "No," she replied. "I'm not sure."

Reilly took a deep breath. "Your truth deserves truth in return. I'm going back into the white man's world to try to stop the killing that will come with this Indian uprising. I cannot do what I must do if I take you with me, for the hue and cry would be out for you and we would both be fugitives."

"I told you I wouldn't leave Josh—Abbie." The slip only served to reinforce her brother's suspicions. For a moment she was afraid he would let the white men fend for themselves and take Meagan to safety, but the teachings of their father and the love of a budding country was stronger than Reilly's fear for his sister.

"I leave you to try to carve your own destiny then," he agreed. "But if the man cannot or will not protect you, I will come for you. Now go and pack. There is little time to spare."

Without a backward glance he was gone, and Meagan went back to the house to finish hanging out the wash and to try to think of some way to convince Josh that Abbie was in danger.

But it didn't come to that. Meagan had only just begun to get the things together that Abbie would need while staying with the Carmichaels when she came dashing up the path to the house, dodging through the clean clothes hanging from the line.

''Meagan, Meagan! Papa says to come quick. There's people down by the creek.''

''Indians?'' The word burst out of Meagan's mouth. What if Reilly and the friends she'd heard whistling in the trees hadn't gotten away?

''No! Real people,'' Abbie said breathlessly. ''Like us.''

Chapter Nine

The people refused to come to the house. Josh and Meagan took bandages, ointment, food and clothing to them where they cowered in a lean-to near the creek.

"We'll be outta here come morning," the man promised. "Them Indians are probably right behind us. Thought we saw some early on in the day."

"We'll hitch up the wagon and take you to the fort," Josh offered. "Give us a few hours to get our things together."

The man looked doubtful. "Don't want to put you out none," he ventured. "We've stayed clear of everyone since the attack. Haven't seen a soul until you found us."

"Your family is exhausted and sick. They can't go on much farther," Josh pointed out. "We'll carry them in the wagon. If you want to set out on your own you can go at your own pace. I'm going to take my womenfolk to the fort anyway, so it won't be any trouble."

The man nodded gravely. "Long as we can stay ahead of them redskins I guess it'll be all right."

"I'll go and warn—" Josh started to say.

"We can warn anyone whose farm we pass," the man

said firmly. "But I ain't going out of my way to warn anyone until I get my family safe. They've been through enough."

There was no arguing with the man. He was going to protect his family and do so in the only way he knew.

Josh was torn between his loyalty to his neighbors and his urgency in getting Meagan and Abbie to safety. The man, seeing his indecision, drew him aside.

"I know how you feel. You think I'm hard-hearted and uncaring, but that's not true. I care as much as any man does, but I care for my own first. They're all I have left. Everyone else was killed. Most of our possessions were burned or stolen." He shook his head as though to rid himself of the horrible thoughts and images that would haunt him for the rest of his days.

"When we got the word that the Indians were planning to raid, I donned my snowshoes and went out to tell my neighbors. By the time I got back the thaw had set in. The Indians had come and gone. Half my family was dead or taken. Those who survived had managed to hide in the root cellar." He scratched his head.

"Let me tell you, Mr. Daniels. In this life, you can't trust nobody. Not your neighbors, not the weather, and sometimes, not even your own faith in the Almighty. Now if we are going you'd better get your things together, and if we ain't, I'm going to sleep so my family can leave early in the morning."

Meagan moved to Josh's side and placed her hand on his arm. "We must take Abbie to safety. After we've done that we can come back and warn the other settlers."

Josh looked from Meagan to his daughter. The child had become a bright and shining beacon in his life. Her newly found beauty had given him profound happiness, just as Meagan had given him hope. "You're right," he agreed. "Go get packed. We'll leave as quickly as we can."

It was dark by the time the livestock was secured in pens down near the creek and the wagon was loaded. Rather than try to traverse the roads at night they decided to wait until the first light of dawn. Abbie considered the trip to be something of an outing and insisted that Meagan curl her hair.

"This is one time when you needn't indulge her," Josh complained. "Go to bed. We have to get an early start."

"I don't mind," Meagan told him. "I'm too edgy to sleep. I guess some of the nervousness from that poor family rubbed off onto me. Every sound I hear I wonder if it's Old Howling Dog coming after us."

Josh turned slowly. He didn't lift his head or his eyes. "How'd you know it was Old Howling Dog leading the raids?"

Meagan hesitated. Did she dare tell him that Reilly had come to warn her? The arrival of the family near the creek had seemed like a direct act of God. It had eliminated the necessity of her having to appeal to Josh to take Abbie to the fort, and now she had destroyed everything with her own words.

"One of the people we talked to must have mentioned the name. It caught my attention. Old Howling Dog is unusual, even for an Indian. I wonder what his mother could have been thinking of when she named him..." She stared off into space as though contemplating the possibilities.

Josh was not impressed. He lit his pipe. "She was probably thinking of a howling dog. Lots of Indian women name their babies for the first thing they see after giving birth.

Meagan was aware of the unusual and inventive ploys the Indians used to name their children, but she let Josh go on instructing her, pleased to have evaded his inquiries.

She was reluctant to let Josh know that she had a half brother who wanted to take her away.

My sister is no man's slave, Reilly had said, and the vehemence in his voice had not made allowances for the fact that under white man's law, Meagan's only other option had been death.

Meagan put the last of the dishes away. They would board up the house in the morning as they always did when they left for any length of time. Josh had already boarded up the parlor. Meagan turned in time to see his eyes scanning the room, as though saying farewell to an old and dear friend.

She walked over to him and touched his sleeve. "It will be here when we get back," she said. "We'll come back and protect it."

"Little good that did the family out by the creek," Josh pointed out. "I don't want some Indian coming in here and running off with you."

"And I don't want you scalped," she returned, "so we'll just have to watch out for each other, won't we?"

Josh smiled. "Watch out for each other," he repeated. "Yes, Meagan, I guess we will. Now—"

"—go to bed," she finished for him. "We have an early start."

Chuckling, Josh put his hand on her shoulder and gently shoved her toward the curtained area where Abbie already slumbered. Neither Meagan nor Josh was aware that the other held close that light touch, for Meagan slept with her hand on her shoulder where his hand had rested so briefly, and Josh placed the hand that had touched her over his heart as though the memory would bring them closer together.

The wagon rattled through the ruts in the road as the party came down from the mountains into the foothills. Behind them there was nothing but a smoky-blue haze concealing the path they had followed.

The children were silent, and the woman talked to Meagan in a soft voice.

"Once this Indian scare has settled down my man will want to get back home," she said firmly.

Meagan felt her chin drop in shock. "But I thought your husband said you'd been burned out."

"That's right," she affirmed, "but we'll rebuild. Got us a right nice place up there. There's lumber and water. God's own country it is. Good place to raise a family. The land is fertile and rich." She paused for a moment and wiped her eyes with a sun-browned hand. "Besides, my babies are buried up there. I have to go back and tend their graves."

Meagan couldn't think of anything appropriate to say as she drove the wagon around the worst of the ruts in the road. The men had ridden ahead while Meagan and the others followed in the wagon. Everyone kept their eyes and ears open. Everyone except Abbie, and her new friend, one of the little girls in the family. Meagan caught snatches of their conversation from the bed of the wagon behind her.

"Perhaps Papa will let me stay in town," Abbie said primly. "Then we could see each other once in a while."

The other child's answer was covered by the creak of

the wheels as they groaned their way across yet another gouge in the road.

Meagan lost herself in thought, ignoring the idle conversation of the woman on the seat beside her. Abbie would be more than willing to stay with the Carmichaels, especially since she would have a new friend there. That would leave Meagan free to go with Josh to warn the other settlers. Like the woman, Meagan knew that Josh would return to his home whether it was still there or not.

The little party rumbled into town on the afternoon of the second day. Half the townsfolk turned out to meet them. In a matter of minutes the family had been taken in and the men, including Josh and Will, had gone off to the fort.

Meagan went home with Phoebe.

"I don't think there's any immediate danger to Banebridge," Meagan said as she peered out the window at the cluttered street where the townsfolk huddled together in clumps discussing the situation.

"They're not so worried about themselves as they are about their families. Most everyone here has someone dear living out in the wilderness. They must be warned."

"Josh and I will warn those we can on our way home," Meagan said.

Phoebe jumped to her feet. "You don't mean to go back there now, do you?"

Meagan remembered the words of the woman who had ridden in with her. "We left so quickly there was no time to close things up properly. Of course we must go back."

"But the Indians..."

"We've seen no Indians so far. The people we brought with us came from a valley farther up in the mountains. The Indians may not even come this way. Or they may not come so far east until spring.''

Phoebe shook her head. ''I know Josh must go back to see to his land and stock, but you should stay here. There's no reason or you to take the risk. It's not your place…''

''My place is with Josh,'' Meagan said softly.

Phoebe opened and shut her mouth twice before deciding she really didn't have anything relevant to say.

''Well then, show me how to put Abbie's hair up in those little curls you do so well and we'll send you and Josh on your way.'' Her voice broke on the last word. Somehow she felt she might never see these dear friends again, or if she did it would not be the same. There was a deep foreboding in her heart, and she hugged Meagan quickly before turning to her dinner preparations.

When Meagan left the Carmichael house just before dawn there were two horses waiting at the hitching post. Will handed her the bundle of food that Phoebe had prepared as he helped her into the saddle. His eyes met those of Josh and then returned to Meagan. He lifted his hand in one final salute as they cantered down the street, the sound of hoofbeats thrumming through the early morning like Indian drums.

As the sound faded into the shadows Will returned to the house where Abbie cried in his wife's arms. ''But why can't Meagan stay?'' she sobbed. ''Why does she have to go with Papa? Who will help me with my studies? And…and…who will curl up my hair?''

''I'll help you,'' Phoebe promised. ''I'll be right here with you until Meagan and your father come back.''

''But what if they don't come back?'' the child wailed.

Phoebe's eyes caught those of her husband. He looked away, leaving her to cope with the little girl's fears. "Of course they'll come back, and then everything will be just fine," Phoebe said with a firmness in her voice that she wished she could have matched in her heart. "Of course they'll come back."

Meagan was saddle-sore and bone-weary by the time they reached the mountains. They had reached Josh's cabin at nightfall after going miles out of their way to warn every settler in the vicinity. After a brief rest, Josh was up seeing to the stock and gathering food and supplies.

"You don't have to come with me," he told Meagan. "I'm going to have to ride hard and fast," he told Meagan. "From all I can tell, no one has warned the families farther on into the mountains. It's more remote there and they live farther apart. You can stay with the Klinerts until I get back." He worked as he spoke.

"I'll stay with you," she said.

Josh glanced toward the ridge of the mountains. "From the looks of those clouds I don't doubt that the Indians already went back to their village and are willing to wait out the rest of the winter. It gives us the break we need to warn the rest of the settlers."

But as they went deeper into the wilderness they found that Old Howling Dog and his band had come farther than they had imagined.

The acrid smell of smoke crept through the trees as Josh and Meagan reined in their horses and moved silently through the forest. There was little sign of life. A ewe bleated from the far side of the yard, frightened at having the run of the place. The barn and house were but burned-out shells devoid of life other than a singed rooster that sat on what was left of the chimney and shouted obscenities at the top of his lungs.

Meagan put her hand over her mouth. "Do you think the people got away?" she whispered.

Josh gave her arm a little squeeze. "Stay here and I'll see what I can find out."

He made his way into the open, taking in the devastation that had lately been someone's home. He touched the blackened wood where once the house had stood. "You can come out," he called. "The ashes are cold. This must have happened several days ago."

They walked the grounds together but were unable to discover any sign of the family, alive or dead. Some distance from the house was a tiny graveyard. Josh gave a sigh of relief at their discovery.

"They must have made it out of here all right," he said. "There's no fresh graves here."

With a certain amount of hope in their hearts Josh and Meagan continued their search. The next family was dug in for the winter and had no idea their neighbors had been attacked.

"Thought we saw smoke from the other side of the rise, but it was quite a distance away, and there wouldn't be anything we could do by the time we got there," the man told them as his wife slapped heaping spoonfuls of mutton stew into pewter bowls.

"You shouldn't go on," the round little woman asserted. "Weather's going to turn any time now."

"We don't have much choice," Josh told them as he applied himself to the meal. "We have to warn as many people as we can that the Indians are going to attack when the weather breaks again."

"The soldiers should come after them redskins and

wipe them out,'' the man said righteously. ''That's what we got the fort for.''

Josh wiped his bowl with a chunk of bread. ''Soldiers aren't going to come out hunting Indians in the dead of winter.''

''From what you say, by spring it's likely to be too late,'' the man protested.

''Best you try to get to the fort while there's still time,'' Josh counseled.

''That what you intend to do?'' the man asked. ''Leave your livestock, house and land and go hide out at the fort?''

''Not till I have to,'' Josh admitted reluctantly, ''but I took my daughter to Banebridge for safekeeping before I came up here.''

The man nodded sagely. ''That was good. Too bad you didn't leave your wife there too.''

Josh was about to tell the man that Meagan wasn't his wife, but held his tongue. How was he supposed to explain her presence? If he told them she was indentured to him they would think she was his doxy. If he told the truth it would probably set them against Meagan.

''Meagan insisted on coming with me,'' he told them.

''Some women do get their backs up and there's no changing their minds,'' the man agreed, then changed the subject. ''You folks aren't moving on before morning, are you?''

Josh glanced at Meagan. She looked tired. There were dark rings beneath her eyes and her cheeks were unnaturally red from the constant whipping of the wind. ''We'd be most obliged if we could put up in your barn,'' Josh told him. ''We need to leave early in the morning and don't want to be a bother.''

''Hell, you're no bother,'' the man told them. ''Ain't

been anyone over in these parts since the first snow fell. It's right nice to have company even when they come to bring a warning." He chuckled at his own little joke and his wife smiled in encouragement.

"There's a bed up in the loft." She motioned toward the ladder along the far wall.

"The barn will suit just fine, if it's all the same to you," Josh told them. There was just the slightest hint of disappointment in Meagan's expression, and before she could speak he bade his hosts good-night and made for the barn. With one last longing glance at the cozy, warm loft, Meagan followed.

She was wrapped in two blankets and covered with a layer of hay when Josh finally addressed the subject.

"I'm sorry we couldn't stay in the house, Meagan," he said softly. "But they would have expected us to share a bed. And if Ruth ever found out…"

The results remained unspoken. They both knew it would mean Meagan's life.

"It just looked so warm and snug," Meagan mused dreamily.

"Are you cold?" There was a hint of concern in his voice.

There was a slight pause before she murmured, "No."

If she had told him she was cold would he come closer and take her in his arms? Would he hold her as he had held her the night she had tried to escape, so long ago? Would he cuddle her against the lean, muscular length of his body and allow her to mold herself to him? Would he move his hands ever so gently over her body, memorizing each curve and crevice? Would he rest his cheek against her head and would she feel the gentle caress of his breath on her hair?

Would she be allowed to cling to him throughout the

night, and awake, drunk with his nearness...the scent of him, the texture of him, the warmth of his skin, the sound of his heartbeat strong and steady beneath her ear?

Oh, God, how close to heaven could one come, only to have it snatched away with the coming of day? Yet she knew that even those stolen moments were dangerous, for should Josh so much as suspect that Meagan loved him, he would turn away from her. Even the easy camaraderie they had achieved would be lost. Yet to save her soul she could not help but love him, and want him to hold her close through the long, lonely night.

Josh heard Meagan's breathing grow steady as she slipped into the depths of sleep. There was so much more he had wanted to say to her. He wanted to explain that he had not dared take her up to the warmth of the loft. He wanted to make her understand that he no longer held complete control of himself where she was concerned.

The sound of her voice quickened his blood. The scent of her hair made him dizzy with longing to bury his face deep in those thick tresses.

Had they given in to the urgings of their hosts and bedded down in the loft, they would have had to remove some part of their clothing. Josh might have come into contact with that smooth skin that Meagan took for granted.

He remembered how she had come to nurse him during the heat of summer. He remembered how she had bent over him to place cool cloths on his head. And how she had remained only a kiss away.

He concentrated on her face: the high cheekbones, the full, inviting lips, the little sprinkle of freckles across the bridge of her nose. Her neck, soft and often smelling of cinnamon or cloves. And then the freckles repeated once again on her shoulders.

Would it be such a sin to kiss just one little freckle? Or, perhaps, because there were so many, two, or more?

Josh turned on his side, his back to Meagan. He would not face her. He would not look at her. He would not think of her…and he would not sleep. For if he dreamed, he knew he would dream of Meagan and no one else since she was that of which dreams were made. But if, in word or deed she so much as suspected that he wanted her almost as much as he dreaded living without her, she would turn from him in fear and reproach. How could she believe that he loved her when the culmination of that love would ultimately end in the termination of Meagan's life?

With that his thoughts turned to stark reality. Over the months Josh had come to realize that Meagan was not guilty of causing Lily's death, just as he had come to wonder over Ruth Somers's vehemence in accusing her.

If Meagan was telling the truth, why had Ruth not simply said that Lily missed her footing and fell down the stairs? There was no shame in a simple accident, even if it occurred on your property.

Josh had warned Rafe about the Indians as they rode past the Somers place on their way west. Perhaps when they returned Josh would stop and make Ruth give him some answers to questions she had not been asked at Meagan's trial.

It was strange, Josh thought as sleep overcame him, that from the moment Ruth had said Meagan was guilty, no question was asked, nor was thought given to any other person's possible involvement. Everything that had been done, had been done to prove Meagan guilty. Will Carmichael, Meagan's lawyer, who claimed he believed

in her innocence, had had his hands full simply trying
to keep them from hanging her. Even Ruth had not been
able to come up with a good reason for Meagan to want
Lily dead.

They were saddling their horses when the farmer appeared with steaming coffee, hot biscuits and cheese.
"Just to give you something warm in your belly as you
go on your way," the man said. "We'll give heed to
your warning and keep our eyes open."

The man watched them ride away. They last saw him
as they rounded the bend in the road.

"Do you suppose he'll be here when we come back
through?" Josh asked aloud, although the question was
more in his own mind. He was almost startled when
Meagan answered.

"The man will stay to protect his land, and the wife
won't leave her husband. I think that's the way it's supposed to be. Like the people we found by the creek. If
they are forced out, they bide their time until they can
go back home."

Josh nodded. "I wouldn't let the threat of a few Indians drive me out of my place," he admitted. "But I'm
glad we got Abbie to safety nonetheless." He shot a
resentful glance at Meagan. "Just wish you'd had sense
enough to stay there with her. Will and Phoebe would
have treated you right and you'd have been a darn sight
safer than you are chasing over the countryside with
me."

Meagan looked at Josh askance. She had told him she
was coming with him. He hadn't objected at the time.
He'd simply nodded his head in assent and let her have
her way. She had been given to understand that she was
chattel to Josh Daniels to do with as he pleased. It had

never occurred to her that it did not please him to have her with him.

"I'm sorry." She all but choked on the words. "I thought you wanted me with you."

Josh looked to see if she were joking. She wasn't.

"I do want you with me, Meagan. You can stake your immortal soul on that." The emotion in his voice was so great it frightened her.

She fought the tears that threatened to spill down her cheeks. Would he never forgive her for her supposed wrong against his wife? Would he never see that she had done nothing to deserve his animosity? But even as it seemed her heart would break with unrequited love, Josh pulled his horse near hers and reached over to cover her hands as they rested on the pommel.

A surge of strength and something akin to hope flooded through her whole being as she looked into his eyes and saw, not hatred or pity, but caring.... Surely it was true caring that she saw before he urged his horse forward.

"We must hurry," he called over his shoulder. "There should be two more cabins within a day's ride. We must warn them both before night falls." And they clattered over the rocky trail that wound off into the mountain valleys, but deep in their hearts they realized that the road their love must follow would be just as rocky and just as winding and treacherous as that on which they rode.

Chapter Ten

Even though it was early in the day, the clouds were heavy and the sky was dark. Josh and Meagan pulled their horses to a halt above the little valley. Ordinarily it would have been a tranquil scene that welcomed the weary traveler, but today, birds of prey circled in the darkening sky.

"Looks like the Indians got here first." Josh spoke his thoughts aloud. "You stay here. I'll go down and look around."

"No..." Meagan whispered. "I'll go with you. I don't want to stay here alone."

They dismounted and walked the horses down into the clearing. As with some of the other places they had seen, the house and outbuildings were burned. This time the smoke still rose from the embers and the ground was slick in places with fresh blood.

It didn't take long to find the bodies. A mother and child and, farther on, a man. There were signs that several Indians had also been wounded and carried away by their brothers. But there had been no one to look to the bodies of the dead settlers, and although they looked over their shoulders every moment, and jumped at each sound, Josh and Meagan buried the dead.

Josh tied two sticks together in the shape of a cross and pounded it into the ground beside the other two crosses he had fashioned. The three forlorn graves stood alone as the wind began to moan in the trees.

"I don't know any words to say over the dead." Josh wiped the sweat from his forehead and looked to Meagan for advice.

"Say the story of the first Christmas, Josh. You know that, just like it is in the Bible." Meagan stepped nearer, hoping her presence would give him the ability to remember the words.

"It don't seem fitting somehow," he objected, shifting from one foot to the other. "The story of the birth of the Christ Child is a happy story and death is…"

"…the beginning of a new life," she finished his sentence. "A life of peace and beauty. A wonderful new beginning in the Promised Land. And Josh, just think of it, they're all right there, together, starting over in a wonderful new life."

"But, where do I start?"

Meagan folded her hands. "Just start where you feel it's right."

She looked past him into the heavens as a shaft of watery sunlight struggled through the gathering clouds and touched the earth with its blessed warmth.

With her words ringing in his ears, Josh locked his eyes on her shining face and began. "And it came to pass, in those days, that there went out a decree from Caesar Augustus, that all the world should be taxed." He stopped.

This was all wrong. It wasn't a prayer for people who

had surmounted the dangers and hardships of a new land only to die such a horrible death.

He shook his head but Meagan whispered, "Go on...."

He looked into her face as the words spun about in his head. He fought to pluck them from his mind. To hold them, to arrange them into some sense and purpose. But he could not think with her looking at him with trust and love, like one of God's own angels. But then the words came.

"And lo, the angel of the Lord came upon them, and the glory of the Lord shone round about them, and they were sore afraid. And the angel said unto them, 'Fear not: for, behold, I bring you good tidings of great joy...'"

His voice grew stronger as the beauty and the hope of the story surpassed the horror and fear of the moment and hope won out as he lifted his own face toward the sky to declare, "Glory to God in the Highest, and on earth, peace, to men of goodwill."

The world stood silent and still, as though joining in prayer for the little family. Then the sun was quashed by storm clouds, and the wind howled a warning.

In the distance the horses snorted and stamped, aware of nature's impatience.

As though awakening from a deep sleep, Josh grabbed Meagan's hand. "We have to be on our way," he told her as the first snowflakes danced about them. "Bad weather's setting in and we'll be hard put to reach the next cabin before nightfall."

Burying the dead had taken up a considerable amount of time. Josh urged the horses on as quickly as he dared. By this time they were well into the mountains and the storm seemed to be tracking them from all sides.

Meagan didn't complain, although Josh knew she must be hurting after the long hours she had spent in the saddle. The ground was covered with a white blanket when he turned to her.

"Keep your eyes open for a trail to the left of the road," he said. "We should find shelter there, if the Indians haven't got there first."

Meagan nodded. Her hands and feet were numb, and her face was frozen. Only her heart was warm and full of the memory of Josh giving the last worldly prayer for the family they had buried. If only he could have heard himself as she had heard him. If only he could have known how beautiful his words had sounded, filled with comfort and hope. Just as he filled Meagan with comfort and hope.

He had scarcely spoken to her since they had left the graveside. She hoped he was not angry because she had urged him to speak over the grave. Surely those poor, unfortunate people deserved to be sent on their way with the word of God.

She could not take her eyes off Josh as he rode before her, his broad shoulders blotting out the storm, the fear and the world.

The cabin loomed up before them suddenly as they came around a bend in the road. The blowing snow almost blinded them. But the cabin was a welcome sight, even to snow-dimmed eyes.

"Stay here," Josh commanded. "I'll go in and see if it's safe."

It took Meagan's frozen mind to understand his words. "Wait!" she cried before he rode ahead. She pulled her horse nearer to his. "What do you mean, safe? Why wouldn't we be safe? There are no tracks in the snow, and the cabin looks deserted."

Josh was pleased that she had quickly taken in the situation. He hated to burst her bubble of happiness, but knew he must tell her the truth.

"The snow hasn't been falling for more than a few hours. There could be someone holed up in the cabin who doesn't want any company. Understand?"

Meagan nodded and shivered at his next words.

"Besides," he continued, "we don't know for sure whether the Indians are behind us or ahead of us. They might have stayed back to take care of their wounded. For all we know they could still be coming and following our tracks. I want to be sure we don't meet with any surprises."

It hadn't occurred to Meagan that the Indians might not have gone on. She looked toward the cabin with trepidation. What had seemed like a haven had suddenly become suspicious.

She looked back toward the road, not bothering to hide the fear in her eyes. The tracks they had made in the snow had already all but disappeared.

"Let me go with you," she said quietly.

Josh reached out and brushed the snow from her cheek. He dared not take the chance that she might be hit by an errant shot from a frightened tenant. "I want you to stay here with the horses. I'll signal as soon as I'm certain everything is all right." He dismounted and turned away. He could feel the pain in her eyes. Regardless of the outcome, she had offered to stay beside him, as she had been beside him throughout their travails. He didn't look back, but turned his face toward the silent cabin that stood sentinel in the blowing snow. If they did not find shelter there, he did not know where they would go, for the storm was well upon them and there was no time to search for another abode.

The building was small, one room, boarded up on the outside. Josh pried a board loose and peered through the window. The room looked deserted.

He found the door had been nailed closed and pulled it open. Stale, icy air filled his nostrils. His face split into a smile and he signaled for Meagan to join him.

By the time she reached the house he was ready to take the horses to a nearby shed, where he found straw, hay and a meager ration of oats.

"Must have belonged to a trapper," he said as he came in and stamped the snow from his boots just outside the door. His arms were filled with wood, and Meagan helped him lay the fire before going out for a load of her own.

Within a short time the fire burned cheerfully and Meagan had found a tin of beans to go along with the dried meat they had brought with them.

Josh pried the boards from the windows. "I want to be able to see if anyone is coming," he told her as he looked through the window into the snow-filled night. "The only thing we have going for us is that this is a trapper's cabin and the Indians are more tolerant of trappers."

"But what if the trapper comes back?" Meagan wanted to know.

"The ashes in the hearth were cold. Looks as though it's been a while since anyone lived here. I doubt the trapper will be back soon. And if he shows up, we'll invite him in to supper."

He gave her a weak smile and turned back to the window and placed his hand against the wooden frame. Whom was he trying to fool? It wasn't the trapper they had to worry about, it was the redskins.

If the Indians were behind them they were dead. He knew it, and Meagan knew it too.

He felt her move to stand close beside him and draped his arm over her shoulder.

"We'll take turns watching," she said, "just in case they see the smoke and come to investigate."

His fingers squeezed the warm, pliant flesh. She felt so good, so solid there beside him. It seemed almost as if when they were together nothing could defeat them. But he knew that wasn't true. A band of hostile Indians would burn them out in a matter of minutes.

"I'm sorry, Meagan," he told her, "I should have left you back at the fort with Abbie."

She looked up at him. Her face was only a kiss away. "I belong here with you, Josh. This is where I want to be."

"But the danger..."

"I would rather fight and die at your side in this lonely little cabin, than live the rest of my life in safety without you."

He shook his head, denying her words in his own mind. Afraid to believe that which he so longed to hear.

"Do you remember the little family we buried this afternoon?" she asked as she hesitantly rested her hand on his arm.

"Of course I remember," he managed. He didn't want to remember the horror, the blood and the death. Why did she have to remind him?

"Do you think he would have run away and left her? Or that she would have left him to find safety?"

He looked at her, confusion written on his face.

"Without one another their lives would have been meaningless. They lived together and died together, and

I believe with all my heart that they are in heaven right now, together.''

''But it's not like that with us,'' he protested, his mouth dry and his pulse pounding. ''You and I can never be together as they were. No matter what we feel for each other.''

Now it was Meagan's turn to feel her heart skip a beat. Was he saying he truly cared for her, the way a man cared for a woman? The way she cared for him? She had to know.

''When a man and woman live and work together and share all the pain and happiness of their lives, what more can they ask of life?'' she asked.

Her eyes were soft and dewy in the firelight, her lips, moist and full. Josh took it all in. Her words, her demeanor, the pounding of her heart and the slight trembling of her hands where they rested against him. He took a deep breath. He gritted his teeth. He clenched his fists, and then he let everything go to hell and took her in his arms and kissed her hard.

Josh caught his breath and swallowed, his eyes still locked on Meagan's mouth. It was a wonderful, beautiful mouth. Filled with sugar and honey and the heat of new-found desire, but sometimes it came up with some pretty silly notions.

''Meagan, that was a dumb question,'' he rasped. ''There's a lot more to life than living and working together. There's loving, and that's what I've been trying to keep from doing with you. But you just keep on being so danged lovable.'' He sighed. ''I was out of line.'' He stepped back and found himself pressed against the window. ''I'm sorry. It won't happen again.''

Outrage flared in Meagan's eyes. She shoved him

back against the window. "Well, I'm not sorry, and if you don't kiss me again, Josh Daniels, I'll never forgive you."

The wind howled. The fire crackled. The cabin groaned as it stood firm against the elements.

Josh popped his head out of the trapdoor in the floor. "It's a root cellar!" he said, beaming. "There's potatoes, turnips, yams and even some beet wine." He surfaced, and handed Meagan the fruits of his discovery before slapping the dust from his clothes. "With the squirrel I got this morning we should have us a right nice meal."

Squirrel meat wasn't Meagan's favorite, but she knew how to prepare it and didn't argue.

Josh brushed past her, depositing a quick kiss on her lips. From the moment Meagan had let him know that his kisses were not unwelcome, Josh had not missed an opportunity to taste the sweet delights she had so freely offered.

The bustle as they hunted up more food for the horses, spruced up the cabin and prepared dinner kept them busy. However, they couldn't stop thinking about what had just happened between them.

Why did she tempt him so? Josh repeatedly asked himself. Why had she not put him in his place when he had stolen the coveted kiss? Why had she met him with a passion seeming as great as his own? A passion neither had the right to acknowledge. He watched her as she bent over the hearth, her body moving gracefully in guileless temptation, as she fussed with the unfamiliar pots and pans. Did she have any idea how deeply she affected him? Did she know that he ached to touch her?

Just touch her, nothing more. To cup her fair face in his hands and thread his fingers through her hair.

To touch her eyes, her ears, her lips? To taste the budding passion that would burst into bloom between them given half a chance?

How could he continue to live if he were denied her much longer? His body pounded with desire. The blood thrummed in his veins each time she brushed past him. Somehow he had to think of something other than how beautiful Meagan looked in the firelight, and how much he loved her.

Meagan was aware of the scowl on his face. Josh had not been himself since they had buried the settlers. Of course, he must be thinking that but for the love of God, it could have been himself. Himself and Abbie…and Meagan? Or did his mind turn to Lily in his litany of death and sorrow?

At first he seemed to enjoy her teasing and willingly dropped kisses on her lips when they passed each other. Then his demeanor changed and she was aware of a coolness between them, although the kisses did not cease. Indeed, if anything, they became more intense.

Soon it would be time to go to bed for the night. There was but one bed, and that looked lumpy. With the wind howling, the snow falling and the temperature dropping, there was no question of sleeping in the shed with the horses.

Meagan didn't want to sleep in the shed. She didn't want Josh to sleep in the shed either. She wanted to hear his even breathing. To be reassured by his gentle snore that told her he slept peacefully and all was right with the world. She wanted to snuggle into his arms and never leave. How she wished it would snow forever and they would never have to leave. Now, that would be heaven in her estimation. She wondered what he would say should she tell him.

She watched him as he oiled his boots to waterproof them against the snow.

Meagan went to the window and looked out into the night. The day had been exhausting but she knew she was not ready to sleep. It seemed Josh felt the same way.

He set his boots aside and pulled the cob mattress from the bed, positioning it in front of the fire. Bunching it into a large lump he dropped into it and patted the place beside him. "Come sit down. You look tired."

"Compliments will get you nowhere," Meagan said pertly. She wished she felt pert. She didn't. She felt just like Josh said she looked. Bone-tired, and he didn't look much better.

Reluctantly she left the window and sat down beside him. He shoved a warm mug into her hand. "Old trapper who lived here last must have had a hankering for spirits. Found quite a stash in the root cellar. Didn't think he'd mind if we sampled a bit."

Meagan lifted the mug to her lips and took a sip. The liquid warmed her clear to her toes. "I didn't realize it was so drafty in here," she told him.

She closed her eyes and let her head fall back a bit. "I wonder what the trapper who lived here was like," she mused.

"He's probably pretty much like Rafe Somers. Most of the trappers in these parts are French."

She opened her eyes. "Is there some reason for that?"

"Can't rightly say, except that most of the French trappers survived and the others didn't."

"I'm glad you're not a trapper, then," Meagan told him.

He chucked her under the chin. It was a mistake. She was too close. He shouldn't have touched her. Not with the firelight playing on her face and hair and dancing in her eyes. "No." He sighed. "I'm no trapper. I'm just a farmer. I like working the land."

"I would think the Indians would be more friendly to the settlers. All they want..."

"Is the Indian's land," he finished for her. "They favor the trappers because trappers don't take the land and most of them don't bring their families." He glanced around the room. "Take this place, for instance. Unless I miss my guess, the man who lived here had an Indian...wife." He almost choked on the word. It was doubtful if the man had a wife, but he didn't want to hurt Meagan's sensibilities by using any less edifying description.

Meagan sensed his discomfort and searched for another subject. Once again her eyes moved toward the window. "Do you think they will come?"

"The Indians? I hope not. I hope they dug in good and deep, or got back to their village before the storm hit. I hope they're sleeping peacefully in their lodges with their squaws and papooses and they don't wake up until we're back home."

Meagan smiled. "And how much of a chance do you think we have of that happening?"

"Not a chance in hell." He laughed. "But when I hope, I do it big."

Meagan curled her legs up under her. "What else do you hope, Josh Daniels?"

He looked into her eyes. They were like a deep autumn pond. Dark, with just a glint from the fire now and again. He couldn't think of anything but her eyes for a moment, and that was just as well, because when he drew his attention from Meagan's eyes, there was a lot more of Meagan to contemplate. *A lot* more, and she was mighty close, and mighty tempting.

"I hope we get some sleep. If the snow lets up we'll be making an early start."

"I thought you said the Indians were all sleeping peacefully in their village," Meagan protested.

"I said I hoped they were. I don't know where they are, but wherever they are, I don't want to be there."

The images of the family they had buried passed through Meagan's mind and she shivered involuntarily.

Josh got up, poured another mug of spirits and threw another log on the fire. "This drink would be better if it were buttered," he grumbled as he handed her the mug.

"We're lucky to have fire to heat it," Meagan reminded him.

"It's hot, all right," Josh agreed.

Hot wasn't the word for it. He felt as if he could have set the liquid to boiling just holding it in his hand. He couldn't stay so close to Meagan. He was burning up. Burning for her, and God help him, sometimes it almost seemed as though she burned for him as well.

"Go to sleep," he ordered brusquely. "I'll take the first watch."

Meagan's eyes popped open. "Watch? Are we really in that much danger?"

"Just being cautious," he assured her as he turned away so she couldn't see the look in his eyes.

Danger! She didn't know the meaning of the word. She didn't even realize the extent of the danger she was in at that very moment. Not from the elements, or from the Indians, but from Josh himself.

Danger! Danger! Danger! What would she know of

the danger that existed between a woman and a man? He doubted if she could even comprehend how much he wanted her. Never! Never in all his born days had Josh Daniels wanted a woman the way he wanted Meagan.

He closed his fists and leaned against the windowsill. It was going to be a long, hard night, but as long as he didn't touch her, didn't inhale the scent of lavender in her hair, didn't feel the heat of her body searing through his clothing and into his body until it touched his heart and soul…as long as none of those situations took place, they would make it safely through the night. He moved silently between the two windows. One overlooked the clearing in front of the cabin. The other had an open view of the road and the mountains far beyond. Josh didn't believe there was any real threat from the Indians. If they hadn't reached their village it was likely they were dug in deep. But standing watch was the best excuse he could come up with to make sure he and Meagan didn't end up in bed together.

Josh gave a deep sigh and settled into place in front of the window overlooking the road and the pass through the mountains. The snow lessened and the wind let up a bit. He rubbed his eyes, fighting sleep. It was then he noticed movement on the switchback trail through the mountains. He waited, hoping his tired eyes had deceived him, but it was not to be. He got to his feet and went to wake Meagan.

She was sleeping soundly, her lips parted ever so slightly. He wished he dared awaken her with a kiss like the people in one of the books that Lily used to read aloud to Abbie. He started to bend down, every fiber of his body yearning to touch her sweet mouth, but at the last minute he drew back. If they were going to get through this night it would be through the will of God, and Josh didn't think he should tempt the Lord's better nature by stealing a kiss.

"Meagan." He nudged her shoulder instead. "Meagan, wake up. Come on, now. Wake up. That's my girl." He helped her into a sitting position and made sure her eyes were open, if a bit unfocused.

"Is it time for my watch already?" she asked groggily.

"No, it isn't, but there's movement through the pass. I can't tell who it is or if they're coming or going, but I'm not about to take a chance. Grab a pan. We're going to have to douse the fire and drown the smoke. If they don't know the cabin is here they'll go right by, and if they know it's here and come around and there's no smoke, they may just continue on."

Meagan nodded and pulled on her shoes. The thought of staying in the cabin without the benefit of the fire filled her with dread. "It's going to be awfully cold in here when we put the fire out," she said as they poured water over the logs.

Josh covered the rest of the logs with snow until the smoke had died satisfactorily. "We're not going to stay in here," he told her. "We're going down in the root cellar. If they don't know about the cellar, they'll never find us."

Meagan gasped. "We'll smother."

"There's a pipe that brings fresh air in from somewhere. I saw it when I was down there. Now get all your clothes and gear and come on."

He moved the rag rug and opened the trapdoor. Without further ado he grabbed Meagan's arm and shoved her into the dark recesses below. A moment later he followed, his arms full of clothing and a bucket with hot stones from the fireplace. The heat of the stones mingled with that of their bodies took the chill from the air. He handed Meagan a lighted candle, carefully secured the rug to the door of the cellar and gently pulled it closed above them.

"If the Indians set fire to the place we'll be trapped down here," Meagan shuddered at the thought.

"Let's just pray that the Indians will pass by without ever knowing the cabin is here."

The ceiling of the root cellar was high enough they could walk, though bent over. They spread their belongings on the dirt floor and began their vigil.

Josh leaned against the wall, stretching his legs out before him. Meagan sat next to him, but it wasn't long until he saw her head nodding as she fought sleep.

His mind on the sounds, or lack of them from without, Josh pulled Meagan against him, resting her head on his shoulder. "Go to sleep. I'll blow out the candle in case we need it later. There's nothing we can do now except wait and pray."

Meagan didn't resist. If she was going to die, there was no place she'd rather spend her last moments on earth than in Josh Daniels's arms. She leaned back and relaxed against him, glorying in his nearness.

The darkness enveloped them like a cocoon. They seemed to be in an embryonic state where all that they were or could ever be was only just starting to develop. Each of them realized it in their own way. This was perhaps the only time when they could say what was in their hearts without embarrassment or fear. This was the moment when they must confess, each to the other, the love they had harbored in their hearts for so long.

"I shouldn't have let you come. No matter how much I wanted you with me. I should have left you where you were safe. I could have faced death without regret if only

I knew you were safe." He turned his face and dropped a series of little kisses along her hairline.

Meagan was stunned. If she was dreaming, she was going to make the most of it and dream for all she was worth.

She reached up and ran her hand down his cheek. "You couldn't leave me behind. You're responsible for me, Josh. I belong to you by right of law, and I belong with you because I love you and with you is where I want to be."

He turned his face into her hand, pressing kisses against the palm. It was not the soft, cherished hand of a lady. This palm was calloused and rough from hours of hard work…work Meagan had done for him and with him. He loved the texture of her hand.

"I wish you were back in town with Phoebe and Will," he insisted. "At least there you'd have a chance."

"No," she said gently. "There is no chance for me. There is no life for me without you. I am where I want to be, at your side, whether you want me or not."

Something snapped in Josh's brain. He felt the blood rush to his head, drowning out her words and his noble intentions as only two words managed to bob to the surface and float on the brink of reality.

"Want you! Want you! God in heaven, Meagan. I want you more than I've ever wanted anything. If it were *my* life that was at stake for making love to you I would have done it months ago and died gladly having known the magic of your love."

Meagan's heart all but stopped beating, so intent was she on hearing his words. She shifted her position until she was kneeling beside him and could frame his face in both her hands. "Oh, Josh!" The words caught in her heart but she managed to push them forth. "Don't you realize that I feel the same way about you? I long to know your love. The only reason I haven't tried more diligently to prove my innocence and reverse the sentence is because deep in my heart I know that once I am free I can no longer stay with you."

A few months ago the mention of the crime for which Meagan had been convicted would have dampened any thought of romance, but now, in this moment of truth, Lily's death no longer stood between them.

"I need you with me Meagan," Josh admitted. "I don't want to live without you, not now, not ever."

Meagan ran her thumbs over the bearded stubble on Josh's face. It was then she felt the little rivulets as the tears slipped from his eyes. Tears he shed out of love for her. And it was beyond Meagan's ability to do more than search the earth-scented darkness until she found his lips and murmured against them again, "Oh Josh, oh Josh…"

There was no question, no hesitation, no guilt between them. They had waited for this moment for too long. They had lived and worked side by side, each giving of themselves to the other in all ways but this one.

Together they had met with death and buried its remains. Together they had defied the elements to try to save those who would be saved. And together they had come to understand each other in all ways save one, and now that knowledge would also be theirs.

Josh did not hurry. He did not need the light as he kissed Meagan's clothes from her body, covering her in a cloak of love.

So enchanting was the game that Meagan joined in, matching him kiss for kiss until they were breathless from their labors.

Josh slipped Meagan's stocking from her foot and started retracing his path of kisses from her toes up. His quest was halted but halfway to her lips. For Josh would make love to Meagan in every way he had ever dared dream. In every way a man can make love to a woman.

All the years with Lily were wiped away. All the times Lily had called him an uncouth clod and pushed him away when he had desired her were no longer of importance. Only Meagan was important. Meagan, who writhed beneath him in joyous abandonment and urged him on with her hands and her lips. Meagan, whose little cries of pleasure were muffled against his body, though they vibrated against his skin and sent shivers clear down to the soles of his feet.

And Meagan, who gave him her virginity, her love, her whole being in wild abandon that transcended anything Josh had ever thought possible.

They drifted back to earth as their souls once more joined with their glistening bodies and they slept in each other's arms. It was impossible to know when they awoke, for there was no time, no night or day in their cocoon of love. There was only fulfillment and wonder, and the perfect peace of loving and being loved in return.

Chapter Eleven

The sounds of reality filtered through into the midnight world they had created for themselves. Sounds that heralded fear and sent them searching for their clothing.

Horses stamped and nickered. Yet neither of them could tell whether the house itself was occupied.

"I'm going to lift the trapdoor and take a look." Josh shifted his position impatiently. "We can't even tell whether the storm has passed from down here."

"Please wait," Meagan cautioned. "We've heard the horses. Someone must have come around. Wait until they leave."

But the sounds of the horses did not lessen and Meagan stubbornly refused to allow Josh to open the trapdoor.

"I wonder what time it is," Josh said, sighing as he looked longingly at the door above him.

"It's still daylight," Meagan told him calmly.

"How do you know that?"

"There's a tiny bit of light through a chink in the back of the cupboard against the wall there."

Josh banged his head against the top of the root cellar as he clambered to his feet. "Hold this," he said, thrusting the candle into Meagan's hand. A moment later he struck flint and steel and the wick caught, giving a wavering light.

"Hold it high," he ordered as he examined the shelves which were all but empty. It was only when he placed his fingers through the knothole and pulled that the shelves moved forward.

"It's a door," Meagan gasped.

"It's our way out of here." Josh gave her a little hug as he pulled the door open, revealing a narrow passage. "Stay here while I see where this leads."

He returned quickly. The smile on his face told her his survey had been successful.

"It ends up in the shed. Those were our own horses we heard. Let's get our gear together. The storm's passed. I want to be out of here by nightfall."

"But the Indians…"

"Indians don't usually travel at night. Something about evil spirits. We should be able to see pretty well with the snow. We'll be at that settler's cabin by tomorrow." He stopped gathering up their gear and put his arms around her. "And Meagan, this time if they offer us the bed in the loft, we're going to take it."

Meagan laughed deep in her throat. "But Josh," she said, "we might be happier in the barn. We wouldn't want to disturb the poor people's sleep."

Josh crushed her to him, covering her face with kisses before settling on her lips. "If you don't stop we'll never get out of here," he warned.

Meagan returned his kisses hungrily. "I'm not sure I want to get out of here," she told him. But they both knew there was no choice. They had to go back home. They had to be there for Abbie, and they had to find some way to keep their insatiable love for each other a secret until they could prove Meagan's innocence.

They went through the tunnel into the shed. The horses made no sound as Josh saddled them. They saw no one, but the snow through the pass was crushed by many hooves.

"Come." Josh handed Meagan the reins of her horse. "We'll walk the horses."

The only sound was the scrunching of the snow beneath their feet. The air was crisp, but the immediate threat of snow was gone, and hopefully with it the threat of the Indians, at least until the next thaw.

Josh stopped at the top of the hill and looked over the vista below. "The Indians are camped over there," he said, pointing to a distant column of smoke. "They must have come right past us during the storm."

"How far away are they?" Meagan wondered aloud.

"Too damn close for comfort," Josh assured. "Now lead your horse down to the bottom of the incline and once we get there we'll mount."

Meagan hardly noticed his words as her whole attention was fixed on this handsome, authoritative man who had made such unbelievably wonderful love to her only a few hours before. "And then?"

Josh had no idea what Meagan was thinking. His full concentration was on getting out of there with their skins and their scalps intact.

"And then, we'll ride like hell until we're well out of the area," he said as he gave her a little nudge to send her on her way before falling in behind her horse.

They reached Josh's land the morning of the third day. The snow had fallen in the mountains and the ground was lightly covered near the cabin.

Although nothing was said, both of them breathed a sigh of relief that the cabin was still standing, untouched. The Indians had not yet come this far.

Through the long days they had ridden hard, and for the most part they had tried to find shelter with some of the settlers during the night. The closer they got to home the more chance there was that someone would know of Josh and Meagan and the situation that had thrust them together. They dared not spend the hours of darkness for anything more than sleep. Only in their dreams did they come together in love, but each time their eyes met love blossomed anew.

They had conformed to convention and not made love since those wonderful hours in the root cellar. Now, with the haven of the house that Josh had built beckoning before them, they urged their horses forward and headed for the barn.

Together Josh and Meagan pulled the saddles from the horses' backs and rubbed them down quickly before giving them a supply of fresh food and water. At the barn door they paused and took the time to look deeply into each other's eyes.

"We're home, Josh! We made it home."

Josh grabbed Meagan's hand and the next moment they were running toward the house. He didn't even bother to take the boards off the windows. He pried the nails out of the door and pulled Meagan into the kitchen and into his arms.

He forced himself to pause long enough to light a fire on the hearth, and as the flame flickered and caught, so their passion flared and burst into a flame of its own.

Clothing dropped in a heap on the floor and two bodies burrowed deep between the feather beds, cozy in their private nest of love.

"I've dreamed of this every night," Meagan said as they cuddled together. "I would lie here and think how wonderful it would be if I could just reach out and touch you in the night."

"You can do more than touch me," Josh promised. "In fact, there isn't much of us that isn't touching right now."

Meagan ran her hands over his back and down his slim flanks. God, how she loved him. Just the feel of his flesh beneath her palms was enough to send her heart hammering in her throat. And he must feel the same way, for his body quickened at the touch of her hands.

She held him close as he peppered her face and neck with kisses, and her whole body arched to meet his when he found her breasts, tender and yearning, and lost himself in their sweetness. No one had ever made her feel this way, and she could scarcely believe that any two other people in the world could have possibly known a love as beautiful and fulfilling as that which they shared.

Their coming together was as joyous as it was spontaneous. The need so long denied burst into the flames of love, warming their bodies, hearts and souls with ecstasy.

It was late in the day when they managed to pull themselves from the warm nest they had made between the thick feather beds. The room was cozy now, as warm and inviting as the love that overflowed their hearts.

Amid laughter and gentle kisses they dressed each other and made their way toward the creek where the animals were waiting.

It took very little time to herd them back toward the barn. Meagan gave them grain and mash while Josh tossed fresh hay from the mow, laughing as it drifted into Meagan's hair.

"You won't think it is so funny when you have to comb it out," she scolded, but the smile on her face belied her words.

Josh removed the boards from the windows on the part of the house in which they lived. The parlor remained boarded tight.

Meagan looked at him questioningly, but she didn't want to hear his explanation. She understood his reasoning. They could not know when they would be forced to flee, and the less they had to do when the time came the better off they would be.

"I'll take the planks off the door if you want to go in for something," he offered, as he caught her glancing over her shoulder toward the boarded door.

"I don't need anything in there," she told him. "But I may have to go in to clean up a bit."

Salt pork and yams were sizzling in the skillet when they heard horses nearing the house. A moment later Rafe Somers was banging on the door.

"I saw smoke, and I said, 'Rafe, either my friend Josh is back or the Indians have burned out his house.' So I came to see which it was." He clapped Josh on the shoulder. "I'm glad to see it is you."

"The way you came clattering up sounded as though you were pretty sure of your welcome," Josh told him.

"Oh, no," Rafe protested, his white teeth gleaming through the darkness of his beard. "I did not know yet it was you, but if it was Indians I wanted to give them good notice I was coming. Then, if they shoot at me I will run away quick before they can catch me."

They all laughed together, but Meagan saw Rafe glancing around the room. The curtain had not been pulled and it was obvious that only one bed had been slept in. Meagan cursed her lapse in not making certain the bed in which they had so recently made love had been put in order, but it was mussed and rumpled, and the hollow where two bodies had lain was obvious.

"Will you stay to dinner?" Josh was asking. "We're just fixing to sit down."

"I must get back to my woman. She is very nervous with all the talk about Indians." He paused, knowing he must ask the question, but dreading to hear the answer. "Were the rumors true? Are the Indians out to get us?"

Josh nodded his head. "I'm afraid so. We found a couple of places already burned out. Buried the dead where there was a need and warned everyone who would listen. We would have been back sooner but we got caught in a snowstorm. Seemed like the Indians got caught in it too. We managed to slip out before they knew we were anywhere around and hightailed it back here."

"They didn't follow you, did they?" Rafe's eyes peered through the murky light into the shadows.

"They went on to their own village. With any luck they'll stay there until spring. By then maybe we'll be able to get enough men together to scare them off."

"Hah!" Rafe snorted. "I don't know about you, friend Josh, but in this case it is Rafe that is scared. When Indians go on the warpath I don't want to be anywhere around."

"I think we're all a little scared," Josh admitted, "but that doesn't mean we're going to run away."

Rafe shrugged. "Sometimes it's better to run while you still can and come back later to pick up the pieces. You listen and take Rafe's words to heart. Because I don't want to bury you and Meagan, and I sure as hell don't want you burying me!''

Meagan and Josh stood silently as they watched the French trapper ride away. It wasn't until he was out of sight that Meagan spoke.

"He saw the bed," she said bluntly.

"He wouldn't think anything of it. There's just one groove in it."

"One *big* groove," Meagan pointed out.

"Men don't notice things like that." Josh turned away impatiently. *He* would never have noticed how big the dent in a bed was, but what about other men? It was definitely beneath him to talk to another man about something like that, so, in truth, he didn't know. That fact scared him half to death.

He put his arm around Meagan's shoulders. "There's not a whole lot we can do about it right now," he told her. "Why don't we have some dinner and then we can mull it over before we go to bed." But even at the mention of going to bed Josh caught the shadow of fear in her eyes. Would it come to the place where they couldn't even talk to each other without causing doubt and fear? Had their brief and passionate lovemaking brought them to this impasse?

He wanted to take her in his arms and assure her that everything was going to be all right. That, somehow he would make it right if it took his last ounce of strength to do so. He wanted to, but he couldn't.

Rafe's appearance had put a blight on their happiness. All Josh could do was to hope that the man would keep still about what he had seen, or thought he had seen, because the garrulous Frenchman didn't have the sense of a bedbug when it came to keeping his mouth shut.

Meagan set the plates on the table. They were piled

high with savory-smelling food, but neither of them was able to do justice to their meal. They picked at the food and moved it around their plates before dumping it in a metal bowl to be taken out to the dog and the pigs.

"Meagan, I'm sorry," Josh began. His heart ached with his sorrow. He should have been more aware. He should have seen how incriminating the bed looked. He should never have put her in danger through his love for her.

Meagan put the dishes in the pan and turned the lye soap in the dishrag until the water began to show signs of suds. "Wasn't your fault, Josh. I should have made up the bed when we got up. Don't blame yourself. It's a woman's place to keep the house. I didn't tend to my job."

"He can't prove anything," Josh pointed out. "We were both right in the middle of the room when he came to the door."

"That's right, we were," she agreed. "But does he need to prove anything? They found me guilty of murder without any proof other than the word of a woman who had more reason to kill than I did."

Josh jerked around. "What are you saying?" he demanded. The possibilities began spinning in his head.

"I'm just saying that Rafe doesn't need proof that we were in bed together. If he says he thinks we were, everyone, including Judge Osborne, will believe him, regardless of what we say."

Josh sat down beside the table and buried his face in his hands. "I'm going in to town day after tomorrow. I'm going to see Abbie and get some supplies. I'll talk to Will and see if he can get the judge to change the sentence." He lifted his head and looked into her eyes. "Do you want to go with me?"

Meagan shook here head. "I'll stay here and take care of the place until you get back. Just leave me one of the horses, and if I see any sign of trouble I'll make for the Klinerts' place."

"I wish you'd come with me," Josh told her. He wasn't going to plead, but the thought of leaving her behind scalded his very soul.

She came toward him and placed her hands on his shoulders and gazed into his face. "Josh, I can't even look at you without everyone seeing how much I love you. All I'd do is make it harder for you and impossible for Will. I can't go with you. If you love me, let me stay here."

Josh nodded his head. The love in her eyes was so obvious he didn't doubt for a moment the truth in her words. "I'll go on alone. Will and I can work something out. I'll stake my life on it." *And yours, too,* he thought as he reached out and took her hand in both of his. "We might as well go to bed. We've already done about as much damage as we can. Might as well reap some of the harvest."

To his relief she answered him with a smile and grasped his hand in a grip that spoke of love and trust in his ability to change the future.

But even as Meagan lay in his arms, her breath warm and sweet against his cheek, Josh could not relax. He knew, now more than ever, that he couldn't live without this woman, even if it meant pulling up the roots he had so carefully planted and moving far beyond the mountains to the frontier, where the laws of the Carolinas did not apply. If all else failed, he would take Meagan so far away that no one would ever find them.

Josh didn't say anything to Meagan about the decision he had reached in the darkness of the night. He knew she would protest if he mentioned abandoning his home to go farther into the wilderness. Perhaps he would never have to tell her. Perhaps Judge Osborne would temper justice with mercy and allow them to live together in peace and love.

It was with real hope in his heart that Josh kissed Meagan goodbye and set out toward the fort. He paused on the rise above the cabin and looked back. Meagan was heading for the washhouse toting a basket of dirty clothes, with a flintlock precariously balanced on top.

He smiled to see her, and was pleased that she was living up to their agreement and carrying the gun with her at all times.

As she reached the door, she glanced up through the trees to the ridge above and blew a kiss on the wind, knowing somehow it would reach her love. And even though Josh knew she couldn't see him, he sent a kiss down to her in return, then looked about, hoping that even the animals had not witnessed his loverlike lapse. But it was with a lighter heart that he left Meagan behind and hurried away.

Having experienced the horrors of Indian attack so recently, Meagan found herself very aware of her surrounding. She prided herself on carrying the gun with her at all times and on being alert to any danger that might exist. Even the dog was more aware than usual, yapping and barking at every strange noise. Therefore, Meagan was doubly surprised when she came out of the barn the evening of the second day and found Ruth Somers standing in her path.

"Mrs. Somers! I...I didn't hear you drive up," Meagan stammered.

"If I'd wanted you to know I was coming I would

have announced myself. My Rafe told me what's been going on around here. You and Josh have been bundling.''

Meagan almost laughed at the woman's accusation. They had done a lot more than bundling, which was acceptable deportment on a cold winter's night. But the laughter died in her throat when she saw the hatred in Ruth's eyes.

''You can't fool me, like you can some. The minute my man told me about the goin's on around here, I knew what you were about. You're trying to use Josh to lighten your lot. Well, it won't work.''

''I carry my share of the work, Mrs. Somers. Josh has no complaints.'' Meagan defended herself briefly, then went on the attack. ''Besides, I thought you had sworn never to come back here again when you forbade me hospitality on your property.''

''Well, I never!'' Ruth puffed herself up like an outraged partridge. ''I came over to see to the welfare of my nearest neighbor and you insult me. Wait until I tell Josh about this!'' She jerked her head around, surveying the property. ''Where *is* Josh, anyway?''

Meagan bit her lip. It was against her disposition to lie, but she dared not tell this woman the truth.

''Josh is running some errands. He'll be back later this evening.'' Without asking the woman into the house, Meagan made for the door, but Ruth was too fast for her.

She poked her head into the kitchen and sniffed the air. ''And you're a liar, too, but then I always knew you were. If Josh was coming back tonight you'd have his dinner cooking. There's no dinner fit for a man on that hearth.''

Meagan felt her heart sink. What Ruth said was true

and she had been caught telling a falsehood by her worst enemy.

"For all I know you may have killed him and were out in the barn burying his body." Ruth warmed to her theme.

"That's ridiculous. Josh is fine and he should be back here any time now," Meagan said. She stuck to her premise, hoping the woman would go away.

"It's not ridiculous for a murderer to kill again," Ruth asserted. "If Josh is really all right then you shouldn't object to coming down to the barn with me to prove I'm wrong." She grabbed Meagan's wrist and jerked her toward the door.

"I was in the barn feeding the livestock," Meagan told her as they struggled across the yard. "Going to the barn isn't going to do any good."

Meagan wondered if she should have tried to snatch up the gun before leaving the house. If the Indians should pick this particular time to attack, the women would be defenseless. Josh had specifically told her to keep the gun with her to guard against danger. But even if Meagan had the gun in her hand at this moment she wouldn't dare use it on Ruth, although in Meagan's opinion, Ruth was most likely more dangerous than most Indians would ever be.

The two women all but burst through the doors into the barn. Startled, the horse reared and bucked at the sudden invasion of his privacy. Meagan stepped toward his stall in an effort to soothe the animal. The moment she turned her back on Ruth the woman snatched up a shovel and brought it down on Meagan's head.

Chapter Twelve

It was dark and Meagan was cold. She tried to move but found her stiff body would not respond.

She could hear the blowing of a horse. Perhaps she was still in the root cellar. Perhaps she was stiff because of the weight of Josh's body on her own. But Josh was warm, and there was no warmth. Only the icy air that sent chilled tremors through her body.

She tried to open her eyes, but they seemed to be glued shut. Had she become ill? Had Josh left her here in the darkness of the root cellar and gone to get help?

No, that didn't seem right. She tried to remember all that had happened from the time they had descended to the soft earthy darkness and found love.

They had returned home, and Josh had gone to the fort to talk to Will and make certain Abbie was all right. Josh had not wanted to leave her alone. He had warned her to watch for Indians.

Had the Indians come? Was that why her hands were tied high over her head? And if that was so, where had they taken her?

She didn't remember any Indians. She only remembered Ruth Somers demanding that they go to the barn.

The horse, neighing and bucking, and then darkness. A darkness that did not cease.

Head throbbing, Meagan rubbed her eyes against her arms and finally managed to open them. In the icy moonlight she could see that she had been trussed up and left in a barn stall.

Her feet were bare, and she had been stripped to her petticoat. The winter air permeated every pore of her body and she shivered uncontrollably. It was Ruth who had done this to her; of that she had no doubt. But why? How much damage must the woman do to sate her hatred? And why did she hate Meagan so vehemently?

Meagan tried to stand and found it impossible. She huddled against the wooden stall. As soon as it was light she would find some way to get away. Somehow, she must escape before Ruth returned. But by afternoon Ruth had not returned, due to problems of her own.

"Where are you going?" Ruth demanded as Rafe shrugged into his coat.

He ruffled the hair of his oldest son as he marched toward the door. "I go over to see if the livestock of my friend Josh needs looking to," he told her.

Ruth was at the door before him. "Why can't Josh take care of his own livestock?" she demanded.

"Because Josh has gone to the fort. He left me a sign when he passed this way. I find it this morning. So I go and make sure everything is all right." Again he started off.

"Rafe! Wait…" Ruth hurried after him. "I'd better go with you. I don't think you should be over there alone with that murderess."

Rafe shrugged. "If you want to come along, go and

get your coat. And move yourself, woman. Night comes
early. I do not like traveling in the dark.''

He watched his wife disappear into the house and
scratched his head, wondering what made Ruth think
that Meagan had stayed behind. With a little sigh he
went out to unsaddle his horse and hitch up the wagon.
It would have been a lot less trouble if Ruth had stayed
behind.

''Come here, Frankie. Good goat. Take a taste of that
nice rope,'' Meagan coaxed, gritting her teeth together
to keep them from rattling.

The little goat looked at Meagan and then at the rope
knotted on the hasp of his stall. He had been scolded for
chewing on ropes and blankets by Meagan often enough,
and the animal seemed confused. He'd never understand.
The goat took another step forward and sniffed at the
rope. It was too tempting to be denied. With half-closed
eyes, he began munching away.

Meagan tried not to move her hands, for her wrists
were already raw and bleeding from her efforts to free
herself. The more she tried the tighter the rope became.
Where had Ruth learned to tie a knot like that? It was
no wonder the woman had wanted Meagan hung. Ruth
had probably hoped to tie the hangman's noose herself.

Balanced precariously, Meagan watched as the little
goat chewed his way through the rope.

He was halfway through when Meagan heard a horse
ride into the yard.

Her heart jumped to her throat. Had Josh come home
early? Or was it Ruth coming to gloat over Meagan's
misery? Or, God forbid, were her visitors the Indians
she so dreaded?

The horses' hooves gave a soft, almost hollow sound

on the frozen ground. White men shod their horses, and the shoes clattered against stone and ice. Her heart leaped to her mouth. She felt tears spring to her eyes. She had come so close to being able to free herself with the help of the goat. So close…

There was silence. Even the animals in the barn held their breath, except for the goat, who kept gnawing away at his tidbit, oblivious to the drama or the danger.

Meagan watched as the rope became thinner. In a few moments she would be able to give it a jerk and free herself. Just a few more minutes. *Oh, please, God, whoever is out there, just let them stay for a few more minutes, and make that goat keep chewing!*

Meagan tried to grip at the rope above her numbed fingers. The pain was excruciating. She bit her lip and held her breath against the pain.

Then the goat stopped chewing and looked back over his shoulder. A gust of icy air wafted through the already cold barn. Meagan closed her eyes. If she jerked the rope and it didn't break all the circulation to her hands would be cut off. But there was no more time. She had to make her escape now.

She closed her eyes and gave a mighty jerk. The pain sent her to her knees. The rope held.

"Meagan! Who has done this to you? When I get a hold of the man who did this I'll kill him!"

Meagan's eyes flew open. The outline of a man wavered before her and she opened her mouth to speak but only a little sob came out. It was enough. In the next moment the rope was cut and she fell in exhausted relief into her brother's arms.

"Meagan! Talk to me!" Reilly demanded. "How did this happen? Where is the man who has done this to you?"

"It wasn't a man, Reilly," Meagan managed. "It was the woman whose testimony convicted me of murder. Ruth Somers tied me up this way."

Reilly checked out the rope. "She is a clever woman. Clever and cruel, a bad combination." He turned to his sister. "Where are your clothes? We must leave here right away."

"Is Old Howling Dog coming? I can't leave until I warn Josh."

"If Josh was worth his salt he would have taken you with him and not left you to the mercies of a madwoman. You will come with me. I'll not take no for an answer." He helped her from the stall and out into the frosty air. "Old Howling Dog is not coming—yet. Your precious Josh will have plenty of time to make himself safe, but I will not leave you here to be murdered. Get your clothes together and write the man a note if you must. But when I leave here you will go with me."

Meagan had never seen her brother so forceful. Somehow she must find a way to make him understand that none of this was Josh's fault, but her head was throbbing and the world was spinning crazily by the time they reached the house. She staggered against the table and Reilly was again at her side. He dipped her wrists into a pan filled with snow and quickly bandaged them with soft leather.

Realizing Meagan was in no condition to get her things together, Reilly dug through her chest and came up with a bundle of clothing. He helped her into her smock and fastened her skirt over her petticoats.

"Are you going to leave a note?" he asked.

Meagan shook her head, trying to escape the ringing in her ears. "There's no use," she said quietly. "Josh can't read."

Reilly raised his eyebrow. It was unconscionable that a man not be able to read, in the opinion of a schoolteacher's half-breed son. But he remained silent, suspecting that even in her weakened condition Meagan would cut his tongue out should he made a disparaging remark about the man she so obviously loved.

The fire was down to embers and the only food was day-old mush. Reilly added a little water and stirred. "Eat this and then we'll go." He offered her a spoon but she only stared at him with fever-glazed eyes.

Reilly put his hand against her forehead and swore under his breath. He dipped the spoon into the mush and placed it against her mouth. "Try to eat, sister, and then we must go. If the person who has done this to you comes back we will both be in trouble. I do not want to kill a white woman, but I will before I let more harm come to you."

"No, Reilly, you mustn't. It would mean your life. Ruth Somers isn't worth it." Meagan had never loved her half brother more than she did at that moment. But she still had to make him understand that she couldn't go with him. Josh would think she had left him. He would never understand, since he didn't even know that Reilly existed. Meagan had not wanted her brother to be involved with a convicted murderess and had purposely kept their relationship a secret.

She'd figure out something as soon as she stopped shaking and felt stronger. She'd explain to Reilly how much she loved Josh, and how much Josh loved her. She had to get her strength back. She had to, for Josh and Reilly....

Meagan accepted another bite of the food and coughed, gagged and slumped forward. "I can't eat any more," she whispered, pushing the spoon away.

Reilly finished the rest of the mush, slipped her bundle over his arm and picked up her cloak. "Come on, Meagan," he urged. "It's time to go."

"Reilly, I told you, I can't go with you."

A dog howled in the distance, followed by the cry of an owl. Reilly grabbed his sister's arm. "Meagan, stop this foolishness. We have to get out of here now. Someone is coming."

"It's Josh!" she cried, staggering toward the door. "Everything will be all right now. I'll tell him who you are and what has happened. He'll be glad...."

"We can't wait around for explanations." The owl hooted again. "And neither can you."

Reilly swung himself up on his pony just as a wagon lumbered into the yard. A short man sat on the seat next to a woman.

"Is that your man?" Reilly asked, but the horror on Meagan's face gave him the answer.

"That's Ruth and Rafe Somers," Meagan said with a gasp. She didn't want to leave the house and run off with Reilly. She wanted to wait for Josh to return. Josh with his warm eyes and warm lips and... But Josh wasn't here. It was Ruth Somers who was approaching her. Ruth Somers, with her unwarranted hatred, whom Meagan feared more than Old Howling Dog himself.

She stepped back into the room and Reilly feared that she would try to bar the door against him as well as the unwelcome visitors, but she reappeared quickly, the flintlock clenched in her hands. "Go! Get out of here!" she shouted.

Reilly's horse danced nervously. He had to gain complete control of the animal before he dared move closer to his sister. Ruth took one look at Meagan, now holding a gun, and dived unceremoniously over the back of the seat into the bed of the wagon. Meanwhile Rafe observed the whole scene with amazement. He could not comprehend his wife's actions and had no idea that Meagan's threats were not meant for the Indian.

"No shooting," Reilly warned Meagan quietly. "If you hit either of them both our lives are forfeit."

Meagan hesitated momentarily. Reilly leaned down and scooped her into his arms. The gun dropped to the ground and discharged into the air. Cursing roundly he put his heels to his pony and thundered across the yard and out onto the road, away from the farm, away from civilization and away from Rafe and Ruth Somers, who stared after him.

It took only a few seconds for Ruth to find her voice.

"There! There!" she shrieked through the evening shadows. "I told you so! I told you that woman was up to no good. You saw as well as I! She just ran off with a filthy Indian."

Rafe clapped his hand over his wife's mouth. "Shut your face, woman," he said as he tried to see into the falling shadows. "The Indian may not have been alone. You will bring the whole tribe down on us with your hollering."

She shook his hand away, her eyes gleaming with self-righteous malevolence. "I was right," she said in a hushed voice. "I told everyone that girl was up to no good. Now she's brought the Indians down on us. We'll be lucky if any of us come out of this alive."

"It looked to me as though the Indian came here and stole the poor girl," Rafe argued. It had seemed that Meagan took one look at Ruth and rode off with the Indian without a fight. Of course, Ruth sometimes had that effect on people. He had been a lonely man when he had first built his cabin far in the wilderness. When he met Ruth she seemed to be everything he needed in a woman. She was young and strong with enough intelligence to learn quickly. If she did not fulfill his needs in bed he did not complain, for she had given him two fine sons.

For that alone he had been willing to overlook her vindictiveness, but her hatred of Meagan Reilly had become an obsession and Rafe knew in his own heart that his wife wouldn't be satisfied until the girl was dead.

Rafe stopped the wagon near the barn and climbed to the ground, his wife's ceaseless haranguing ringing in his ears.

"Aren't you going to go after them?" she demanded.

"I don't chase Indians and I don't want them chasing me," Rafe told her.

"But she'll get away. She'll go live with the Indians like a free woman."

Rafe tied the horses to the hitching post. "I doubt the life of a white woman with the Indians is anything to be envied. Now, you go and make sure the house is shut. I'll take care of the animals."

But Ruth wasn't done with her tirade, even as she walked toward the house. "Meagan isn't just any white woman. She's a murderess. She should be punished. I demand you go after her!"

Rafe didn't bother to answer as he lumbered into the barn. Perhaps he should go after Meagan. Maybe the Indians would make him a swap. Ruth for Meagan.

"Hah!" he said aloud as he filled the horse trough and slapped the animal on the rump. "If I gave those Indians my Ruth for Meagan they would find out their mistake pretty quick and come back after my scalp, for sure."

As he made certain the other animals were fed, Rafe

noticed the cut rope hanging loose above his head. The other end was frayed almost to a thread and still fastened to one of the iron rings on the stall door. The arrangement looked much like the way they trussed up pigs when they were butchered and cooled.

Rafe looked around again. There was blood on the cut rope, and what looked to be clothing in the corner of the stall. He didn't like what he saw. More than that, he didn't like what he was thinking. This was not the kind of thing an Indian would do, and Rafe could not believe Josh would tie Meagan in the barn in the middle of winter and leave her there while he was gone.

No, there was only one person who might do such a thing, and she would take some careful watching.

He narrowed his eyes against the night wind and shut the barn door behind him.

"Well," Ruth demanded, "were the animals all right? Or did the Indians steal them all?"

"The animals are fine, but it looks as though someone was held prisoner in there." He didn't bother to look at his wife as he spoke. "I don't think Meagan went willingly with that Indian."

Ruth huffed, "Of course she did. It's just as I said. If anyone was held prisoner it was probably Josh. The poor man may be lying somewhere bleeding to death at this minute."

"I'll come back tomorrow and have a look around," Rafe promised. "If he isn't dead, he should be back by then. If he isn't back we'll go to the fort and find him."

"We'll go to the fort, all right," Ruth contended. "We'll go get the men together to go after Meagan and that Indian before we're all murdered in our beds. We shouldn't wait another minute!"

Ruth continued her tirade while Rafe wrapped his

scarf tight over his ears and clucked to the horses as they headed home.

A twig snapped against the night but there was no other sound. Shadows slipped through the trees and into the yard. A rawboned Indian with hard quick eyes slipped into the barn. Old Howling Dog looked around and saw what the Frenchman had seen. It was the short, plump squaw who had done this. He lifted the end of the rope and smiled. The woman knew many things. A woman like that would be of much use in the village while the men were gone. Of course, something would have to be done about her raucous voice, but that, too, could be taken care of with little trouble.

He must give this some thought. He did not want to put his own people in danger because of a vindictive white woman. Still, she piqued his interest. She would be a challenge, and he would enjoy breaking her to his will. He would enjoy every moment of it, even if she didn't.

He slipped through the woods, staying far enough from the wagon to keep out of sight until the couple reached their own land.

So this was where the woman lived! He would remember, and if he decided he wanted her, he would come back.

His mind returned to the girl that Reilly had taken. She was young and strong, but so were the women of his village. Reilly's woman would have to be taught how to survive the Indian way of life, while the woman Old Howling Dog was considering was self-sufficient.

Yes, he had made a wise choice when he had come upon the place yesterday and seen the two women together. By waiting and watching, he had discovered a plump little woman who would fit nicely into his way of life.

Without a sound he made a gesture of farewell, and disappeared into the trees.

Josh Daniels was feeling pretty good about himself and the world in general as he finished loading supplies on his horse and the pack mule Will Carmichael had insisted he borrow. Abbie watched from the kitchen window, her face still a bit petulant in her disappointment at not being allowed to return with him. But he had promised that both he and Meagan would come back for her soon and then they would all be together. Will had been downright encouraging about getting Meagan's sentence changed so they could get married. He was going home where Meagan would be waiting for him with open arms.

He sighed in anticipation as he tightened the girth on the saddle. If he rode straight through he could get home early the next day. Maybe they'd just skip dinner and get right to the important things, like making love.

He enjoyed making love to Meagan in the daylight. He liked looking at her creamy white body and following the little trail of freckles that seemed to lead to wondrous exciting places. Yes, daytime was a right nice time to make love.

Meagan would be surprised when he told her that they wouldn't need to eat for a long while because there were more important things that needed to be done. Like taking her in his arms and kissing her until she was breathless and then carrying her over to the bed and...

A wagon careened down the street and came to a stop before the general store. People jumped aside to get out of the way and grumbled loudly over the recklessness of the driver.

Josh's eyes opened wide when he realized the woman driving the lathered horses was Ruth Somers. Concern hit at the same moment. He started toward the street along with most of the townsfolk.

"Ruth!" Josh called. "What are you doing here? Where's Rafe? Is everything all right?"

"If everything was all right, I wouldn't be here," she declared breathlessly. "Meagan is gone. Indian came and took her away just before dark yesterday afternoon."

"Why didn't you stop them?" Josh demanded.

"You didn't hear me," Ruth said, although she was shouting. "I didn't say Indians, I said Indian. One Indian. She jumped on his horse and rode off with him. She's run away and it's up to every man in this town to go after her and find her and shoot her down."

Josh felt the blood drain from his face. The thought of Meagan being pursued and shot down like a wild animal was more than he could bear.

"Meagan wouldn't have run off with an Indian," Josh said defensively.

"I know what I saw," Ruth declared. "She sold us out to the Indians for her freedom. There isn't a one of us that's safe now. She saved her own skin, but the rest of us will all be killed. I tell you, I saw her run to that Indian's horse and practically climb into his arms."

The gathering crowd muttered nervously over Ruth's accusations. Seeing her advantage, she was about to launch into an even more detailed account of the situation, when her husband shoved his way through the crowd.

Rafe Somers's face was red and streaked with sweat,

despite the cold. His clothes were mud spattered and there was anger in his eyes as he approached his wife.

"You dumped me from the wagon and left me to walk into town. Why did you do this, woman?" he demanded.

"It was necessary that we get our news to the people as quick as possible," Ruth contended self-righteously. "We don't want any more bloodshed."

"What bloodshed?" Rafe shouted. "There won't be any bloodshed until I get my hands on you!"

Ruth shrank back and Rafe caught sight of Josh. "Friend Josh, I'm afraid the Indians have taken your woman," he said.

"She ran off with them," Ruth contended, but she kept her distance. "I knew you wouldn't want to hurt Josh's feelings and that you'd try to keep the truth from him." She gave an indignant toss of her head and turned her full attention on Josh. "You're better off without her," she told him. "I'm going to go tell the authorities at the fort. They should know that a criminal is loose and be ready to shoot her on sight."

"Silence your tongue, woman. Josh has enough pain. He does not need to hear your clacking." He turned to Josh. "They rode west. Go on your way and see if you can pick up their trail. I would come with you, but I think this one—" he jerked his thumb toward his wife "—should go home."

"I'm not going home," Ruth shouted him down. "I'm going to the fort and I'm going to tell the authorities that woman has sold us out to the Indians. We're all in grave danger."

Before either Rafe or Josh could speak again, Will Carmichael stepped forward. "If everyone is in imminent danger of being killed by the Indians, why did you leave your sons behind?" he asked smoothly.

"My boys can take care of themselves," she contended once she found her voice.

"Don't seem like a mother would leave her young'ns behind if she thought there was a real threat of an Indian attack," one of the old men mused in the loud voice of the partially deaf as he sat whittling on the bench in front of the store.

"How dare you!" Ruth bristled. "Are you insinuating that I'm not a good mother?"

The old man got to his feet and looked the woman up and down. He hadn't liked her when she had taken such pleasure in testifying at the murder trial, and he didn't like her any better now. She reminded him of his mother-in-law, now long dead, and he hadn't liked *her* either. "I'm just saying you're trying to make a tempest in a teapot. You're a busybody and should be at home raising your own children and minding your own business instead of running all over the countryside trying to get other people into trouble."

"You'll thank me when the Indians come. Then you'll see that I'm telling the truth. I pride myself on always telling the truth."

"What was that story you told about Lily Daniels's ghost playing the organ at the Daniels house?" Phoebe piped up from the old man's side.

The crowd mumbled and nodded their heads as many of them remembered Ruth's wild tale of being driven out into a stormy night by a haunted organ. Will smiled at his wife. Ruth's credibility had been satisfactorily impugned, but it didn't bring Meagan back, nor would it make Will's job any easier when he tried to get Judge Osborne to lessen her sentence.

Realizing that nothing she said would be effective after Phoebe's revelation, Ruth marched into the store and slammed the door behind her. Josh started back toward his horse, with Rafe hurrying along beside him.

"I would have gone after them, but there was no time," Rafe apologized. "I had the wagon with my woman in it. The Indian took off across country. I could not catch him."

"But Meagan! What about Meagan?" Josh agonized. "She wouldn't have run away. Not from me. Not now."

"I tell you true, Josh Daniels. I do not know that your Meagan did not want to go. She took one look at us and the next thing we know she is up on the horse with the Indian and they ride like hell to get out of there."

Josh shook his head. "But that doesn't make sense," he told the other man.

Rafe knew it would make more sense if he told Josh of his suspicions about what had taken place in the barn, but he had only suspicions and he didn't want to cast aspersions on Ruth. There was already bad blood between them and it had caused Rafe a lot of sorrow, trying to choose between his wife and his nearest neighbor.

Josh sensed the man was holding something back. "We will talk when I return," he said.

"He went through the trees to the west of your property," Rafe volunteered. "He was on a pony and I think there were other Indians with him. We will form a posse and go after them."

"I'll go after him alone," Josh said before even Will could object. "I don't want any trigger-happy militiamen taking a potshot because he believes in your wife's lies."

Rafe didn't even try to defend his wife. "I'll tell you all I know when you come back with your Meagan. But Ruth's lie is not that Meagan went with the man willingly." He sighed as Josh untied the mule and handed the lead rein to Will Carmichael. He knew that neither of the men believed either him or his wife. "Sometimes I think I would go off with the Indians just to get away from Ruth." It was the best explanation he could give Josh without going into detail that would have caused himself trouble and Josh serious delay.

Josh did not seem to notice. He shook Will's hand and mounted his horse. Within minutes Josh was out of sight.

"Are you going to tell me what you meant by that last remark?" Will asked the Frenchman.

"Right now I am going to go and try to silence my wife before she causes more trouble," Rafe said evasively. "We will talk later."

"That we will," Will agreed, and caught the quick look Rafe sent him as he walked away.

Will had some questions to ask Rafe. Questions that had not come out at Meagan's trial in deference to Josh's grief. Questions like why Rafe Somers was in the upstairs portion of his house in the middle of the day while his wife had gone to town, and how come Lily Daniels was upstairs with him? And while Will didn't like to think that Lily might have betrayed Josh, he knew that it was possible. He also knew that had he tried to bring this possibility to light during Meagan's trial, he would probably have been tarred and feathered for his efforts.

Lily was a beautiful woman and well liked in the community. The townsfolk held firm to their belief that people shouldn't speak unkindly of the dead. Now, however, Lily had been laid to rest for many months, and it was time to think about the living. And Will's concern at the moment was not over what Lily might or might not have done, but what had happened to make Meagan run away.

And, if there was any truth at all to what Ruth and Rafe had told them, what would Josh do when he finally caught up to her? And, for that matter, what would Meagan do when Josh found her?

No matter the outcome, Will decided he'd better be there when things came to a head. He started toward his house to tell Phoebe that he was going to the fort with the Somerses to make sure they didn't turn out the whole militia by making everyone believe they were faced with a full-scale Indian war.

Chapter Thirteen

Josh picked up the Indian's trail near the edge of his property. There were several horses, and one of them left deeper imprints as though it was carrying double. He was a good tracker and had often helped out the militia with his abilities, but never before had he used his abilities for his own purposes.

His head swam with the accusations and innuendos that had been thrown at him by Ruth and Rafe Somers. His heart ached with despair, for he had only just found hope and it was hard to lose it so quickly. The newness of the love he had found with Meagan was hardly tapped and now it had been taken from him. He would not believe that Meagan had gone willingly from his arms to those of an Indian. He would never believe it unless he saw it with his own eyes and heard her tell him with his own ears.

Night fell and the moon ascended, casting an eerie light over the land. Josh stopped to rest his horse and then moved on. He could not rest until he knew Meagan's fate, and his own.

On the morning of the fourth day he was bone-weary.

The cold had permeated his soul. He lolled listlessly in the saddle although he knew he should stay alert.

His senses quickened as he heard the sharp cry of a bird. By rights, the creature should have taken flight after such a sound, but there was no stirring of branches or fluttering of wings. Josh quickly became aware and surveyed his surroundings. He could see nothing out of the ordinary, but sensed danger.

He left his horse in a copse of trees and climbed silently to the crest of the hill. Below him was an Indian encampment. A fire burned against the night, and while Josh longed for its warmth he did not move. The Indians had not yet retired. It was a small band, and he could only hope that Meagan was with them.

He lay pressed against the frozen ground, fighting sleep until a tall Indian came out of the tepee. A moment later Josh's heart stopped as Meagan stepped into the firelight.

He leaned forward, straining to catch their words, but it was impossible. He was too far away.

Meagan did not seem to be at odds with her captor. She talked to him with ease. Indeed, she even laughed with him. Perhaps Ruth had spoken the truth.

Josh remembered how Abbie had told him she had thought she heard Meagan talking to someone the night he lay caught in the trap. Until now he had never questioned Meagan's explanation that she was singing to herself. The man looked familiar and yet Josh was fairly certain he didn't know him.

He pulled back, fighting the jealous rage that threatened to undo him. What did it matter if Meagan knew this young Indian? She belonged to Josh and he would wait until the Indians slept, then go down and take back what was his.

With this thought in mind, Josh settled back to wait. It wasn't until they bedded down that he was again overcome by anger. While the braves spread their blankets around the fire, their leader took Meagan into the tepee. And Meagan went willingly.

As soon as the Indians settled down for the night Josh made his way into the gully behind the camp. He moved silently and settled down to wait until it was time for Meagan's friend to take his turn as sentry.

The watery moon had hardly found its way above the trees before the man left the tepee and went to relieve the others. Josh crept to the back of the tepee and slit it open with his knife. The next moment he was inside.

His hand slipped over Meagan's mouth. He saw her eyes fly open in terror and then relax in recognition.

"Josh," she mouthed the word as he relaxed his grip.

"Be quiet," he ordered as he pulled her toward the slit.

"Wait! You don't understand," she spoke more loudly this time, and Josh knew he must take drastic measures.

Without wasting another second, he neatly knocked her unconscious, threw her over his shoulders and headed for the hills.

In his place as lookout Reilly saw the man as he burst through a patch of moonlight. He thought of going after them but decided against taking action. His sister had spent most of her days and nights trying to make him take her back to her precious Josh. Well, Josh had come after her and she was with him just the way she wanted to be. Reilly could only hope the man had sense enough to take care of her, because there were signs that Old

Howling Dog was on the prowl and Reilly would have his hands full trying to keep track of him.

Above the ridge on the far side of the campsite, Reilly saw the man ride off, Meagan cradled in his arms. It was only after they were well away that he realized that even though Josh had Meagan on the saddle in front of him, he was also leading a horse. A quick perusal of the ponies confirmed his suspicions. "I hope you're as good a man as you are a horse thief," Reilly said under his breath. His braves wouldn't be pleased when they learned that one of their horses was gone.

"Take care of her," he charged, "for if you do not, you will reckon with me, white man."

"There was no need for you to knock me out," Meagan told him as she nursed her aching head later that day. "Those Indians wouldn't have harmed either one of us."

"I could see that you were getting along pretty well with one of them," Josh said dryly.

Josh had been surprised at how close they were to his cabin. It seemed the Indians had taken a roundabout trail. Or perhaps they were lost and traveling in circles, but somehow he didn't think so.

"Josh, let me explain." Meagan tried for the fifth time to tell Josh that Reilly was really her half brother.

"You can explain once we get home," he told her. "I can't listen while we're riding and I'm not about to stop." It bothered Josh that Meagan was able to ride the pony bareback without any difficulty. Most women had a great deal of trouble staying on a horse without a saddle, but Meagan didn't seem to mind at all. Josh had planned to offer her his horse but decided against it when he discovered she rode bareback better than he did.

The winter thaw had begun in earnest. Springs and rivulets sprang forth and tumbled over the rocks, biting ridges out of the land. The air had turned warm during the day and Josh's mind turned to the work that must be done to prepare the land for the spring crop. Planning the crop was all that kept him sane as Meagan rode silently, no longer trying to make any kind of explanation for her defection or her behavior with her captor.

The cabin was cold, but it still stood and had apparently not been touched while they were gone. They left their muddy shoes outside the door and went into the chilly room.

Meagan remembered her panic the night she had left. Had Ruth and Rafe Somers not appeared when they did she would not have gone willingly with Reilly and heaven only knew what Ruth would have tried next. She shivered at the thought.

"I'll have the fire going in just a minute," Josh told her as he bent over the hearth.

True to his word the flame fluttered and caught. Josh fed it bits of kindling until the first bit of heat permeated the chill of the room.

They looked at each other, remembering the day they had come home and barely lit the fire in the hearth before their desire had burst into flame and they had made love amid the feather beds before the fireplace.

Josh dragged the bedding from the corner and dumped it unceremoniously in front of the fire.

"Josh, we have to talk," Meagan began. She didn't want their lovemaking to be ruined by anger and distrust, and she knew Josh was seething with both emotions.

"Is there any reason why we can't be warm and talk at the same time?" he asked.

"Is there any reason why you have to be so angry?" she returned.

"You tell me," he said as he pulled off his shirt.

The warm fire glow touched his skin, caressing him as Meagan longed to caress him.

"I've been trying to tell you all the way home."

"Well, now I've got time to listen." He dropped the rest of his clothing beside the cot and crawled between the feather beds. "Now get in here and start talking before we both freeze to death."

"There's no reason for you to be jealous of Reilly," she began.

"Reilly? Who is Reilly? I thought you were going to tell me why you ran off with the Indian."

"I didn't run off. And you have no right talking to me like that." Meagan started to move away, but Josh was too quick for her. He seized her wrist and she cried out in pain.

Josh drew back and removed his hand. He could see the fresh rope burns on her wrists, still red and raw.

He examined both of her wrists closely. "Forgive me, Meagan," he said humbly. "I shouldn't have doubted you. I was just jealous. I didn't want to believe you'd gone off and left me of your own free will, but Ruth and Rafe Somers both said..." He took a deep breath and pressed his lips against her wrists and then moved up her arms to her shoulders and neck. "I shouldn't have believed them. I'll never believe them again." His lips followed the curve of her neck and the planes of her face. "I'll never doubt you again. I'll never let anyone hurt you again. We'll pack up and leave here. We'll go far beyond the mountains to territory where white men haven't even been before. We won't have to worry about courts or laws or judges and their stupid sentences. We'll love each other forever, and I'll never let you go."

"And I'll never let *you* go either," Meagan assured him.

They came together in an urgency that surpassed anything either had dreamed, much less experienced. They drained each other of the last magic dregs of love and still wanted more, until finally, sated, they fell back in exhaustion.

He brushed her hair from her glistening forehead and kissed the place where it had been. She wiped a droplet of perspiration from his cheek and touched her finger to her lips. It was then he once more noticed the wounds on her wrist.

"If I catch those dirty redskins I'll make them pay for what they did to you," he vowed.

"But, Josh, that's what I've been trying to tell you," Meagan said patiently. "It wasn't Reilly who tied me up. It was Ruth Somers. She trussed me up and left me in the barn. My brother Reilly found me when he came to warn us about Old Howling Dog."

Josh had no chance to reply as the door burst open and Ruth stepped into the room.

"There! What did I tell you? She's seduced him! Seduced him and is lying there with him in the throes of sin! She must be hanged according to Judge Osborne's order! And Josh should be sent to jail."

Ruth tugged at the nearest men, urging them to enter. Several men glanced inside and then backed away, shamefaced with embarrassment.

Josh snatched up the gun that lay at the side of the bed. "Git out, and git out fast," he ordered. "The first person who takes a step toward this bed is dead."

"I...ahem...I think we ought to step outside and let

them get decent,'' one of the men suggested. ''Then we'll reckon about what we ought to do.''

Will Carmichael rode into the yard in time to see the men backing away from the door. His horse had thrown a shoe and he had found it impossible to keep up. From the sound of the shouts from the men clumped together at the door of the house the horse might well have cost him his friend as well as his client.

''I say we should hang her now just like the judge said,'' Ruth shouted as the men pulled her forcibly from the Daniels house into the yard.

''I say it's unnatural for a woman to want to see her neighbor get out of his bed buck naked,'' one man grumbled. ''I wouldn't put no mind to anything a woman like that had to say.''

''You saw them as well as I,'' Ruth sputtered. ''They were rolling around in the bed like they were in heat.''

The man shook his head. ''All I saw was a couple doing a bit of bundling to try to get warm.''

''But *you* saw them.'' Ruth pointed to the man who had grumbled about her perversion in wanting to see Josh get out of bed. ''You said yourself they were naked and rutting like—''

''*You* said they was naked,'' the man protested. ''I didn't get close enough to see anything but your *be*hind blocking the whole doorway.''

Will pushed through the men and stood before the closed door. When he spoke, his voice was quiet and calm, forcing them to be silent to hear his words. ''We'll take Meagan and Josh back to town, find Judge Osborne and see if we can sort this all out.''

Several of the men added their voices in agreement. Will folded his arms and leaned against the door, giving his friends a few moments to get themselves together.

* * *

Josh pulled on his boots and headed for the window at the back of the room. "If we're lucky they won't be looking for us out back," he said. "Now, what did you say that Indian's name was, and where can we find him?"

"His name is Reilly."

"Reilly what? What is the rest of his name?"

Meagan finished dressing and wrung her hands. "His Indian name is Standing Wolf. He's my half brother. Why do you want to know?"

Josh gave her a look of skepticism mingled with relief. Reilly. Meagan Reilly. Her half brother. It made sense to him, but maybe only because he wanted it to.

"Whoever he is, he's the best chance we've got of getting you away from here. I'm not going to take the chance of some damned fool listening to that Somers woman's viper tongue and believing what she says. I'll find a way to get you to safety. We'll go to the other side of the mountains where nobody knows us. We'll build a life together, just you and me and Abbie. And somehow I'll find a way to clear your name if it's the last thing I do. I'm only sorry that I compromised your safety because of what happened today."

"You're sorry?" Meagan choked on the words. The last thing in the world she wanted was for him to be sorry for the most wonderful moments of her life.

He took her face in his hands and kissed away the newly fallen tears. "I'm sorry I couldn't control myself until I was sure we were safe. I'm sorry Ruth Somers and her posse came when they did, but Meagan, to save my soul from hellfire, I'll never be sorry I made love to you, or that you love me enough to make love to me."

"Then we've got nothing to be sorry for, do we?" Meagan managed a smile.

"Guess we don't." He bent down and kissed her gently, disregarding the voices just outside the door.

"Josh." Her voice broke as she spoke his name. "You'll have to go without me. I'll only slow you down. If they catch us they'll put us both in jail and we'll never be able to prove my innocence."

Meagan knew she couldn't outrun the mob that waited outside the door. She was still weak from loss of blood and half-sick from spending the nights in the cold. Somehow she had to convince Josh that he must go without her. No matter how bad it was, she could face it knowing he was free.

Josh felt her tremble against him and knew that what she said was true. She would never be able to keep up the pace and they'd both be caught.

"Meagan, we'll find a way," he tried again, but she shook her head.

"Go without me, Josh. Find Reilly and come back for me. Will won't let anything happen to me. You know he's on our side."

Josh saw the courage in her eyes. The courage and the self-sacrifice. He rubbed his fingers across his eyes hoping she didn't see the sudden tears. It wouldn't do for her to remember him blubbering like a baby while they were apart. He was the man. He had to be brave. But how could any human being be more brave than Meagan was at this moment when she sacrificed herself and sent him away?

"You're right." He sighed. "They'd chase us to ground like a pair of cur dogs." He slipped his leg over the window ledge. "Try to slow them down. I'm going to drive off their horses so they'll have to walk at least part of the way back to town. Don't let them rush you. Force them to make the journey as slow as possible and give me as much time as you can to find your brother.''

With one last kiss Josh climbed out the window and disappeared into the trees. The pounding on the door became more insistent.

Meagan secured the window and pulled her hair into one braid that hung down her back. She smoothed her dress and glanced in the mirror that hung by the door. If only her face wasn't still flushed with lovemaking, and her lips still swollen with the memory of Josh's kisses. But there was nothing more she could do. With tears in her eyes she opened the door to Will Carmichael.

It took only a moment for Will to ascertain that except for Meagan, the room was empty.

''Where's Josh?'' He mouthed the words, shocked that his friend would leave Meagan in such dire straits.

Meagan moved her eyes toward the window, hoping Will would get the message. She might have said more, but her words were lost in the sound of horses being driven away from the house.

The cries of the men augmented the noise, with Ruth shrilling above them.

''I told you! I told you! They're guilty as the devil and have taken our horses and run away.''

But her voice was drowned out as the horses stampeded across the fields and down toward the creek.

''We'll go to my house,'' Ruth declared. ''There are horses there. It's only a few hours away.''

And though the men had no choice but to agree, they all knew that a few hours on horseback turned into many hours on foot.

Ruth didn't bother to mention that the Somers family owned two horses; one had been driven off along with those of the men, and it would most likely take a direct act of God to make Rafe part with the other.

"One horse don't do you no good," Rafe told his wife. "You got too many men. I think it's better that you all walk."

"I don't care what you think, Rafe Somers. I'm not walking all the way to the fort."

"Then don't go," Rafe suggested. "Stay here at home where you belong."

"I'm going to see that justice is done and I intend to ride into town like a lady." She glanced around, defying anyone to argue. "Now, let me see..." She left the men milling around the yard and made for the house. "I need clothing and money for a room at Mrs. Timmons's boardinghouse."

"You need to keep out of other people's business," her husband grumbled as he followed her into the house. "I give you enough money to keep you for a week. You cannot have the horse. I need him. If you want to ride, ride the oxen."

Ruth looked as though she might explode, then she realized that the oxen meant she could take the wagon. "Very well," she agreed. "I'll do that."

Josh watched as the horses scattered across the countryside. He hoped some of them would find their way home. He felt sorry about taking Will's horse, but it couldn't be helped. He'd done what he had set out to do. With any luck he would find Meagan's Indian half brother and they'd steal her away before the mob reached the fort. He needed all the time he could get to find help to set Meagan free.

He couldn't keep a smile from his face as he silently

congratulated himself on his success. Now, if only he was as successful in finding Reilly. What kind of name was that for an Indian? he mused as he rode along. But Reilly was Meagan's surname. He knew that for a fact. And if Meagan had a brother, Reilly would be his name, too. Now all Josh had to do was to find Reilly before hostile Indians found Josh, or before it was too late to save Meagan.

He returned to the area where he had taken Meagan from the Indian camp and began tracking from there. The Indians had done nothing to hide their tracks, apparently believing that no one would be looking for them now that Meagan was no longer with them.

They were setting up camp when he came upon them. He crept forward, hoping to somehow figure a way to find Reilly without the others knowing. Before he had covered half the distance to the camp a red blur dropped from one of the trees. They rolled across the frozen ground until a voice rang out, "Do not kill him!"

Both men let go their grip and jumped back, knives still clenched in their hands. Neither bothered to look at the young brave who came toward them. Each knew that they would be killed if they broke eye contact.

"Who are you?" the brave demanded.

"Where is Reilly?" Josh returned.

"Why should I tell you of Reilly if you won't tell me who you are?" the Indian answered.

Somewhat surprised at the Indian's command of the English language, Josh replied, "I'm the man whose farm you raided, and whose woman you stole some days ago in the valley on the other side of the mountains. I must find the Indian called Reilly. I need his help to get my woman back."

"If you do not take good care of what is yours, Josh Daniels, you do not deserve to keep it."

Josh's eyes opened wide. He forgot about the Indian with whom he had fought and turned his attention to the other man, for the second man held the intelligence and the danger.

"I am Meagan's half brother, Reilly," the Indian said. "Now, you will come with me and tell me what has happened to my sister."

On the cliff high above, a sharp-eyed, hook-nosed Indian watched and assessed the situation while his braves waited some distance away.

Old Howling Dog knew Reilly had stolen a white girl. The white man had stolen her back and then a posse, led by the cackling turkey-hen woman, had stolen the girl from both Indian and white man. It looked as though the two men would join forces to free the girl before they fought each other for her. It was obvious they found her worth their lives. But the girl did not interest him. Old Howling Dog wanted something more than youth and love. He wanted a woman who could set a trap or skin and gut a deer. A woman who could work without his constant supervision. One who would understand without being told that she must work to survive. It was time he made his move and took the little turkey hen, before she got herself killed by sticking her nose where it didn't belong.

Ruth Somers was in the height of her glory. She was riding in a wagon, albeit drawn by oxen, but riding nonetheless, while Meagan and the men walked behind. Of course, Ruth found it irritating that Meagan laughed and talked with the men, as well as the fact that she never complained, even though she limped pitifully and was forced to sit down often. It never occurred to Ruth that Meagan's lameness was all a ploy to buy more time before they reached the fort. Time in which Josh could find Reilly and they could come to set her free.

Meagan dragged her feet, limped, hobbled, feigned dizziness and begged to be allowed to go and rest. Anything to prolong their journey.

Will Carmichael was well aware of what she was doing and coached her whenever a new ploy was needed. Will suspected the past days had taken their toll on Meagan and had he been able to convince her to do so, he would have insisted that she ride. It wasn't until she quietly pitched forward in a dead faint that she was put into the wagon.

At first Ruth chose to hit every bump and rut in the road, but after breaking a wheel and making herself terribly uncomfortable she relented and tried to find the least furrowed path.

As it was, it took five days for the group to reach Banebridge, and Josh and Reilly were already there.

Chapter Fourteen

It wasn't until Meagan reached her destination that her fears began.

Throughout the journey she had believed that Josh would help her escape before she reached the fort. Even Ruth's vicious taunts had not fazed her throughout the weary miles, but now, faced with the prospect of having to go through another trial, again with Ruth as the prime witness, Meagan felt her heart sinking.

Was Josh and the love they shared equal to the test they must face? How could he hope to prove her innocence when the only witness to Lily's death held fast to her story and never wavered in her determination to see Meagan punished? And what had she done to deserve the hated of Ruth Somers?

Meagan was taken to a small, secure room that would serve as her quarters to await the arrival of the judge. But it was not Judge Osborne whom Meagan waited for, it was Josh, and with him were all her hopes.

Hopes that might have been vanquished had Meagan seen him slip into Will Carmichael's house in the middle of the night.

"Where is she?" Josh asked without preamble.

"They've taken her to the fort." Will allowed weariness to enter his voice. "Phoebe has gone to her." He held out his hands in mute appeal. "It was the best we could do. Ruth Somers raised holy hell when I asked to bring Meagan here. The magistrate didn't want to deal with it and gave in without question." He walked across the floor, running his hands through his hair. "Maybe it's just as well. This way I won't be held responsible when she escapes."

"You think it would be hopeless to appeal to the judge then?" Reilly asked.

It was the first time Reilly had spoken, and Will looked up in surprise. He had seen the dark-skinned man come in with Josh, but he had not expected the man to use the king's English, and with better diction than Will himself.

Josh put aside his concern for Meagan long enough to introduce the two men. "Reilly is Meagan's brother," he added.

Will looked at the Indian and cleared his throat. "Of course, I can see the resemblance," he managed to say.

To his surprise, Reilly laughed aloud. "There is no resemblance between my sister and myself," he admitted, "but we share the same blood through our father. The blood and the education were his only legacy, but it was enough." He didn't bother to explain that when he lived with the Indians he thought and talked like an Indian, and when he was in the white man's world he easily adapted to their ways and language. "Now, what must we do to get Meagan out of here?" he asked.

"There is little we can do tonight," Will told them. "Phoebe will stay with Meagan until morning. The best thing for you to do is eat and get some sleep. If the judge refuses to listen to reason there will be little time for rest.''

Josh glanced around the kitchen. A rag doll lay in the corner near the hearth next to Abbie's pet kitten, which she had managed to smuggle from home.

"Where is Abbie?'' Josh asked. "Can I see her?''

"She's already in bed,'' Will said as he followed his friend's gaze. "She leaves her doll to sleep with the kitten so it won't get lonely. You can go up if you want to, but I'll wager none of us gets any sleep if that young'n wakes up and finds you here.''

Josh grinned and took the bowl of beans and ham that Will spooned out of the pot. "I'll look in on her before we bed down for the night,'' he promised.

Will would have put them up in the spare bedroom, but both Josh and Reilly shook their heads.

"We'll sleep here next to the hearth,'' Reilly told him.

"That's all well and good,'' Will agreed, "but if you're going to sleep by a hearth in my house you'd better use the one in the parlor. If Phoebe comes in and finds an Indian in her kitchen she's likely to raise the whole town.''

They chuckled in agreement before turning to more serious conversation, which carried on far into the night.

Judge Osborne didn't want to go to Banebridge. He took his time on the road and stopped for any feeble excuse. Now he had run out of excuses and the fort lay before him. He grumbled under his breath as he half-heartedly nudged his horse forward. The time was at hand.

He rode through town early in the morning when most of the people were still in bed. If he was recognized it was not remarked upon and he made his way directly to the building where Will Carmichael had his home and law office. Without further ado, he dismounted and went inside.

Will, an early riser, heard the jangle of the bell on the office door and almost tumbled into the room where he conducted his business, stopping short only after he recognized his caller. He quickly closed the door behind him. It wouldn't do at all for Judge Osborne to discover an Indian sleeping on the hearth of the town's foremost young lawyer.

"Judge Osborne! What are you doing here?" Will and the judge were not friends on a social basis and Meagan was the only reason the man would come to Will at this time.

"What I'm doing here is not the point," the judge told him. "I wish I were anywhere but here, but *here* I am. Now, where is that Reilly girl, and why haven't you whisked her out of the colonies? God knows I've given you enough time."

Will felt the heat of blood flow into his face. "I planned to petition the court to reverse Meagan's sentence and set her free," Will admitted. "Everyone knows she didn't purposely kill Lily Daniels. She's risked her own neck to warn the settlers about the Indian uprising, and besides, Abbie loves her, and so does Josh."

The judge harrumphed. "*Everybody* doesn't love her. *Everybody* doesn't want her set free. I had word that the Somers woman was lying wait for me at the Widow Timmons's house on the edge of town so she could get her licks in before I talked to anyone else." He brushed the morning dew from the sleeve of his coat. "Had to go half a mile out of my way to avoid the old peahen. Then, once I get here I discover that after all the time

I've given you and your friends to spirit that girl off, here you are, sitting on your thumbs thinking I'm going to bend the law and lay my own reputation on the line in order to set her free.''

"Josh and Meagan don't want to have to spend the rest of their lives running from the law," Will explained. "They want to go back to their land and raise Abbie like a regular family. They have a right to be heard."

The judge slapped his hat against his leg. "Oh, I'll hear them all right, but beyond that I can't promise a thing."

"But you must see that Meagan couldn't have murdered Lily," Will argued. "She swears she didn't even go into the upper regions of the house."

"And Ruth Somers swears she did," the judge reminded him.

"Meagan had no good motive to kill Lily Daniels," Will said firmly.

"And there's no good reason for Mrs. Somers to say the girl did it if she didn't!" the judge fired back.

"It's Ruth's word against Meagan's," Will reiterated.

The judge sighed, sank into a chair and folded his hands on his lap. His brow furrowed in thought. "If you can give me one good reason why Ruth Somers would lie about Meagan I'll suspend the sentence," he finally said.

Will rubbed his hands over his face. He'd gone over every ploy he could think of as to why Ruth hated Meagan so much and nothing made any sense.

"And if I can't?"

"Then you'd better get the girl out of the colonies, because if you don't, there's going to be a hanging."

"I need time," Will hedged.

"That's another thing I haven't got," the judge said.

"I'll give you until the day after tomorrow. Until then, I won't make my presence known. Do what you can, and good luck."

The judge got to his feet with a grunt and hobbled toward the door. "And you can tell your friends they could hear better if they'd open the door a bit more." He gestured toward the door leading to Will's living quarters as he went out into the morning light.

"You heard," Will said as Josh and Reilly came into the room.

"He meant what he said, didn't he?" Josh almost choked on the words. He had hoped the judge would listen to reason, but there was no hope of that now. The chances of them getting Ruth to change her story were almost nonexistent.

"He meant it," Will told them. "I think we'd better make plans to get Meagan out of here and have her long gone before the hearing takes place."

"I can take her away tonight," Reilly offered. "There is word that Old Howling Dog and his braves are raiding again so if my friends make a disturbance Old Howling Dog will be blamed."

"I'll go with you," Josh offered. "We can be out of legal jurisdiction by the end of the week."

"What about Abbie?" Will reminded the man of the little girl who asked for her father and Meagan on a daily, if not hourly, basis.

"We'll come back for her," Josh promised.

"You come back and you'll get yourself hung. The minute people figure out both you and Meagan are gone you're going to be as guilty in the eyes of the law as she is." Will put his hand on his friend's shoulder and looked him in the eye. "Once you go, you can't come back."

"I have to save Meagan." Josh tried to clear his thoughts and understand what his friend was trying to tell him, but all he could think of was that Meagan was in danger and somehow he had to get her out.

"You're not going to save Meagan by getting yourself killed," Reilly told him. "Let me take her away. No one will suspect me. No one knows I exist. We'll try to get word to you once Meagan is safely away." His eyes were steady and his voice firm for all his youth. "After all, that *is* the reason you sought me out, isn't it? To take Meagan away."

Josh clenched his teeth. "Yes, it's true," he admitted. But he didn't want to leave Meagan now. Not without seeing her. Not without holding her and calming her fears.

Desperately he clutched at straws. "The judge said he'd let her go if we could figure out why Ruth hates her so." He turned quickly to Reilly. "Do you know the woman? Did you meet her somewhere? Did Meagan, or you, or even your father slight her in some way sometime in the past? Think, man! You must remember something. There has to be a reason why she hates Meagan."

But Reilly only shook his head. "I made it a point to look closely at the woman who condemned my sister, and she means nothing to me."

The men sank into the chairs around the desk, a cloud of gloom surrounding them.

Josh was the first to speak. His heart was in his throat but he knew the words must be spoken. "If you take Meagan beyond the mountains, we both know there isn't much chance of my finding you. If I go asking for you there's a good chance that someone will follow me and

I'll lead him right to you and endanger Meagan's life. If I wait until you send word and then pack up and take Abbie to join Meagan, Ruth Somers or some other nosy do-gooder might get suspicious and have us followed." Tears filled his eyes and he brushed them aside. "Don't seem like there's any way this is going to work out."

He turned to Reilly. "Take your sister and get out of here. Don't send word back. Don't try to get in touch with any of us. I want to go myself, but I can't take the chance with Meagan's life. If it ever seems safe I'll find you."

Will nodded. "That's the best way," he agreed, and neither of them seemed to realize that they had decreed that the young Indian give up any plans he might have had for his own future in order to save his sister.

Reilly didn't bring it to their attention. He would do what he must, just as they all did, and now it was his duty to save Meagan's life. He could only hope that the "safe time" would come sooner rather than later, so Josh and Meagan could live out their lives together. Then Reilly could be free to follow his own pursuits.

There was a clattering on the stairs and the next moment Abbie, clad in her long flannel nightgown and a frilly bonnet, came bursting into the room.

"Papa!" she cried as she clambered onto her father's lap. "I knew I heard your voice, but at first I thought I'd dreamed it, and then when I kept hearing it I knew you were here, and you *are* here."

Josh laughed and kissed his daughter. "You have ears like a fox," he told her.

Abbie put her hands on either side of her bonnet. "I hear real good, but my ears don't have hairs on them," she said soberly while the men laughed.

The laughter drew Abbie's attention to Reilly. She

gazed at him speculatively. "Hello," she said finally. "I'm Abbie Daniels." She held out her small hand.

"My name is Reilly." He took her hand in his and bowed over it.

Abbie took in the difference in the color of their skin as white rested on reddish-tan. "Are you a red Indian?" she asked.

Josh, embarrassed, would have silenced the child, but Reilly shook his head ever so slightly.

"Partly," he said. "My mother was an Indian. My father was white, like yours."

The little girl sighed deeply. "I'll bet you got teased about that worse than I did about my ears." She leaned forward and placed her hand against his cheek. "But don't you worry. Meagan says it's just words, and they can't hurt you unless you let them."

Touched by the child's perception, Reilly swallowed the lump that had formed in his throat. "She told me that, too," he said. He didn't add that it had given little comfort at the time when the half-breed boy had fled from the merciless teasing of his peers.

"She did?" Abbie pounced on the words. "Meagan did? You know Meagan?" Now she was off her father's lap and jockeying for position on Reilly's lap. "Where is she? Is she with you? Is she still in bed? Can I go and wake her up?"

Josh detached the child from her perch on Reilly's knee. "Meagan isn't here, sweetheart," he told her. "She's gone away on a long trip. We won't be seeing her for a while."

"But who will teach me to read?" Abbie protested. "And who will take care of me while you're working in the fields? And...and...who will curl up my hair?" And on the last, drawn-out word, Abbie burst into a flurry of tears. "I want my Meagan!" She sobbed. "I want my Meagan!"

The men tried to quiet her, but Abbie only cried louder, tears squirting from her eyes as she swiped the sleeve of her flannel nightgown over her face.

She had to think. She knew her father wasn't telling her the truth. At least not all of the truth. Since returning to Banebridge with her new hairdo Abbie had made friends with several of the little girls, and heard the gossip. She knew that it had been no accident that Meagan had come to her house to live and work. Meagan had been sent there by a man named Judge Osborne.

Judge was a funny name for a man and so, when Abbie, whose room was situated over Will Carmichael's office, had heard Will talking to someone named Judge she had pulled herself from her sleep long enough to listen before she dozed off. And it was due to the placement of her room that she had heard her father's voice and realized he was in the building.

She continued blubbering to the consternation of the three men. All the while she tried desperately to remember exactly what Judge had said about Meagan. If she could just remember maybe Meagan wouldn't have to go away. And she'd better remember fast, because from the look on her father's face, she was afraid he was going to cry, too.

Ruth Somers…that was one of the names Judge had mentioned. Something about how Ruth hated Meagan, but that was nothing new. Auntie Ruth didn't like anybody. Everybody knew that. People were only nice to her to keep her from getting even with them.

Maybe that was what Auntie Ruth was trying to do to Meagan…get even…but for what?

Abbie had never even seen Meagan before that day at

Auntie Ruth's when Abbie's mother had fallen down the stairs. And Meagan hadn't even been in the room until after Mama lay at the bottom of the stairs and Meagan came running from the kitchen to see if she could help her.

Maybe Auntie Ruth hadn't wanted Mama to be helped. Maybe that was the reason she was mad at Meagan. Maybe if Abbie told her papa and Uncle Will and the Indian named Reilly that Auntie Ruth hadn't wanted Mama to get any help, maybe they wouldn't send Meagan away. Then again, if Abbie told, maybe Auntie Ruth would try to get even with Abbie.

The absolute frustration of the situation brought Abbie to a whole new level of hysteria. Her sobs became louder and she choked on her own cries.

Unnerved by the screaming child, the three men tripped over one another trying to quiet her.

"I'll send for Phoebe. Abbie needs her right now, and I don't know what else to do." Will made for the door, but the child only screamed louder.

People had stopped on the street and stood open-mouthed, wondering about the turmoil within the lawyer's office.

There was a sharp knock on the door. Without permission Ruth opened it and filled the doorway.

"What in the world are you men doing to that child?" she demanded. In one fell swoop she plucked Abbie from Josh's arms and held the struggling child against her buxom bosom.

"There now, this is no place for you. The strain has become too much. I told you, Josh Daniels." She turned on the girl's father. "I told you that Abbie should have been living with me all this time. Just look what you've done to her, making her live with a criminal."

"Ruth, it's not like that," Josh tried to explain. "It's not what you think. Abbie isn't homesick, she's just upset, and you're not doing anything to help."

Abbie began throwing herself backward, causing the woman to give the little girl her full attention. To Abbie's satisfaction she saw Reilly slip out the door. She hoped he could get out of town before anyone saw him and teased him about the color of his skin.

Auntie Ruth would have teased Reilly had she seen him, Abbie knew. Auntie Ruth's sons always teased Abbie and didn't care how much she cried when they stole her bonnet and threatened to cut off her ears so they wouldn't stick out.

Pleased that she had been able to keep Reilly from being tormented for something he couldn't help, Abbie burst forth with another screech and threw herself backward again, almost knocking Ruth Somers off her feet.

Ruth righted herself and shook the child vigorously. Abbie continued screaming. She'd show everybody that Auntie Ruth wasn't the nice person some of them thought she was. The townsfolk were gathering around the front of the building, peering curiously through the door and windows.

Good! The more they stared at Abbie and Auntie Ruth, the more chance Reilly had of getting away without being teased.

Abbie burst forth with a series of loud sobs.

Ruth slapped the child across the face and slammed her hand over Abbie's mouth.

Abbie bit her.

Ruth let go her hold. Her face turned red and her eyes glared venomously. "There! There, you see? She's just like a little animal. I'll take her home with me and teach her some manners before she is beyond hope."

Abbie scrambled into her father's arms. "Don't let her take me," she begged.

"If you don't hand her over to me right this minute, I'm going to petition the judge for her custody. She shouldn't be allowed to live alone with a man of obviously loose morals even if the man is her father," Ruth declared self-righteously. "You know the child is out of hand and what I am proposing is to her benefit."

"Don't let her take me!" Abbie cried again as she felt her father's grip loosen.

How she wished she had gone with Reilly. Anything was better than having to go to live with Auntie Ruth. She wondered if she could break away and find him. But no, she'd only get him in trouble, and she was in enough trouble for both of them.

Fear beyond all reason filled her little body. Fear greater than anything she'd ever known. She stared at Auntie Ruth from the haven of her father's arms. "Please, don't let her take me," she begged.

Josh held her close. Because of Ruth Somers he had lost every woman he'd loved, and now she was threatening to take his child from him. He was filled with fury and only Will Carmichael's steadying hands pressing down on his shoulders kept him from leaping at her throat.

"Steady, Josh," Will said quietly. "Just stay calm and I'll get her out of here."

He walked around his friend and started toward Ruth.

"Don't you dare touch me!" She held out her arms as though defending herself against Will, although he had not so much as lifted a hand against her.

"I think you'd better leave, Ruth." Will kept his voice soft and even the child's screams quieted as she tried to hear what he was saying.

Realizing she was getting nowhere, Ruth moved toward the door. "Very well then, I'll go. But I'll be back, and when I come I'm taking that ill-behaved child home with me."

Ruth charged out the door, slamming it behind her, and swept off down the street, leaving little clouds of dust in her wake.

"Perhaps we should take her up on her offer." Will chuckled, unmindful for once of the child. "Taking Abbie back to the farm would take Ruth at least two days and might keep her out of town during Meagan's hearing."

Abbie didn't know what a hearing might be, but she knew she didn't want to go home with Auntie Ruth. If Auntie Ruth took her home she might never see Meagan again. For that matter, she might never see her papa again. She wasn't going to go with Auntie Ruth no matter what she had to do.

Drawing a ragged breath, she clutched her father's arms.

"No! No! Papa, you can't let her take me. I won't go. I won't go live with Auntie Ruth. She'll push me down the stairs like she did my mama!"

Chapter Fifteen

The room rang with stunned silence. The men looked at each other and then at the child. Will moved toward Abbie, intent on questioning her, but Josh kept him back with a simple shrug of his shoulders.

"What do you mean, Abbie?" Josh asked quietly. "Did you see your mother fall down the stairs? Were you there in the house that day? Do you know what happened?"

Josh had never given the possibility any thought before. He had assumed that Abbie had been out playing with the other children, but from her words it was obvious he had been wrong.

Will leaned forward, watching the child closely, and Abbie wished she had been able to think of another way to keep from going to live with Auntie Ruth and keep Meagan from going away at the same time.

From the look on her father's face she was well aware that she had no choice but to tell him the truth. There was life and hope in his eyes, and the expression on his face reminded her of the way she felt just before Christmas.

Her father would believe anything she said, but Uncle

Will would know if she lied, so she had to stick to the truth as closely as possible.

Her tears stopped. She blew her nose and swallowed. Her mouth felt dry. What if they didn't believe her? They'd send her to Auntie Ruth's and heaven only knew what they'd do to Meagan. The tears started again, but Uncle Will's voice caught her attention as he gave her some direction that she could follow.

"Just tell us what you remember about that day, Abbie. Start at the beginning and tell us all about it."

Abbie could do that. She closed her eyes and remembered the last day of her mother's life, and the first day she had seen Meagan Reilly.

"Well, I was sleeping real good that morning when Mama woke me up," she said, following instructions as only a child can and starting from the very beginning. "She said I had to hurry because we were going for a buggy ride and if I didn't hurry and get dressed she was going to make me go without my bonnet and everybody would laugh at me.

"If I had known we were only going to Auntie Ruth's house I wouldn't have bothered picking out a clean bonnet, because the boys always took my bonnet off my head and laughed at me anyway, but I thought maybe we were really going somewhere, and I hurried as fast as I could. I hurried so fast I didn't even get anything to eat.

"We didn't get to Auntie Ruth's until after lunchtime. I didn't see Auntie Ruth so I don't guess she was there, but she wasn't usually there when Mama called.

"Uncle Rafe was there though. He told me to go on and play and Uncle Rafe and Mama went into the house.

"I didn't much want to play with the boys, and when I didn't see them anywhere around I went to the orchard to find something to eat. The apples were still green and hard but I ate some anyhow. Then I sat down where I could see the door so I would be ready when Mama came out to call me to go home.

"I waited a long time and my tummy began to hurt. Pretty soon it hurt so bad I could hardly keep from crying, so I started walking toward the house. I was afraid to go around back to the outhouse. Mama had said plenty of times that if I wasn't ready to go when she called she'd leave me at Auntie Ruth's—and we'd been there a long time."

Abbie looked up at her father. He had a strange expression on his face and his teeth seemed to be sinking into his lower lip the way people did when they were trying to keep from laughing.

"Don't laugh at me, Papa," Abbie said indignantly. "This isn't a funny story."

He bowed his head so she couldn't see his face. "I'm not laughing, sweetheart," he told her. "Believe me, I'm not laughing." Why hadn't he seen it? Josh asked himself. Why hadn't he realized that Lily no longer loved him and was having an affair with another man? How could he have been stupid enough to allow Abbie to go through this terrible situation?

Josh tried to clear his head and at the same time find some words that would comfort his child, and perhaps, himself, but it was Will who spoke.

"Nobody's going to laugh at you, Abbie," Will assured her. "Now go on with your story. How did you manage to get to the house when you had such a bad stomachache?"

Reassured that they understood her plight and believed her words, Abbie prepared to continue.

Josh kept his head bent. The knowledge that Lily, his

wife, had been betraying him with his friend could not assuage the joy that filled his heart at the realization that came closer to reality with each word the child spoke. Meagan was not guilty. Meagan had not killed Lily, either on purpose or by accident. And in a matter of hours Meagan would be free…free to love him as he loved her.

He forgot to breathe as he waited for Abbie's next words.

''I hadn't hardly got into the house when I heard a wagon come into the yard. Mama and Uncle Rafe weren't anywhere around, and I knew I wasn't supposed to be in the house alone, so I crouched down under the sideboard and hoped I could slip back out the door without anybody seeing me.

''Then Auntie Ruth came in with her arms full of bundles. Meagan came in right after her, only I didn't know it was Meagan. I didn't know who Meagan was. But I knew it wasn't Auntie Ruth because she came in first.'' She nodded her head in affirmation and then looked at the men and realized they were listening to every word she said. It was a heady feeling and she was tempted to make her story a bit more interesting, but the silent warning in Uncle Will's eyes kept her to the bare bones of the subject.

She coughed and returned to her recital. ''Meagan followed Auntie Ruth into the kitchen. I got ready to run out the door, but Auntie Ruth came back into the room right away. She took off her bonnet and carried it up the stairs.

''My tummy hurt something awful and I knew I had to get out of the house or I would have an accident right under Auntie Ruth's sideboard, so as soon as Auntie Ruth disappeared down the hall I started to crawl out.''

Will found it impossible to keep from interrupting the child. "Where was Meagan?" he wanted to know.

"I guess she was still in the kitchen. I don't know where she was. I was hoping she wasn't in the outhouse, because that was where I was going."

Josh gave Will a disparaging look. He didn't want Abbie's account interrupted in case she became self-conscious and stopped talking.

"Go on, honey," he said gently.

"Well, before I could get to the door there was a lot of noise from upstairs. Mama and Auntie Ruth and Uncle Rafe all came running out into the hall.

"Then Auntie Ruth started shouting about a war. I couldn't think what she was talking about because Mama didn't even know how to shoot a gun, but Auntie Ruth was saying 'War, war,' again and again. When Mama started to walk away Auntie Ruth grabbed at her and then Mama fell down the stairs, and Auntie Ruth was screaming and Uncle Rafe came kinda run-hopping down the hall."

She looked at the men to see how they had taken her account of the situation. They stared at her as though they didn't understand her words, and she plunged on.

"Meagan ran in from the kitchen and squatted down beside Mama at the bottom of the stairs. That's when Auntie Ruth started screaming at the top of her lungs, but I couldn't understand anything she said. I just knew that if I didn't get out of there I was going to have an accident and when Mama woke up she'd make me walk home behind the wagon, so I ran out the door, and—" she shrugged her shoulders eloquently "—that's what happened."

The men were silent for a long while. Such a long

while that Abbie began to fidget, wondering if they believed her.

Then her father spoke. ''Abbie, why didn't you ever tell anybody about this before?''

Abbie had to think about that for a moment. ''Well, at first I was afraid to tell anybody for fear Auntie Ruth would push me down the stairs, too.'' The little girl squirmed in her chair, sensing her answer wasn't acceptable to the adults. ''Besides,'' she said in a firm voice, ''nobody ever asked me.''

Her answer left the men speechless as they, too, recalled the hours following Lily's death. Abbie had cried hysterically with what everyone had thought was grief, but now it seemed that fear and possibly a major amount of pain had been the cause of her distress.

In an effort to keep the child from having to go through the rigors of the trial and trying to adapt to life without her mother, she had been sent to stay with relatives. Relatives who were sworn to see that nothing was mentioned regarding the death of Abbie's mother.

Josh reached back and grasped his friend's hand. ''What do you think?'' he asked.

''I think we'd better go see if we can find Judge Osborne because we have quite a story to tell him.'' He turned to Abbie. ''Do you think you could tell Judge Osborne your story, just the way you told it to us?''

Abbie nodded her head, then shook it violently.

''What's the matter?'' her father asked. ''Don't you want to tell the judge so Meagan can come home to live with us?''

Abbie didn't want to admit to her father that she was afraid of both the judge and what Auntie Ruth would do when she found out Abbie was a tattletale. She seized on her father's last words, ignoring the fact that everything hinged on her willingness to repeat the story to Judge Osborne. "Can Meagan go home with us tonight?" She jumped to her feet. "Are the Indians our friends so we can go back home?"

"It won't be long before everything will be back to normal," Josh told her. "You just tell the judge your story the same way you told Will and me, and everything will be fine."

Abbie gave her father a hug and ran off into the other room to give her kitten the wonderful news.

Josh didn't even bother to tell her not to run in the house. It was all he could do to keep from jumping up and down himself. Everything was going to be all right. Meagan would be free.

"I'm going to ask the judge to marry Meagan and me before we go back to the farm," he told Will. "I'll take her home as my lawful wife."

Will sat down on the edge of the desk and observed his friend. Josh had been through so much misery that Will hated to burst his bubble of happiness, but there was a lot that had to be done before Josh could take Meagan home.

"I've got a pretty good idea where the judge is staying," Will said. "We'd better get to him fast while the story is still strong in Abbie's mind. I don't want her to get carried away in telling it again and start embroidering on the facts, or worse yet, get cold feet and refuse to say anything."

But Josh ignored his friend's warning, for his mind was racing ahead. "We'll see if we can't make peace with the Indians. Reilly has some great ideas on how to do that. He talked a lot about them while we were riding back...." Josh looked around. "Where *is* Reilly?" he asked, his throat suddenly dry.

Will slammed his hand down on the table. "I don't know, but we'd better find him quick because the last he knew he was supposed to find a way to help Meagan escape and get her so far out of the territory that nobody would be able to find her."

The men rushed into the main house, tripping over Abbie, who was sitting in the middle of the floor playing with her kitten.

"Sorry, honey," her father apologized as he stopped to see if she was hurt. "We have to find Reilly. Did you see where he went?"

"I saw Reilly leave when Auntie Ruth came in," Abbie told them. "He went off toward the fort."

"Good girl." Will patted her head. "I didn't even see him leave. You saw more than I did."

"Well, just because my ears are too big doesn't mean I can't see good," the little girl told him indignantly.

Both men laughed, and, oh God, it felt good because Josh had wondered if he would ever feel like laughing again.

"I'll go look for Reilly," Josh said. "You take Abbie and look for the judge."

And Will Carmichael realized that even in the throes of happiness over Meagan's innocence, the man didn't want to hear again the story of his wife's infidelity and betrayal.

The men parted after allowing Abbie to dress and put on her prettiest bonnet. She fussed all the while because neither Meagan nor Phoebe were there to curl her hair. "I suppose it's just as well," she said with all the airs of a fashionable lady. "After all, curls would be crushed under the bonnet, and it just wouldn't do to go calling without one."

Josh headed toward the fort, stopping to peer into deserted stables and sheds on the possibility that Reilly might have holed up in one of them to wait until nightfall when he would have a better chance of taking Meagan and making an escape.

He didn't notice Ruth Somers arrogantly marching down the street, the feather on her bonnet standing erect as though at full military attention. For it hadn't taken long for the news of Judge Osborne's arrival to reach Mrs. Timmons's boardinghouse where Ruth was staying. She had no more than entered the dining room when the judge's arrival was mentioned. Forgoing breakfast, Ruth had turned on her heel and left the establishment. She was going to see the judge to tell him she wanted custody of that ill-behaved Abbie Daniels. She'd make the child straighten up all right. There's be no chance that Abbie would end up a loose woman like her mother.

All Ruth had to do was talk the judge into giving her Abbie and make sure he followed the letter of the law and hanged Meagan.

The sooner Meagan Reilly went to meet her maker, the better, because Meagan Reilly was the one person Ruth feared. Meagan had been in the house the day of Lily's death. The girl had never accused Ruth of pushing Lily Daniels down the stairs, but it was just a matter of time before she did, and Ruth wasn't about to allow that to happen. Not while she had breath in her body and justice on her side.

After all, Ruth rationalized, she was just an instrument of the Lord. If that weren't true she never would have returned home early enough to catch her poor, weak husband and her erstwhile friend in the upper regions of the house, scrambling into their clothing. And, although she had suspected there was something going on between the wife of her neighbor and poor, weak Rafe, Ruth had never been able to catch them together. But that particular day...she knew it had been meant to be. Not only did she catch them, but when Lily fell down the stairs and broke her neck, Meagan Reilly had been there to take the blame, and no one ever needed to know that Rafe had betrayed his wife.

Now *that* certainly was the hand of God at work. And Ruth Somers believed in God. Yes, she did! Just as much as she believed that it was wrong to air one's dirty laundry among one's neighbors. As long as she protected the honor of her family, she was doing what she had been set on this earth to accomplish.

"And God help anyone who tries to stop me from seeing that girl hanged," she whispered in self-righteous fervor.

It didn't take Will long to learn where the judge was staying. The man was still sleeping but, at Will's insistence, the alderman's wife sent a servant to wake him up.

"Just tell him I have the information he wanted," Will instructed as Abbie peered around his leg to look inside the house.

It only took a few minutes for the man to return with the promise that the judge would be down presently.

The alderman's wife led Will and Abbie into the parlor, which overlooked the veranda along the front of the house. There was some question in her mind as to whether the child might leave fingerprints on her precious rosewood furniture, but the little girl seemed well behaved and the woman decided to go against her instincts and allow Abbie to sit on a low stool as long as she kept her hands to herself.

Since Will was not an invited guest, and his wife was

not with him, she did not offer refreshment and went to answer an insistent knock on the door as soon as the judge appeared.

The man was still tucking his shirtwaist into his trousers when he came into the room. "I hope this isn't a tempest in a teapot," he grumbled as he sank down into one of the gentlemen's chairs across from the settee.

"I assure you, it's not," Will said, making a silent prayer that the child wouldn't be frightened into silence by the strange man questioning her. He would have felt more at ease if Josh had been there with them, but with things as they were, it was impossible. Will would have to trust to providence that Abbie would be able to repeat her story with conviction.

"Well, go ahead, man! What is it?" the judge urged, raising his voice to be heard over the insistent yelping of female voices in the entry hall. He wished he could slam down his gavel and demand silence, but the noise in the hallway persisted even after Will began speaking.

"Abbie has something she needs to tell you," Will said, rather more loudly than he had planned, but it was imperative that the judge hear him. "It seems she was in the Somerses' house the day her mother was killed."

There was immediate silence in the hall. The front door closed firmly and the judge breathed a sigh of relief tinged with impatience.

"Very well, child. What do you have to say?"

Abbie wasn't sure she wanted to say anything to this man. He was gruff and talked loud and she wasn't at all certain he wouldn't go right out and tell Auntie Ruth everything she told him. Auntie Ruth would *get* Abbie for telling, even if it was the truth.

Sensing the child's reluctance, Will spoke up. "I want you to understand, Judge Osborne, that Abbie didn't come forward with this information on her own. She has never known the reason Meagan Reilly came to live in the Daniels household, since she was visiting relatives during the trial and for the first months of Meagan's tenure.

"It wasn't until Ruth Somers suggested that Abbie be sent home to live with her that the child made her revelation."

"And what exactly did you say?" the judge turned his full attention on the little girl.

Abbie felt her insides turn to jelly. "I said…" She swallowed and bit her fingernail. "I said I didn't want to go home with Auntie Ruth." She wasn't sure she liked this surly man. She wasn't sure she wanted to tell him anything. She shut her lips tight.

The judge included Will in his exasperated glance. "And why didn't you want to go home with Mrs. Somers? Haven't you been to her house before?"

Abbie squirmed. She bit at another fingernail and pulled her bonnet more snugly over her ears. She tried not to cry. She didn't want this man to see her cry.

"Answer Judge Osborne, Abbie," Will urged gently.

"I've been to Auntie Ruth's house lots of times, but I don't want to go anymore because…I'm afraid."

With that admission the tears popped out of her eyes and trickled down her cheeks. The judge reached into his pocket and pulled out a handkerchief. He dabbed at the tears. Maybe he wasn't such a bad man after all, she mused as she took the handkerchief and blew her nose.

"Why are you afraid?" he asked as he stuffed the handkerchief into his pocket. "I'd think Mrs. Somers's house would be a fine place for you to stay until we get things ironed out with your father."

Abbie's heart jumped into her throat. She swallowed

twice before she dared say a word. If this judge man didn't believe her story he was going to send her off to stay with Auntie Ruth.

With true desperation in her voice she all but shouted her words, running them together as they tumbled from her mouth. "I'm afraid Auntie Ruth will push me down the stairs like she did my mama…and…and…and…" Desperately Abbie tried to think of something else to say.

Not that being pushed down the stairs wasn't bad enough, but people, especially old men, sometimes didn't think little girls were all that important.

She had to say something more. Something that would make everyone think of another subject so she wouldn't have to talk about Auntie Ruth, or the day of her mother's death anymore. "And…and I've never heard of anybody named Judge before. Are you sure your mama didn't mean to name you Judd?"

The two sentences, so far apart in context, gave the man pause. He realized very quickly that he was dealing with a child and that she must be coaxed along if she was going to tell her story. With patience that his contemporaries would have found unbelievable, Judge Osborne put his best foot forward and began making friends with the little girl by explaining the difference between a name and a title of authority. And while it was questionable if the child understood the man's premise, she appreciated the attention paid her and responded politely.

A few minutes later when Will asked Abbie to tell her new best friend what had happened the day her mother died the little girl managed to recite the whole story, even to the part about eating the apples and the discomfort they caused her.

"Are you sure Rafe Somers was in the house?" the judge inquired. "Did you see him?"

Abbie nibbled at her finger again, intimidated by the pressure of the questions. "I saw Uncle Rafe when he came out in the hall with Mama and Auntie Ruth. He was kind of limping and dragging his trousers like he'd hurt his leg or something."

Will's eyes met those of the judge. Both men wished the questions didn't have to be asked. Both were glad that Josh wasn't there to hear the child's answers.

"And where was Rafe Somers when your mama fell down the stairs?" This time Will asked the question.

"Uncle Rafe stood between Mama and Auntie Ruth while Mama started down the stairs. Then he went back down the hall to his room. That was when Auntie Ruth…did it."

"Did what, honey?" Will almost pleaded. "You have to tell us what she did."

"I told you already." Abbie gnawed on her fingernail. It began to bleed.

"Abbie, do you want Meagan back?"

Abbie nodded and sucked on the wounded finger.

"Then tell us exactly how your mother fell down the stairs."

Abbie almost cried in frustration, augmented by the pain in her finger. But from the look on the men's faces she knew if she wanted Meagan back she would have to answer. "Uncle Rafe went back into his room but Auntie Ruth still wanted to fight."

"How do you know she wanted to fight?" the judge asked.

"Because Auntie Ruth yelled 'war…' and pushed Mama down the stairs. And when she finds out I told on her, she'll push me down too." And all the little girl's courage collapsed as she began to cry in earnest.

Realizing the depths of the child's sacrifice in giving this information to save Meagan, the judge lifted Abbie onto his lap and again offered his somewhat soggy handkerchief. Abbie's sobs quieted but the judge shook his head.

"It just doesn't make sense. Why would Ruth Somers refer to a war? There was no Indian attack reported at that time."

Abbie sniffled. "Auntie Ruth called Mama a war. She kept saying woor…woor—" Abbie drew out the middle of the word imitating the sound she had heard "—and then she pushed her down the stairs."

"Whore," Will said under his breath, and this time the judge nodded in understanding and agreement. Still, just as Josh and Will had done, the judge asked, "But why didn't you tell someone before this?"

Abbie shrugged her shoulders. "I didn't know it was important. I thought everybody must know what happened. I knew, and most always I don't find out about things very fast."

The judge sat back and watched the child. "And why do you suppose that is?" he asked.

"I suppose it's because it's not my business," she answered bluntly and the judge laughed aloud.

"Well, I wish I had known sooner," he said, "but it wasn't your fault that I didn't. I'm glad you told me, Abbie."

Abbie twisted the ribbon from her bonnet around her finger. "Can we have Meagan back now so we can go home?" she asked.

The judge was about to give her a positive answer, when he realized how greatly the circumstances had changed. "I'll see to it that Meagan is set free, but I'm afraid it's up to you and your father to convince her to go back home with you, because Meagan Reilly is a free woman."

There was a thud near the front window. Will reached it in time to catch a glimpse of a skirt disappearing around the corner of the house as quick footsteps faded into silence.

"I take it we have an eavesdropper," the judge mused. "The whole situation will no doubt be all over town before dinner. I'd better get over to the fort and have Meagan released before someone does it for me."

In all truth the judge was in no hurry to release Meagan, because once he had declared her innocent, he would be forced to tell of Ruth Somers' guilt. Dealing with women criminals caused problems and embarrassment. He wished the whole gender would behave themselves. It would cause himself and the world in general a lot less trouble.

He had no more than reached the door when his hostess greeted him. "Won't all of you please stay for breakfast," she offered with reverberating courtesy. "I'm sure you must be famished." Her invitation took in Will Carmichael as well as the child, for she had managed to hear part of the conversation and was sure she could ferret out more information over a hearty meal.

The judge smiled, accepting for Abbie and Will as well. "Does a man good to start the day off with a full belly," he said heartily. "And a child, too. We won't take no for an answer, will we, madam?"

And his hostess beamed in agreement.

Although Will knew he should go after Josh, the smell of food overruled his better judgment. Within minutes he had convinced himself it was his hostess who had been listening from the porch, for her questions were too obvious for her not to have heard some of what had been discussed privately. However, Will would not have been so sure of his deduction had he seen Ruth Somers, hat askew, trotting down the road as fast as her legs would carry her.

Chapter Sixteen

Had she had the time, Ruth Somers would have gone to the fort and demanded that the men get up a lynching party for Meagan Reilly.

Had she had time, Ruth would have waited at the alderman's house until Will Carmichael came out with little Abbie, snatched the child away and taken Abbie home with her, judge or no judge.

But Ruth Somers had no more time. Time had run out.

It was only luck that had sent her to the alderman's house so early in the morning. Had she not been there she would never have heard their heinous plot to try to shift the blame for Lily Daniel's death from Meagan to herself.

Well, she'd just see about that little story. Once she got back home and told Rafe, he'd make sure no harm came to her. After all, Rafe was her husband and the father of her children. He was sworn to protect her, even if he didn't always approve of the things she did.

Ruth cut across the yard of Mrs. Timmons's boarding house and yelled at the stable boy to hitch up her ox and wagon. Then she went to her room, threw her clothing into her traveling basket and bolted out the door, almost colliding with the Widow Timmons in her haste.

"But I thought you'd be staying much longer," Mrs. Timmons called as she followed her departing guest down the stairs.

"Things have changed. Seems the judge has lost his last ounce of good sense and is going to set that Reilly girl free." Ruth hefted her basket into the bed of the wagon and clambered up onto the seat. "I'll not stay in a town overrun by murderers. You won't be safe in your own bed."

"But you've paid for the full week," the Widow Timmons protested.

"Keep it! I'd rather stay alive than stay here another minute." Ruth slapped the whip against the rump of the oxen and lumbered off.

A tired Phoebe Carmichael trudged down the street and into the widow's path. Noticing Mrs. Timmons standing alone, curiosity overpowered fatigue and Phoebe paused to speak to the woman.

"Wasn't that Ruth Somers driving down the street in the wagon?" she asked. At this point Phoebe really didn't care if it was Ruth Somers or the king of England, but it would ease Meagan's mind to know that Ruth was gone.

"It most certainly was," the widow affirmed. "Took out of here like a bat out of hell, she did. Didn't even eat her breakfast. All that food going to waste. It's a sin, that's what it is. She'll rue the day she was so wasteful."

"Did she say why she was leaving?" Phoebe asked.

"Well, you should know as well as anyone. Miz Somers said they was settin' that Reilly girl free and she didn't want to be here when that happened."

"Setting Meagan free?" Suddenly all the tiredness left Phoebe's body.

"That's what she said," the old lady reiterated. "Now why don't you come in and have some breakfast? The Somers woman paid for it and I've made sugar buns and hot coffee."

"Oh, thank you, Mrs. Timmons, but I really can't stop right now. I have to find my husband. And then I have to get back to Meagan, right away."

"Well, wait here a minute and I'll get some of my sugar buns for you to take to her. No sense in facing the world on an empty stomach." The old woman shuffled into the house while Phoebe shifted restlessly on the street and watched for Josh or Will, or even the judge himself, to come by and tell her what had happened to produce such miraculous results.

Reilly had taken shelter in the stable behind the boardinghouse, not realizing this was the establishment where the formidable Ruth Somers was staying. He heard the stable boy come in, grumbling, and lead an oxen out of a nearby stall. Realizing that the boy would be coming back to perform his morning chores, Reilly slipped out of the building. He had hoped to be able to stay hidden in the stable until nightfall, but the activity had driven him out. He rounded the house just in time to see Ruth drive away.

His heart lurched. What if she was going into the fort to make more trouble for Meagan? He looked around, hoping to see either Josh or Will, but the street was empty except for two women standing in front of the boardinghouse.

Without further hesitation Reilly disappeared into the

bushes and was soon following the creekbed while keeping the road and the Somers woman in sight.

He ran easily, his long strides keeping pace with the wagon as it labored over the winter-rutted roads.

When she had passed the last turnoff to the fort, Reilly slowed his pace. He would go to the lookout point just to make certain she did not decide to return.

He watched the wagon as it wound its way toward the mountains. Satisfied that she would not turn around, Reilly was about to start back. He must find Josh and Will and tell them that Ruth Somers had gone and would not be there for the hearing. It was a good sign. It was more than they had hoped for. He chuckled to himself as he headed back into the trees.

Then the sky opened and blackness fell as Reilly was struck on the head.

A hook-nosed Indian rolled the half-conscious man to his back.

"Go back to your friends at the fort, Wolf Reilly," the Indian said. "Go back and steal your woman away from them. But that little fat hen in the wagon is mine, and if you try to take her from me, you are a dead man." He gave Reilly a shake. "You hear and understand?"

"I hear," Reilly managed as the world spun around him. "I swear I will not take your livestock."

Old Howling Dog snorted back his laughter. This brave had been around the white men too long and forgotten how the Indians spoke. Either that, or Old Howling Dog had hit him too hard.

Before he could speak, his thoughts were interrupted by the vibration of the earth.

He looked around, seeing nothing but feeling it in his feet, while Reilly, who lay prone on the ground, was instantly aware of the significance of the trembling.

"Horses," he said, still dizzy from the blow. "Many horses."

Old Howling Dog dropped to his knees and placed his ear against the ground. "Many horses, yes," he repeated. "You stay here," he ordered.

Reilly had no wish to move, as the man had dealt him a telling blow and his head still reeled. He managed to get to a sitting position by the time Old Howling Dog returned.

"What is it?" Reilly asked.

"Many men. Soldiers. They ride toward the rising sun," the Indian said.

"They're going to the fort, and after they get their orders, Old Howling Dog, they're probably going to come after you. They are angry because you kill their people and burn their houses."

"The white man takes my land. He builds his cabin where I pitch my tepee. He plants his seed where I build my village. He kills my game and digs up the ground where the stag and fowl feed. I have sworn to drive him out."

"And instead you have forced the white men to send more soldiers to protect the settlers. Many of those soldiers will see and like the land to which they have come. They will stay and bring their families. For every settler you kill a hundred will come to take his place."

Old Howling Dog grabbed Reilly by the hair, jerking his head back until he looked the man in the face. Nose to nose they stared at each other.

"You dare speak to Old Howling Dog in this manner?"

"I dare to speak the truth. Take your people and go up past the high mountains. It will be a while before the white man follows. Perhaps not even in your lifetime.

Enjoy your way of life, for it is at an end. You may be the last of your kind to have this chance, Old Howling Dog. Do not jeopardize it for the lives of a few white settlers who want only to live in peace.''

Old Howling Dog let Reilly's head go after giving it a jerk. ''Bah! You are half-white yourself. Of course you would try to protect your people.''

''I have no people,'' Reilly told him. ''The white man will not accept me and the Indian looks on me with suspicion. I have come to the conclusion I share with you because this is also what I intend to do.''

Old Howling Dog watched the younger man closely. He had heard his words and knew them to be true. ''I will not run away. The white men as well as the Indian hear my name with respect and fear.''

''The white men will hunt you down.''

''And if they do, I will kill them. I will kill you, too, Wolf Reilly, if you cross my path again. I do not listen to the white man or the red man. I listen only to the voice of the spirits and those spirits tell me to kill the white man and drive him from the land.

''You tell them. You tell the white man if they stay, they will die. The spirits have told me it must be so.''

''I will tell them, but it's not going to stop them from coming.'' But Reilly was talking to himself, because Old Howling Dog had gone.

Meagan stood by the tiny window for a long while after Phoebe left her. She heard pounding in the distance and her heart thudded with every beat of the hammer. Was it a scaffold they were building? And was it for her?

How she wished she and Josh had never returned from the tiny cabin high in the mountains. How she wished they had stayed there and built a life together. A life filled with love and trust. All that had happened since their return had been on the brink of disaster, culminating with the final appearance of Ruth Somers and the men from Banebridge.

Had Meagan and Josh been in the mountains they never would have been discovered, especially in such circumstances. There had been no way to explain that situation. Ruth had caught them and she had taken advantage of their dilemma.

Once again Meagan tried to comprehend why the woman hated her so violently. There was no rhyme or reason for Ruth's hatred.

Meagan's only sin was to have loved Josh and his daughter. She would have dedicated the rest of her life to making them happy, and done so gladly, but it seemed it was not to be. The downcast eyes of the guards told her that there was little hope. Even Phoebe, who believed in her husband's abilities only slightly less than she believed in the power of God, could not look Meagan in the eye and give her encouragement.

Perhaps there was no encouragement. No more than there was hope, for neither Josh nor Reilly had come to her.

It seemed that Meagan must face her accusers alone. She could only pray that she could do so with courage, and that Josh would continue to try to prove her innocence, even though she might no longer be around to enjoy vindication.

She allowed the tears she had held at bay for so long to course down her cheeks as her hands tightly clasped the bars on the window.

Suddenly her fingers were enclosed in warmth and her eyes opened wide as Josh's face appeared before her.

"Josh! You shouldn't have come," she whispered. "But, oh, I'm so glad you did."

She pressed her face through the bars until she could feel the touch of his lips against her own.

"You have to get out of here. Ruth said she'd have you arrested for contempt of court. They'll lock you up, too. What will Abbie do then?"

Josh placed his finger over her lips. "Abbie told us what happened to Lily. She's known all along. Will has taken her to Judge Osborne."

"What happened to Lily? What do you mean? Abbie wasn't there. I didn't see anybody except Ruth, until Rafe and the hired hands came in answer to her screams."

"Believe me, Abbie was there and Ruth won't trouble you anymore. I'll see to that, Meagan. Ruth will be out of our lives forever. From now on, it's just you and me and Abbie."

"But I thought we were going to have to go away...."

"I thought so too, but that's all in the past. Abbie told us what happened, and..."

There was a snap of orders and the sound of marching feet. Josh flattened himself in the shadow of the wall until the men had past.

"If there's nothing to worry about then why are you hiding?" Meagan wanted to know.

"Until you're free, I'm worried," Josh admitted. "Will and the judge should be here soon. I'm on my way to meet them. It's going to be all right, Meagan. I promise. We're doing everything we can." He kissed her once more while Meagan wondered if "everything they could do" was going to be enough.

Suddenly she reached out and grasped his collar.

"Please don't go, Josh. Please, don't leave me alone. Stay with me now. I'm so afraid."

And Josh stayed, even though he could hear Will's voice in the distance along with that of Judge Osborne and the bright laughter of a child. Even though he would have given half of what he owned to learn what had happened in the meeting with the judge and to find out if Will had word of Reilly. Josh entwined his fingers through Meagan's and stayed with the woman he loved above all else.

"Don't worry, Meagan," he told her. "The only way they can separate us is to drag me away."

And although Meagan didn't say so, she was afraid of that, too.

"I want the courtroom set up immediately," Judge Osborne told the adjutant. "I made a mistake, and I want the same setting in which to correct it. No hole-in-the-wall justice for Meagan Reilly. I was at fault and I intend to see that she is vindicated legally and with proper jurisdiction."

The adjutant scurried away to comply with the judge's orders, while Will and Judge Osborne tried to answer the questions of the bystanders.

"Don't you think one of us ought to go in and tell Meagan?" Abbie asked cautiously as the men became garrulous with their chronicled explanation of the circumstances.

Will started toward the door, only to be stopped by the voice of his wife.

"Will! Will! Wait a minute, I must speak to you!" Phoebe came running through the gates of the fort and didn't slow down until she was caught, breathless and gasping, in her husband's arms.

"What is it, Phoebe? I thought you'd either be with Meagan, or at home in bed."

"I was on my way home when I saw Ruth Somers. She was driving her buggy right out of town, and Widow Timmons says she isn't coming back."

"If she does, the woman is subject to arrest," the judge declared.

"Ruth Somers? Subject to arrest?"

"Yes," the judge affirmed. "Arrest! For the murder of Lily Daniels."

"But I thought you found the Reilly girl guilty of Lily's death," a bystander called out.

"That's right," the judge said, "but I was wrong. New evidence has come to light and we now know that Meagan is not guilty. I've come here today to see that she is again a free woman."

"But what about the Somers woman?" one of the men asked. "Are you going to hang her now?"

"We'll come to that decision when the time comes," the judge declared, as he prayed to heaven that the time would somehow never come.

"Now, the adjutant tells me that the courtroom is ready. Perhaps Will Carmichael would be kind enough to escort Miss Reilly to the courtroom."

The judge took the hand of little Abbie and led her through the crowd to the impromptu courtroom that had been set up in the schoolhouse.

Though it was not widely known, and seldom mentioned, Judge Osborne was a grandfather several times over, and although he usually found children of little interest, they were not unfamiliar to him. At the present time he'd rather listen to childish prattle than think about the situation that faced him once Meagan Reilly had been freed.

* * *

The keys rattled in the door and Meagan jumped. Her fingers dug into Josh's hand and she bowed her head, unable for the moment to turn and meet her fate.

Will stepped into the room and caught a glimpse of Josh's face through the barred window. "Josh!" he called. "Did you find Reilly?"

"No sign of him," Josh replied. "How about you?"

"Nothing, but it's a moot point now. The hearing will take place this afternoon."

Meagan's heart sank as she realized her brother must have been given the task of implementing her escape and had not yet been given the opportunity he needed to free her. She caught her breath several times and lifted her chin. She would not go to her fate a blubbering coward. But the tears continued to stream down her cheeks even though her face remained expressionless.

Will realized Meagan had no inkling of her fate. "There, there," he said, patting her shoulder, for she still clung to Josh's hand through the bars. "Everything is going to be fine. Ruth Somers has left town, and the judge wants to set you free."

Meagan's fingers slipped from Josh's hands and the next thing Will knew he was holding her erect.

"I think I'd better come in and give you a hand," Josh told his friend. "I guess I didn't rightly prepare her for the shock of freedom. Not that she's going to enjoy being a free woman very long."

Will awkwardly held Meagan upright until Josh joined him outside the little cell, while Phoebe and half the women of the town flapped around trying various ways to bring Meagan back to her senses.

"Just what did you mean by that remark about Meagan not staying free very long?'' Will asked as the women hustled Josh and Will out of the room.

''I meant that as soon as she is able to say 'I do' we're going to get married, and nobody's ever going to take her away from me again.''

''And amen to that,'' Will said fervently as a pale but smiling Meagan appeared in the doorway under her own power.

Judge Osborne was glad that Meagan Reilly was innocent of murder. He was pleased that the little Daniels girl had come forward to set things straight. He was even happy to learn that Meagan and Josh had learned to love each other despite the circumstances under which they had been thrown together. But the fact that Ruth Somers had been responsible for Lily Daniels's death cast a dark pall over everything as far as the judge was concerned.

It irritated him no end that he would be forced to deal with the trial and sentencing of yet another woman. With this in mind he went into his makeshift courtroom with a scowl on his face that sent a message of gloom to all those involved.

Even Will was taken aback at Judge Osborne's facial expression. He stopped Josh and Meagan outside the door to tell them that he intended to attempt to discover the judge's disposition, but his plans were thwarted by Abbie. She had caught a glimpse of Meagan and rushed to throw her arms around both her father and the woman who would soon be her mother.

''Oh, Meagan, Meagan, I missed you so much.'' Abbie closed her eyes and scrunched herself against Meagan's skirt, getting as close as she could and hanging on tight.

"And I missed you, too." Meagan returned the hug with equal enthusiasm.

"I have so much to tell you," Abbie expounded. "I made ever-so-many friends since I've been here. And one of them is Judge Osborne—only Judge isn't really his name—and the other is the Indian, Reilly. You remember Reilly, don't you? He says he's partly your brother and that you told him the same thing you told me about not being hurt over what people say." The little girl paused, caught her breath and frowned. "I don't think it worked all that well for him either," she said thoughtfully.

"Anyhow, Reilly was going to take you away, but he doesn't have to now, does he? You can come home with Papa and me and…look! There's Reilly now!"

All eyes, including those of the people who had gathered around the schoolhouse out of curiosity, turned toward the young man, who tried to lose himself in the shadows and disappear between the buildings, but Abbie was hot on his trail.

She had pulled free of Meagan's embrace and raced down the street, arms outstretched toward the Indian while the townsfolk gasped in horror.

Trapped by a little girl's love, Reilly dropped to his knee and caught the child in his arms.

He realized for the first time that his sister was among the group gathered on the porch of the schoolhouse. Obviously the judge had moved the time for the trial forward.

It was too late to try to take Meagan away before the hearing, and Reilly could only hope that without the objections of Ruth Somers his sister would be set free.

"What are you so happy about?" he asked the little girl.

"Meagan is going to go and talk to Judge Osborne and then we can all go home. Do you want to come home with us?"

Reilly looked toward the hills. He doubted that Old Howling Dog would heed his warning and stop the raids on the settlers. He wondered if Abbie would have a home to go to, and there was only one way to find out.

"I think going home with you would be a fine idea," Reilly agreed, "but first I'm going to have to have a little chat with the judge myself."

Abbie nodded sagely. "Well, be careful what you say and always tell the truth and he'll like you just fine. And don't worry if he won't let you sit on his lap like he does me, because you're too big anyway."

Reilly choked back his laughter and joined the others with a smile on his face that eased the trepidation in his heart.

To Reilly's everlasting relief there was no reason for him to speak to the judge on Meagan's behalf. He stepped forward only when the question arose as to Ruth Somers's whereabouts, concisely giving his information regarding her impromptu flight.

Abbie, who had grown tired of repeating the story of her mother's death, reluctantly recited an abbreviated version of the circumstances, and Judge Osborne brought down his gavel, making Meagan a free woman.

Throughout the proceedings, Josh stood at Meagan's side, his hand protectively holding hers, but only his body stood firmly beside her for his mind had finally absorbed the facts behind the story that Abbie told.

Josh did not see the judge as the man spoke the words that would set Meagan free. His mind caught and held his daughter's words and he realized again what a fool he had been regarding Lily. He had been disgraced. Duped by his own wife and a man he had considered a close friend. Foolishly he had overlooked the most blatant signs of their betrayal and Meagan had almost paid with her life.

He should have known. He shouldn't have been such a damn fool to think that a woman could really love him and be happy with the kind of life he led. A life that involved working from dawn to dusk every day of your life. What woman in her right mind would want a life that offered nothing more than work and hardship and death?

Lily hadn't been able to survive that life. He forced himself to remember Lily as she had been during the early part of the marriage. It had been Lily's gaiety, tinkling laughter and passion that had attracted him.

Oh, yes, Lily had been passionate, but the passion had faded and finally dissolved to the point where she snapped at Josh when he so much as touched her. It had seemed as though there was nothing he could do that would please her, and he was such a fool he thought that if he could not please her, no one else could either. How wrong he had been. What a fool he was not to have realized that Lily's passion had not faded, but instead been bestowed on another man. Rafe Somers, who proclaimed himself to be Josh's friend.

Again the gavel banged. Josh gave a little start as he realized Meagan was hugging him while Abbie alternately danced around them and hugged everyone in sight.

Meagan, his Meagan, with her warmth and loving passion that gave as well as took in the act of love. He loved to touch her, and to feel her touching him. He longed to know again the miracle of her love, and the comfort he felt when he held her close after their love-making was done, when Meagan snuggled against him, needing his nearness as greatly as he needed hers.

Only in Meagan's arms could Josh shake off the pain and the shame of the past. But how, in good faith, could he expect Meagan to feel the same way about him? How did he know that she, too, would not come to feel over-burdened by the hardships of the life they would lead? And how could he bear it should she turn from him as Lily had done? It would be better to make the break now when only his own life would be destroyed, and allow Meagan to find her own life, a life of social and intel-lectual fulfillment, with someone else.

Meagan left his arms to receive the congratulations of Will and Phoebe Carmichael. He felt bereft and suddenly alone despite the crowded courtroom.

The judge, smiling in satisfaction over the outcome of the situation, cleared his throat. If Josh and Meagan wanted him to perform the wedding ceremony they'd better get under way. Tongues would certainly wag if Josh took Meagan back to his place without marrying her first and all the goodwill they had acquired would be lost, as would Meagan's reputation.

"Mr. Daniels, wasn't there something you wanted to ask me?"

Josh turned slowly toward the judge and lifted his head. There was a glazed look in his eyes. The look of a man who has taken a blow to the head.

"Mr. Daniels?" the judge repeated, wishing now that he had not been so hasty. "Did you have a request of this court?"

Josh looked at Meagan. She shimmered like a living light in her happiness. How could he ask her to return with him to drudgery and hard labor that would be no different than the sentence she had served as punishment for a heinous crime? She should be free to marry a man who would provide her with a home where she could live the sort of life Phoebe Carmichael enjoyed.

His throat worked as he tried to form the words that would free her not only from her bonds of enforced slavery, but also from any obligation she might have felt she had to Josh himself.

Meagan deserved to be truly free. Not saddled with a house out in the middle of nowhere and a child to raise that wasn't even hers, and a man who was so stupid he couldn't even read the signs that his own wife was betraying him with another man.

Read the signs! That was a laugh! Josh was nothing more than a farmer. Until Meagan came, he couldn't even read.

Oh yes, Meagan deserved better than that. Meagan deserved to be free, and it was up to Josh to see that justice was done.

The sharp strike of the gavel brought him back to the present.

"No, Your Honor," he croaked as he swallowed the lump in his throat and tried to fight down the tears. It was bad enough that he had to let Meagan go, he wasn't going to add to his embarrassment by bawling about it. But the very sound of his own voice condemning himself to a lifetime of loneliness was more than he could bear. "Meagan is free and I don't want anything more than that."

His voice caught in his throat and the tears spilled down his cheeks as he pushed his way through the crowd while little Abbie followed in his wake, her voice piping over the noise.

"But Papa, aren't you going to ask Meagan to marry us?"

Chapter Seventeen

The people followed Josh out of the courtroom as though sucked by a vacuum. But it was Will who managed to stop the man before he reached the end of the street.

"What in the hell has got into you?" Will demanded as he jerked his friend to a halt.

"Reality! Honesty! Truth, I guess." Josh shook Will's hand from his arm. "Meagan deserves better than me. Better than the life I can give her."

"Is that what this is all about?" Will ran his hand through his hair in pure frustration. "You can give her a home and you love her. What more do you think she wants?"

"Friends, people to talk to. Meagan would be better off in town, with her own kind of people, educated and sociable."

Will stepped back and looked his friend up and down. "I don't see anything all that different about you, Josh. You're a bit pigheaded and stubborn, and right now you've got the wrong notion about the whole situation, but your heart's in the right place."

Abbie caught up in time to hear Will's last words. She

tugged at her father's coat. "Meagan's crying," she announced, "and you better go back and ask her to marry us, or I will!"

Josh dropped to his knee and looked his daughter in the eye. "Meagan has a right to choose the kind of life she wants, Abbie. Just because we love her and want her to stay with us doesn't mean it's the right thing for her."

"Yes, it does." Abbie stuck her lip out in determination. "We're the right thing for Meagan and I'm going to tell her so."

A soft hand closed on Abbie's shoulder. "You don't have to tell me, Abbie. I already know. Now run along with your Uncle Will. Your papa and I have to talk."

But they didn't talk. They walked down past the stables into the pasture at the end of the road. Somewhere along the way their hands met, and held.

The path ended near the pond where the animals came for water. It was there they stopped and faced each other as well as the issues that had brought them together and at the same time had kept them apart.

Josh looked down at Meagan's face. He placed his free hand under her chin. "I'm sorry I made you cry. I only wanted what was best for you. I wanted you to be free to choose and not feel obligated because… because…"

Meagan watched his expression. She longed to take him into her arms. But it was not yet time. There was so much pain in his eyes. And, having heard Abbie's account of what had happened the day Lily was killed, Meagan could only guess at the pain that must dwell in his heart. Perhaps if he could put his deepest thoughts into words, he would be free, for Meagan knew instinctively that it was not herself that Josh wanted to set free, but Josh.

"Because…" she urged, praying she was doing the right thing.

"Because I love you so much and I'm afraid you won't be happy with me."

The words all tumbled out in a pile. For a moment they lay between them as real and tangible as if they were of solid substance.

"Oh, Josh, don't you understand? I couldn't be happy without you." She stepped into his arms, crushing into nothingness the words and the fears that stood between them.

He held her for a long time in his arms. He held her close, without passion or desire, but in the embrace of true, undeniable love.

She relaxed against him, knowing that the worst was over and even though the ghost of past pain would undoubtedly someday raise its grisly head, she would be there to stave off the darkness. She would be there beside him, as his wife.

She stepped from the circle of his arms and took his face in her hands. "Josh Daniels, will you marry me?"

He kissed her. Tiny kisses running over her lips, her eyes, her cheeks. "Yes," he murmured between the kisses. "Yes, yes, yes…" Then it was Josh's turn to back away. "Wasn't I supposed to ask that question?" he asked in mock wonder.

"I couldn't wait," Meagan told him as she took his arm and they started back to where Abbie anxiously waited.

Word of Meagan's innocence and the injustice that had been done to her due to Ruth's testimony had spread among the townsfolk who came en masse offering their apologies and sympathy. When it became known that a wedding was imminent, they brought not only their best wishes, but some of their own keepsakes as wedding gifts.

Meagan was rushed from Josh's arms to Phoebe's house, to which Widow Timmons came parading down the street followed by her stable boy, who lugged a small trunk containing the widow's own wedding dress.

"It came from France," she announced with pride, "and hasn't been worn but the one time."

"Oh, but I couldn't..." Meagan began, somewhat overwhelmed by the woman's generosity.

"You can and you will," the widow insisted. "Don't let it bother you that I'm so portly. It wasn't always so and I think with a few tucks here and there the dress will fit to perfection."

While the widow and the alderman's wife tended to Meagan's hair and clothing, Phoebe dressed Abbie in her Sunday best. They both lamented that there was no time to secure a lasting curl in her hair.

"But I'd have to wear a bonnet in church anyway," Abbie said stoically, "so I guess it doesn't really matter."

For once, the little girl gave minimal thought to her appearance. Today she would gain her heart's desire and her Meagan would belong to herself and her papa forever. Had the truth been known the child would have braved the whole congregation without either bonnet or curls rather than miss out on being there when Meagan became part of her family. Still, she was glad when Phoebe brought out Abbie's most lavish and frilly bonnet to be worn for the auspicious occasion.

As soon as Abbie was properly attired she slipped to

the window and glanced out to the street, wondering if the Indian—Reilly—would come to his sister's wedding. It would be very nice if Reilly was there. Meagan would like it, and Abbie would be able to stand beside Reilly and let him hold her hand during the ceremony. And that would be nice, too.

The ceremony took place at twilight. The chapel was filled with candles and the judge looked regal as he waited before the altar. It seemed right and fitting somehow that the judge who had agonized so much over having to pass the sentence, was now given the opportunity to set things right and join Meagan, Josh and little Abbie together as a family.

As the judge intoned the words, Abbie spied Reilly. At first she did not recognize him, for he was dressed like a real gentleman, and only the rich mahogany hue of his skin gave notice to his heritage. Abbie's breath caught in her throat, for she knew she would never behold another man so unbelievably beautiful if she lived to be a hundred.

After she remembered to breathe again, Abbie sidled toward Reilly and deftly slipped her little hand into his. He smiled down at her and kept his hold on her hand throughout the rest of the ceremony. Together, they followed Meagan, Josh, Will and Phoebe out of the church.

It seemed that everyone in the town had come to offer their congratulations. The hour grew late and Abbie fell asleep on Reilly's shoulder. He relinquished her to her father, carefully making certain that her bonnet was secured in place so she would not face embarrassment.

Meagan and Josh planned on spending their wedding night at the Carmichaels' house and, amid shouts of good wishes, the party went out into the street.

Meagan slipped her hand through her husband's arm. "Just think, Josh, tomorrow we'll go back to our own home."

He kissed her lightly, for his joy was yet too great for passion and his arms were filled with his daughter. Shifting the child to his shoulder, he placed his free arm around his wife as she looked toward the hills and the road they would take home.

Her sudden gasp caught him off guard as Meagan's hand clutched Josh's shirtfront and her eyes opened wide in panic.

"Look!" she said, never taking her gaze from the sky.

It was in the reflection of her eyes that Josh saw the cause of her fear. He stared, unaware of the revelation, then turned to face the inevitable.

"Heaven help us," he said as the voices silenced around them.

Cries and moans from the settlers replaced the joyous celebration that had ensued only moments before.

"My God, have they left anything?" one of the men asked, as far to the north yet another fire flamed into the sky.

"I don't know," Josh admitted, "but I'm sure as hell going to find out."

Will went to the fort to alert the militia while Josh and Meagan packed up their belongings in the wagon.

"I don't want you to come with me," Josh told her. "It's too dangerous. Stay here with Phoebe and Abbie."

"I'm your wife, Josh Daniels, and I belong at your side, for better or for worse."

Josh glanced up at the reddening sky. "Let's hope it don't get much worse than this," he muttered, realizing that regardless of what he said, Meagan would come along anyway.

Meagan and Josh started for home with an escort of soldiers and settlers that wound along the road like a giant snake.

They reached the first cabin at midday.

"Them redskins burned my barn but left my house untouched," a man said as he rubbed his head in frustration. "Took some of my livestock, too."

"Did you recognize any of them?" Josh asked at Reilly's prompting.

"My woman says it was Old Howling Dog. Saw him good and close last time he came this way. He burned the cabin then. We just got it rebuilt and I thought I'd have to put it up again sure, but it didn't turn out that way."

"Then everybody is all right?" one of the soldiers asked.

"Right as rain," the man affirmed. He was shaken but grateful that the damage had been minimal.

"When you get your lumber ready you let me know, and we'll have a barn raising," Josh told him as they rode off.

Over the next few hours they discovered various dimensions of destruction, but wherever they went only a portion of the buildings had been burned. Few if any of the settlers had been killed, and no scalps taken.

"Almost seems as though Old Howling Dog is playing with them," Josh remarked to his new brother-in-law as they rode along.

"In the first place, Old Howling Dog isn't an old man. Far from it, he's probably not yet your age," Reilly said thoughtfully. "And I doubt that he's playing. Instead, he's making certain that the white man won't forget him, without infuriating anyone to the point where they'll chase him down in vengeance.''

Josh shrugged. Coming from a man who had not yet seen his eighteenth birthday the sage words seemed almost ludicrous. "I don't know, Reilly. I'm going to feel pretty vengeful if I find my property burned to the ground.''

But before they could travel to Josh's property they had to deal with the Somerses. Even in the happiness Josh had found with Meagan, he dreaded meeting the people who had so blatantly befriended and betrayed him.

The sun was hidden by the trees and shadows crept over the land by the time the party reached the Somerses' house. Smoke hovered over the trees and the air was acrid.

"We're too late," Josh said aloud. "The Indians have already been here.''

The buildings were burned to the ground and the men lit torches as they searched for bodies.

Meagan buried her face in Josh's chest. "I didn't wish her dead," she told him. "Truly, I didn't.''

"I know." He stroked her hair as he spoke. "Nor did I.''

Josh hadn't even found it in his heart to want Rafe dead, even though he had betrayed Josh with Lily. It had obviously taken two, and the fact that Lily had come to the Somerses' house, and often, left little doubt that she was a willing party to the betrayal.

His fists clenched as he wished he could get hold of his erstwhile friend. But when a group of soldiers dragged Rafe from the trees, Josh held his peace. It was not the time or the place to bring up the past.

"It was Old Howling Dog and his war party," Rafe was saying. "They burned my house, they drove off my livestock, they trampled my newly planted crops. I could not stop them." He looked at the embers, glowing like red eyes in the night.

"What happened to your children?" Josh asked.

"I had sent them over to check on your livestock. They were not here when the Indians came."

"The Indians have struck many of the settlers, but yours is the greatest damage. I am surprised, given the amount of damage, that you are unharmed," the captain remarked as he surveyed the scene.

"They said if I promised not to follow they would leave me my life, my scalp and my sons. I agreed."

"Where are the Indians now?" the captain wanted to know.

"They took Ruth and headed south." He gestured toward the trees.

Meagan gave a little gasp.

"What's wrong?" the captain demanded.

"My land is to the south," Josh said as he grabbed Meagan's hand and pulled her toward the wagon.

"I go with you," Rafe called, and one of the soldiers gave him an arm up onto his horse.

Within moments the thunder of hooves drowned out the sound of Indian drums that echoed through the night.

The dim glow in the sky portended no good as Josh pushed onward, followed by the rest of the men. They burst into the clearing in time to see the flames licking upward as the Indians ran to and fro in the euphoria of destruction.

Unwilling to give up their advantage both Indian and white men took cover, fighting one another while the fire bit into the wall of the house.

"The whole thing will be lost if we can't get them out of there," one of the soldiers growled as he jammed the rod into his flintlock.

Meagan's heart sank as she realized the truth in his words. And the Indians had the advantage, for they could defend their position until the little structure was nothing more than a memory.

"I'll slip behind the lines and see if I can speak to Old Howling Dog," Reilly said as he stripped off his shirt. "Maybe I can make him see reason. He seems drunk with destruction."

Meagan grabbed her brother's arm. "I'd rather see the house burn to the ground than have you risk your life to save it. If you go to the other side and the Indians don't kill you, it's likely the soldier will."

"I don't intend to get killed." He tied a bandanna around his head as he spoke.

"No one ever does," Meagan pointed out without releasing his arm.

"Do you have a better idea, sister?"

The wind picked up and the fire flared.

"No," Meagan admitted. "Nothing but a direct act of God is going to save the house now."

As if in answer to her words, the wind whipped through the trees, slapping at everything within its reach. The flames raced along as though pursued. Then, an ethereal moaning filled the night. It was the sound of a soul in torment. The moan became a shrill cry and finally a shriek, fading into a guttural groan before rising again.

Reilly grabbed his sister's hand. "What is it?" he whispered as his eyes searched the shadows. "It sounds like the souls of the damned."

"It's not the souls of the damned," Josh assured

Reilly as he handed his gun to Meagan to reload. "It's just that damned organ."

"The fire has burned through the wall behind the organ," Meagan explained, as Reilly looked from one to the other askance. "What you hear is the wind blowing into the organ bellows. It happened before and almost scared me to death."

Meagan's thoughts turned to the night when she had run to Josh's arms to find comfort, safety and love, but Reilly grabbed her arms and brought her from her reverie.

"You're sure it's the organ?" he demanded.

Meagan nodded, surprised at her brother's vehemence.

"How long do you think it will last?"

Meagan watched the flames engulf the outside wall of the parlor. "I suppose until the organ burns up," she said with a sigh, "along with the rest of the house."

"Then there's not a moment to lose." Reilly took to his heels and, despite Meagan's objection, disappeared into the night.

The wind grew stronger. The screeching became more predominant. Lightning crashed through the night.

Men on both sides stopped firing. The smell of fear was as strong as that of fire and smoke. Brave men trembled in terror as the unknown entity cried out for vengeance, and while the white men managed to hold their ground, some of the Indians bolted with fear of the unknown.

Old Howling Dog's guttural voice could be heard as he fought his own men in an effort to continue the attack, but their superstition was too great and the fear of the howling spirits surpassed their fear of Old Howling Dog.

An Indian lifted a white flag and rose to his feet from

the shadows. "Get water. Put out the fire. We will help you. The spirits demand it."

Within moments, everyone fought together to subdue the flames. Then, as if in answer to their prayers, the rain came pouring down. The cries of the damned faded into nothingness as the men stood together, shoulder to shoulder, to survey their work in mutual satisfaction.

The parlor was gone, and half the dogtrot, but the rest of the house was untouched. Meagan, breathless and soot-covered, rushed forward to gauge the damage to her house, exclaiming over everything that had been spared as though it were an old friend.

"It's just the parlor that's burned." Meagan gave Josh a little hug. "The rest of the house is still standing."

Josh pulled her into his arms, his eyes dancing. "I'm afraid everything in the parlor is lost, even the organ."

The only thing that kept him from laughing aloud was the wild-eyed and wary expressions on the faces of the men who had joined forces to fight an unseen foe.

Meagan hugged him and buried her face in his chest to hide her girlish giggle. "I think we can say the ghost of the organ has been exorcised."

As soon as it was obvious that the fire was out and the crying spirit was silenced, the Indians disappeared.

"We must go after them and free the Somers woman," the captain told his men, but his men hadn't the heart or the strength to move.

Before the captain could urge them to action, Reilly returned from the Indian camp.

Spying an Indian, the sentry jumped to his feet, gun at his shoulder.

"Stop! Don't shoot!" Meagan screamed. "It's my brother."

"Shore looks like a bona fide Indian to me," the sentry said as he lowered his gun and glared at the young man. "I almost shot you, boy," he growled. "You better call out first if you're going to run around looking like that."

"I've got to talk to your captain," Reilly told him. "It's about Old Howling Dog."

"What about Old Howling Dog?" the captain asked.

"He wants to talk. He wants a treaty. But he won't talk to anyone but Judge Osborne."

The captain rubbed his eyes. He was tired. His eyes burned and his body ached. "Tell Old Howling Dog to surrender the woman and he is free to go."

"There's no question of that," Reilly told him. "He will take the woman deep into the mountains and when you try to follow, your men will be killed, one by one."

"Do you believe he is capable of this?" the captain asked.

"Don't you?" Reilly returned.

The captain bowed his head in submission. "Go to the fort and get the judge. We'll keep the Indians at bay until you get back."

Rafe approached Josh with an inner reluctance that he would not allow to be seen. He knew now that Josh had learned the truth of the situation between himself and Lily. And realized that their friendship was at an end. However, being Rafe Somers, the little man felt he somehow had to vindicate himself.

"Your animals are still hidden in the pens by the creek," he said with pride. "I take good care of them."

"Your boys took care of them, just like they always do," Josh corrected without looking up from the gun he was cleaning.

From the set of Josh's face, Rafe wished he had picked a different time to have this conversation. Confronting a man who was holding a gun about having had an affair with his wife was foolhardy to say the least. And Rafe was not a foolhardy man, except where women were concerned.

"I am sorry for the lie my wife told about Meagan. I am sorry Ruth made the accidents happen so you would think Meagan was incompetent. I am sorry she set the trap for Meagan that caught your arm."

Josh stared at his gun, unable to believe what he was hearing, as Rafe, having made his apology, blatantly continued. "I congratulate you on your wedding. You and Meagan will have a good life together."

"Is that a promise, or a prophecy?"

"It is truth. Meagan will be a good wife to you. She will work hard and she will not complain nor will she want more than you can give her. You will be happy together."

Josh didn't answer, just kept his head bowed and cleaned his gun.

"Lily, your other wife, was not happy here. She was lonely. She wanted friends and excitement. She wanted to leave you and the little girl and return to the home of her parents. She told me this."

Rafe wished Josh would put the gun down. He wished Josh would say something, anything, even if it was just to swear at him. The man's expression had not changed from the moment Rafe had started talking, and since Rafe didn't know what else to do, he continued.

"You did not care that your wife was lonely. You would not take time from clearing the land and planting the seed to spend time with her. So Rafe did it for you. Rafe kept her happy, and Rafe kept her here." He thumped his chest proudly. "I did it for you, friend Josh. I keep your family together."

Had it been anyone other than the French trapper, Josh would have loaded his gun and shot him, but, having known Rafe for several years, Josh knew that Rafe believed every word he said to be true.

Josh did not answer and he did not look up. He continued cleaning his gun, and when he had finished he filled it with powder from his horn and pounded it down. When he had done that he looked up. Rafe had chosen retreat as the better part of valor and was walking away.

Unable to hold his temper another minute, Josh vented his spleen by slamming the butt of the gun down on the ground. A shot rang out and Rafe Somers broke into a run and scampered down the road and out of sight.

Josh was immediately surrounded by curious faces. "My gun accidentally went off," he told them. "I guess Rafe thought it was another Indian attack."

"He sure took off like the devil himself was after him," one of the soldiers chortled as the men continued on toward their camp in a clearing some distance from the house.

Chapter Eighteen

The judge arrived the afternoon of the second day. Assured that the danger was over and the Indians were ready to parley, he had brought Will, Phoebe and little Abbie along with him.

It was Abbie's laughter that brought Meagan running from the house to take the little girl into her arms.

With her family firmly in place, and despite the fact that her house was filled with company, Meagan set about cleaning up the house and washing clothes while Josh went down to the creek to bring back his livestock.

Abbie sat on the doorstep, while Reilly squatted before her.

"But why do you have to go live with the Indians?" she asked. "Why can't you just stay here?"

"I made a promise and I have to keep it," Reilly told her. "I promised Old Howling Dog that if he would stop burning the settlers' homes and talk to Judge Osborne, I would go with him to help him build a new place for his people to live."

"When will you come back?" the child asked, trying to understand and fight back her tears at the same time.

"I don't rightly know, but I *will* come back, I prom-

ise.'' He chucked her under the chin. ''Now give me
that pretty smile to remember you by.''

''I don't have a pretty smile,'' Abbie said. ''My front
teeth are too big and the rest of me is too little, except
for my ears.'' She all but choked on the admission. More
than anything in this world Abbie didn't want Reilly to
think she was any uglier than she already was. ''Besides,'' she blundered on, trying desperately to change
the subject, ''you say you won't forget me, but you will.
You'll go away and you won't ever think of me at all.
And when you come back you'll just say something like
'the last time I saw you, you were just a little girl with
big floppy ears' and that's all you'll remember.''

''No, it's not,'' Reilly assured her. ''I *will* come back,
and I *will* remember you while I'm gone.''

Abbie scoffed and turned away. She didn't believe
him any more than he believed himself. It was all a
bunch of kindhearted lies people told so that saying
goodbye would be easier. But it wasn't easier. Not for
Abbie. How could she bear it if she grew up and Reilly
came back and didn't know who she was? To add to her
distress tears popped out of her eyes and dribbled down
her cheeks and her nose felt leaky.

Reilly couldn't stand to see Abbie cry. God knew she
had had enough sorrow in her life and he didn't want to
be the cause of any more. Still, he knew that she was
young and, given time, would more than likely forget
all about him.

It occurred to him that he did not want Abbie Daniels
to forget him. He took off his beaded headband and
handed it to the little girl. ''When you see this, think of
me,'' he told her.

There! That was done. He had discharged any duty he

had to make parting easier. He turned away and did not comprehend Abbie's dilemma.

She had nothing to give him. Reilly was leaving now. She might never see him again. And he had given her his beautiful headband. He would go away and fall in love with an Indian princess and never think of Abbie again. She had to give him something. Something of herself. Something that she treasured, that was uniquely her own. Something so unique that when he saw it he would think of her alone.

Reilly started walking away and Abbie made a decision.

"Reilly, wait." She tried to swallow the lump in her voice. "Wait, Reilly. I have something for you too."

She twisted her finger into one of the lovely curls Meagan had fixed to make her look pretty. With a little grunt of pain she tore it from her scalp.

She placed the curl in Reilly's hand, and then turned and ran away.

Reilly stood staring at the russet hair that curled lovingly on the palm of his hand. He thought of going after the little girl but there was nothing more to say. Abbie had said it all.

As Reilly walked toward his horse he could hear Meagan singing while she washed the clothes and Josh whistling to the stock as he drove the animals up from the creek. Reilly felt the love that surrounded them.

He would take part of that love away with him, thanks to Abbie. But more than that, he knew that with her gift Abbie had ensured the success of her request, for as sure as the world was round, and day followed night, Abbie Daniels was one person Wolf Reilly wouldn't forget.

The captain and Judge Osborne sat beside Josh across the small campfire from Old Howling Dog. After greetings were exchanged there was an uncomfortable silence. Finally, unable to contain himself any longer, the captain spoke up.

"We are here to negotiate the return of Ruth Somers," he announced pompously.

Old Howling Dog silenced the man with his own announcement.

"We are here because the spirits called out to us through the fire, telling my people that we must move on and leave the white man in peace. We are here to make certain the white man does not follow."

The judge had been apprised of the history of the organ and realized the instrument's import on his negotiations. He did not contradict Old Howling Dog's premise.

"Once you turn Ruth Somers over to me you are free to go. The settlers will not demand revenge for the loss of their land and property," the judge agreed magnanimously.

"The woman goes with me," Old Howling Dog said flatly.

"Ruth Somers is accused of murder. She must stand trial according to our laws."

"And?" the Indian demanded.

"If she is found guilty she will be hanged," the judge said reluctantly as the Indian glowered at him.

"I will not give her back to you to be hanged. My people understand that she protected the honor of her husband and her house. We take her with us and let her live in peace."

"But she is guilty of murder," the judge argued. "I must take her back...."

Old Howling Dog leaned forward. He had heard much

from the soldiers. He understood what had taken place. "When the woman Meagan was convicted of murder you sent her into service to pay for her crime. Now you have the same problem with yet another woman. I say Ruth Somers goes with me to live the life of a squaw. It will be punishment enough."

Above the drums a woman's strident voice could be heard as Ruth demanded she be allowed to speak to the judge, to Josh, to the captain or even to her husband, whom she was sure she could browbeat into demanding her release.

The judge cringed inwardly at the raucous sound, but Old Howling Dog never even flinched.

"Punishment, yes," the judge agreed. "Perhaps for both of you."

The hawk-nosed Indian grunted what could have been taken for a chuckle. "Perhaps," he agreed as he took a small stick from the fire and carefully lit his pipe, "but my braves are young, and their squaws even younger. I need a woman who can cook and trap and tote. One who can draw and skin the day's kill and show the squaws how to do the same. Ruth Somers is that woman."

"Has she agreed to do this?" Josh asked.

"If she wants to survive, she will see that this is what she must do," Old Howling Dog assured him. "I need this woman. You want only to put her to death. Let her come with me and live a productive life to pay for the sins of her past."

Judge Osborne was forced to come up with an answer. An answer that would benefit everyone.

"So be it," the judge agreed, ignoring the quick intake of breath by the captain.

"Then we are in accord." Old Howling Dog pulled deeply on the ceremonial pipe before offering it to the judge. "My people will stop the raids on the settlers and go to live beyond the far mountains. The woman comes with me and the white man does not follow. It is not the white man's justice and it is not Indian justice. But justice is served."

The judge had to admit the Indian was right. He fingered his watch. He would have taken it out and read the brief inscription but he knew that Indians were attracted by bright objects and discreetly kept his watch out of sight.

There would be a hue and cry among the settlers when they discovered what he had done, but Judge Osborne knew it was in the best interest of the majority, and it saved him from having to sentence the woman to hang.

"Agreed," he said, taking the pipe.

"Agreed," Old Howling Dog repeated. "Let justice be done."

The judge looked up quickly, almost choking on the smoke at the man's choice of words. "Yes, let justice be done, though the heavens fall."

Josh got to his feet and brushed the dust off the seat of his pants. "When Ruth Somers finds out what's happened the heavens just might fall," he said sagely. "Now, if you gentlemen will excuse me, I've got to be getting back to my wife."

As he left the campsite he passed Reilly and paused to bid him a last farewell. "If things don't work out you'll always have a place with Meagan and me," Josh reminded his brother-in-law.

"Thank you, brother," Reilly said softly. "I will remember."

It wasn't until Reilly had returned to the campfire and Josh was on his way home that he realized Reilly was wearing a new headband. A single thong of leather adorned with what almost looked like a lock of some woman's hair.

Josh hoped it was a lock of hair. He hoped Reilly had found someone to love the way Josh loved Meagan. It pleased him to think that the young man who had given so much of himself in trying to secure justice for his sister had the promise of a lifetime of love and happiness.

He hoped the love Reilly had found would survive the storms of time the way the love Josh shared with Meagan had survived.

Yes, it was a wonderful thing having a woman to love, and Josh was glad Reilly had found someone who cared enough to give him a love token. Perhaps someday, if Reilly returned, Josh would find out who she was.

Josh smiled, secure in the belief that all his troubles were behind him as the lighted windows of his house glowed in the distance, welcoming him home.

*   *   *   *   *

"Don't miss this, it's a keeper!"
—Muriel Jensen

"Entertaining, exciting and
utterly enticing!"
—Susan Mallery

"Engaging, sexy...a fun-filled romp."
—Vicki Lewis Thompson

See what all your favorite authors
are talking about.

Coming October 1999 to a retail store near you.

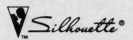

Harlequin® Historical

After the first two sensational books in award-winning author Theresa Michaels's new series

July 1997

THE MERRY WIDOWS—MARY #372

"...a heartbreaking tale of strength, courage, and tender romance...."
—*Rendezvous*

and

February 1998

THE MERRY WIDOWS—CATHERINE #400

"Smart, sassy and sexy...one of those rare, laugh-out-loud romances that is as delicious as a chocolate confection. 4☆s."
—*Romantic Times*

Comes the final book in the trilogy

July 1999

THE MERRY WIDOWS—SARAH #469

"Extraordinarily powerful!"
—*Romantic Times*

The story of a half-breed single father and a beautiful loner who come together in a breathtaking melding of human hearts....

You won't be able to put it down!

Available wherever Harlequin books are sold.

HARLEQUIN®

Makes any time special ™

HHWEST1

 **HARLEQUIN®**
Makes any time special ™

 **WIN A DREAM**

In celebration of Harlequin®'s golden anniversary

Enter to win a *dream!* You could win:

- A luxurious trip for two to *The Renaissance Cottonwoods Resort* in Scottsdale, Arizona, or
- A bouquet of flowers once a week for a year from **FTD**, or
- A $500 shopping spree, or
- A fabulous bath & body gift basket, including **K-tel**'s *Candlelight and Romance* 5-CD set.

Look for **WIN A DREAM** flash on specially marked Harlequin® titles by Penny Jordan, Dallas Schulze, Anne Stuart and Kristine Rolofson in October 1999*.

 FTD

RENAISSANCE. COTTONWOODS RESORT SCOTTSDALE, ARIZONA

K·TEL

COMING NEXT MONTH FROM

HARLEQUIN HISTORICALS

In October 1999,
Harlequin Intrigue®
delivers a month of our
best authors, best miniseries
and best romantic suspense
as we celebrate Harlequin's
50th Anniversary!

Look for these terrific
Harlequin Intrigue® books
at your favorite retail stores:

STOLEN MOMENTS (#533)
by B.J. Daniels

MIDNIGHT CALLER (#534)
by Rebecca York

HIS ONLY SON (#535)
by Kelsey Roberts

UNDERCOVER DAD (#536)
by Charlotte Douglas